DIAMONDS AND DECEIT

The Search for the Missing Romanov Dynasty Jewels

GENE COYLE

authorHOUSE®

AuthorHouse™
1663 Liberty Drive
Bloomington, IN 47403
www.authorhouse.com
Phone: 1-800-839-8640

©2011 Gene Coyle. All rights reserved.

No part of this book may be reproduced, stored in a retrieval system, or transmitted by any means without the written permission of the author.

First published by AuthorHouse 3/25/2011

ISBN: 978-1-4567-4000-9 (e)
ISBN: 978-1-4567-4001-6 (sc)

Library of Congress Control Number: 2011903694

Printed in the United States of America

Any people depicted in stock imagery provided by Thinkstock are models, and such images are being used for illustrative purposes only.
Certain stock imagery © Thinkstock.

This book is printed on acid-free paper.

Because of the dynamic nature of the Internet, any web addresses or links contained in this book may have changed since publication and may no longer be valid. The views expressed in this work are solely those of the author and do not necessarily reflect the views of the publisher, and the publisher hereby disclaims any responsibility for them.

OTHER NOVELS BY GENE COYLE

The Dream Merchant of Lisbon: The Game of Espionage

No Game for Amateurs: The Search for a
Japanese Mole on the Eve of WW II

AUTHOR'S NOTE

Czar Nikolai II, his wife, their children and several personal servants were murdered in the early morning hours of July, 17, 1918 in the basement of the Ipatiev House, in Ekaterinburg, Russia. Despite DNA testing in 2008 on the parts of the exhumed bodies of the Romanov family that were found, there is still debate about whether one daughter, Anastasia, might have survived.

Yakov Yurovsky was the head of the security detail at the house and the chief assassin. He lived until 1938. The Soviet authorities searched for many years to find a large cache of Romanov Dynasty jewels that they believed to exist, but which had not been found on the dead bodies back in 1918.

Ivy Litvinova was the English-born wife of Maxim Litvinov, the Soviet Commissar for Foreign Affairs during the 1930s and the Soviet Ambassador to the United States during much of WW II. She was an author and spent several years in the late 1930's in Sverdlovsk (formerly Ekaterinburg), teaching English.

There is, of course, an Indiana University, located in Bloomington, Indiana, with a world-renowned Slavic Language and Literatures Department. The various campus locations and departments mentioned in the story are real, but all characters of the story are fictional. Indiana University kindly gave its permission for the use of various copyrighted names connected with the university. The CIA's Publication Review Board has reviewed and cleared the novel for publication.

Any similarity between this imaginary account of what happened to the missing Romanov jewels and information that might be held in any classified US Government files is purely coincidental.

CHAPTER 1

BERGEN, NORWAY

Mr. Blackwell turned his collar up against the chilly wind coming off the harbor. The strong, westerly gusts whipped the water of the small bay into a frothy green mixture. The waves crashed against the granite rocks along the shoreline, just as they had been doing since the last ice age had carved the geography of Norway. Though a bright sunny day, it was only early March in Bergen and the temperature in the low 40s. For the locals, however, this first pleasant Sunday after a long, dreary winter was a sure sign that spring was near. The residents of the small city were out in great numbers. Entire families strolled the streets and crowded the small cafés in the center of the picturesque city. There was a festive atmosphere on the square and along the narrow streets that lead to the wharf area of this ancient coastal trading center. Small buds had appeared on some of the trees and the heads of crocuses were just pushing out of the soil in the well-tended flower beds. Theirs was a short growing season, but the Norwegians took their gardening seriously.

Robert Blackwell ambled through the Central Park. His expensive, black leather wingtip shoes made a solid, crunching sound against the small grain gravel in the pathways. Shouts of happy children drifted on the air. He had one hand stuffed in his gray trench coat while the left one held an ice cream cone. He looked no different than many of the people on the streets that afternoon, just another middle-aged man walking about after lunch, enjoying the unusually fine weather. He might have passed for a banker or a prosperous merchant. The broad shoulders and straight back contrasted with his white hair and the number of fine line wrinkles that covered his face.

But he was not a local, nor a citizen of the country. Blackwell wasn't even his real name, though that was who his American tourist passport proclaimed him to be. He had used that document and a matching credit card to register the previous day at the Norge Hotel in the heart of the port city. In fact, he was not a typical member of any society, for he belonged to the small, international fraternity of intelligence officers. He was loyal to his adopted country of America, but often felt more in common with his fellow spies of the world, regardless of their nationality, than with the typical American citizen.

The local people wandering around the park, enjoying their relaxing Sunday, had no idea that a spy was strolling among them. Blackwell appeared to be walking aimlessly, eating his orange sherbet, but his eyes were alert and his mind automatically noted anyone who looked out of place or who might be paying attention to him. A professional like Blackwell was different than the people who surrounded him. He never totally relaxed, nor completely trusted anyone. A stranger on a plane who asked too many questions about him was suspect. Blackwell would automatically wonder what was that person's real motive? He himself often had a hidden agenda when he talked with people and presumed the same of others. Besides, if he were to let himself get too close to anyone, that relationship might someday cause him great pain, as it had once in his life. So Blackwell only floated through on the surface of life. He interacted with people. He used and manipulated people. He just wasn't really a part of society.

He stopped in front of a store window to study the men's clothing for sale and to check the reflection of the glass, to see if anyone was following him. Blackwell took a glance at himself in the reflection. Other than his white hair, he thought himself rather nondescript. He appeared to be about 60 years old, of average height and weight. Some thought he had a handsome face, but he thought it too was just average. Of course, contrary to the movies, real spies don't come in any particular shape or dress in a certain style. Who might be a spy was similar to the question of the existence of aliens from outer space -- perhaps they walk among us now and we simply don't know it. No one in the park on that lovely Sunday suspected he was a spy, so how could one say for sure just who all might have been in the crowd. Perhaps the woman in the blue coat by the fountain was an extraterrestrial, or perhaps the balloon seller. No, he was most likely an undercover policeman. He had a small wire running down from his left ear and was keeping an eye on two swarthy-skinned men under a nearby tree. Blackwell had noticed those two when he had walked past them a few minutes earlier. He had mentally noted them down as pick pockets, looking for a mark, or possibly drug dealers. He veered off in another direction. He wouldn't want to accidentally get caught up in something and find himself a witness, being asked to give his name and a statement to the police. He had another civic duty to perform later that afternoon and couldn't risk being late.

Having finished his ice cream cone, he approached the small ticket kiosk on the dock and bought passage on the 3 p.m. sailing of the tourist ship, the White Lady. This would be a two-hour cruise of the harbor area and nearby fjord with a couple of stops at other locations. The White Lady could carry some 50 passengers. A few locals would occasionally ride it to get to one of the midway stops, but mostly it was for tourists. It was a comfortable ship, though it had a rather noisy diesel engine. They sold sandwiches and beer are on board and the captain would frequently let loose with the loud fog horn in response to waves from children along the shore. Of particular interest to Blackwell, was the window in the men's lavatory that opened for ventilation on the port side of the ship's first deck. If a man of average height stood up on the toilet seat, he could see out that window or even stick something out the window without being observed from anywhere else on the ship.

He still had two hours before the cruise departed. The spy stood motionless at the water's edge, his hands in his pockets. He was thinking about all the people that had sailed in and out of the ancient port, dating back to the days when the Vikings sailed off to England and Ireland for rape, pillage and plunder. He stared at the water lapping against the shore. It reminded him of his days as a small boy, playing along the shore of the river that ran near his home. So many stormy years had passed since those tranquil childhood days. A noisy seagull landing beside him, hoping for a snack, brought him back to the present. He felt weary. Maybe he was getting too old for this business. He returned to strolling through some of the small, cobblestone side streets, continuing to check that no one was following him. He came across a small shop, featuring items from

Russia. Blackwell drifted inside, looking at the collections of hand-painted, wooden boxes, icons and nested *matriochka* dolls, for which Russia was famous. There wasn't much in the store and most of the items were simply sitting on top of the wooden packing crates in which they'd arrived. Clearly a low-budget operation. On the back wall were shelves of allegedly antique books, mostly from Russia as well. There was a battered old set of the Great Soviet Encyclopedia, but it seemed to be missing a number of volumes. A young Russian girl, maybe twenty-five and very pregnant, addressed him in broken Norwegian, then broken English.

"You want Russian dolls? First quality," she said, pointing at a row of hand-painted *matriochka* dolls.

"No thank you, just looking." He pointed at her large belly and smiled. "How soon?"

She grinned proudly, like expectant mothers everywhere. "Two months, maybe."

"Congratulations. I'll take one of these boxes of Russian chocolates." He paid her in cash for the overpriced box and headed for the exit. He stopped in the doorway, as if deciding where to go next. This gave him an opportunity to see if his departure prompted anyone leaning against a wall, reading a newspaper, or staring into a shop window, to move as well. All was still. He'd seen such stores as this one with other young Russians all over Europe. They'd all left Mother Russia to seek a better life elsewhere, with just enough money saved, borrowed or stolen to pursue their dreams in the West. He took out a plain metal pocket watch to check the time. It seemed out of place with his expensive clothing. He looked at the blurry picture of the young woman in the case for a moment, then continued his strolling. He tossed the chocolates in a nearby trash can.

Bergen's glory days as a trading center were long gone, but it was still a very colorful city with brightly painted houses. While still inhabited mostly by Norwegians, a fair number of foreigners from Russia and Eastern Europe had settled there since the end of the Cold War, all looking for a better life. Norwegian immigration laws were very liberal and there was even a small Arab community made up of Iraqis, Palestinians and the odd Egyptian who had claimed political asylum. They all lived very well off the generous welfare benefits of Norway. There was even a small, storefront mosque on the street along the harbor that led north out of the inner city. It's mullah, a self-taught holy man from Egypt named Abdul, was almost a celebrity. He had been arrested previously in two other European countries on charges of supporting terrorist activities, but was released each time on some technicality. In the typical European way of handling problem foreigners, he had been "encouraged" to move on to another country after each previous brush with the law. Supporting terrorist groups by collecting money or encouraging young men to go off to join the Jihad was generally not against the law in most European countries. This lack of initiative to confront people who only supported terrorists, but never raised their own hand in violence, drove the United States government crazy. For the Norwegian government, as long as Mullah Abdul didn't personally go out and shoot at least three Norwegian citizens while the Minister of Justice himself was watching, he had committed no crime. Calling for Jihad, arranging for volunteers to travel to the Middle East to be trained to become suicide bombers and raising money for terrorist groups was considered part of Abdul's civil rights as a guest in their peaceful land. To Blackwell and others, it seemed a cowardly way to buy off such people from carrying out terrorist acts within Norway. Norway could be their safe haven, as long as their bloody acts were carried out elsewhere.

Mr. Blackwell returned to his hotel to rest a little and warm himself before his planned cruise. He settled into a comfortable leather chair in the Bibliotek Bar on the second floor of the modern-looking structure. He read in the menu how for 1170 Kroners one could get a Richard Hennessy cognac, a Cohiba Lancer cigar and your name inscribed on a brass plaque in the bar lounge. The cognac sounded good, but he doubted his employer would appreciate his having his name mounted on a plaque in Bergen. A wisp of a grin came to his lips as he contemplated the humor of an inscribed plaque to commemorate the civic duty he would perform that day.

A white-coated waiter approached him, making the slightest of bows.

"Have you decided yet, Sir?" His accent had a hint of Eastern Europe and his features placed him probably from Bulgaria. Blackwell was no Professor Henry Higgins, but he'd been around the world enough to make educated guesses about people's origins.

"Yes, I'd like a glass of the Hennessy," replied Blackwell with his own slightly accented English.

The young waiter repeated his imitation of an English butler bowing and then retreated across the plush carpeting. After receiving his drink and trying a sip, the tired spy closed his eyes and drifted into a half sleep. Others in his profession would have been reviewing the plan for what would transpire later in the day, but Blackwell had already done that several times on the train that had brought him from Oslo to Bergen. He found it preferable to simply relax, to let his mind drift to other places and other times. His breathing slowed and deepened as his thoughts took him back to a forest of birch trees, a picnic with his wife and their young son.

The sound of nearby voices slowly awakened him. A glance at the wall clock told him that he had an hour before the sailing of the tour boat. He paid his tab and decided it was time to move.

He went up to his room, packed his suitcase and checked around the room to make sure he hadn't left anything behind, like any good traveler would. Then, unlike most tourists, he used a bath towel to go around the room and wipe down any surfaces where he might have left the fingerprints of Mr. Blackwell. He took the elevator down to the lobby, paid his bill and assured the solicitous assistant manager that he had found everything at the hotel most satisfactory. And just in case they were later any police inquiries, he told the clerk how he hated to leave, but he had to get back to his accounting job in Pennsylvania.

He had about five hours before he would catch the evening train back to Oslo. The train would reach the capital early the next morning, leaving him plenty of time to make his SAS flight back to Newark. It was only a half mile or so back to the train station and his bag had wheels, so he decided to walk. Along the way, he passed by the statue of the famous musician and Bergen native son, Edvard Grieg, in a pose playing the violin. Nearby, a young man was playing a violin, with his case on the ground to accept tips. He was no Grieg, thought Blackwell. The elderly spy arrived at the train station with still a half hour before the White Lady sailed. He showed his ticket for a first class, private sleeping compartment on the overnight train to Oslo and was able to check his bag in advance. He then found a table at the station's restaurant. The Norwegians were serious about their coffee and even in a train station, the brew served was quite good. Blackwell carefully placed an out-of-print copy of Birds of Norway near the edge of his table. Another foreigner soon approached his table, coffee cup in hand.

"Is that chair free?" asked the stranger in English, pointing at the space opposite from Blackwell.

"Certainly."

The stranger sipped his coffee in silence. He appeared to be of the same 60-something age as Blackwell. After reading a bit of his two-day old **International Herald Tribune**, he finally spoke.

"Quite a mess there in Iraq, eh," said the man, pointing at a picture on the front page of his paper as he slid it towards Blackwell.

"Quite," was Blackwell's succinct reply and then he returned to sipping his coffee.

"Well, I have a train to catch and then a long flight home to Vancouver."

"Have a safe journey," was Blackwell's polite response.

A minute later, Blackwell picked up the newspaper the stranger had left and began reading the front page. He eventually laid it on the table to open it to page two. He deftly removed the baggage locker key that was taped to the inside page with his left hand as he lifted his cup to his lips with his right.

Blackwell finished his coffee and returned to watching people in the station. He enjoyed watching crowds and guessing at what reason had brought each traveler there. There were a number of university-age youth with backpacks, who had probably come to Bergen for the weekend. There was the usual smattering of young and old. Some had but one small bag; others were seated at benches surrounded with what appeared to be their life's possessions in suitcases of every size and description. The teenagers laughed and flirted as they rushed through the station.

An elderly couple, arm-in-arm, walked slowly through the station, as they had probably done every Sunday afternoon for the past 50 years. The gentleman used a cane and leaned a little on his wife for support. The white-haired spy wondered if he would have someone to lean on when he reached the age when a stroll to a train station was the high point of his day. He took out his pocket watch. Yes, it was time.

He made a quick stop at the men's room, where just before exiting he added a scarf up around his neck and a crushable, cloth rain hat pulled low over his face. He wasn't sure what surveillance cameras there were in the station, but just to be cautious, he added these items. Blackwell then went to the day lockers and using the key he had acquired ten minutes earlier, opened one and withdrew a black backpack. It was a kind commonly seen; a bit longer than some, but nothing to attract attention. He headed purposefully, but at a medium pace, for the main exit of the station. Once out on the street, he walked straight to the White Lady. He boarded and found a seat towards the back of the inside lounge area of the ship, placed the backpack at his feet and stared intently out at the water and surrounding scenery. He now had a small camera dangling from his neck, as proof that he was merely another tourist.

At 3 p.m. sharp, the ship shuddered as the engines revved into reverse and the White Lady moved away from the dock. There were only thirty or so other passengers on board. Blackwell had assessed each as they'd entered alone or in small groups. A few appeared to be locals; the rest were obviously tourists, especially the Japanese. The ship proceeded right down the middle of the bay, headed for the Eastern Channel. The others were busy taking pictures of colorful houses along the shore or were drinking hot coffee. Blackwell remained in his seat. At about the ninety minute mark of the journey, the average-looking man took his backpack and went to the men's room. He carefully bolted the door and opened a small window above the toilet.

Mullah Abdul was standing on a second floor balcony of his home, chatting with members of his flock, as was his habit on Sunday afternoons. He was enjoying the sunshine just like his Christian neighbors. The wives were all in the kitchen and the men stood outside with their spiritual leader. On this occasion, however, it was soccer, not Allah, that was the focus of their conversation. One of Abdul's young sons handed him a small cup of strong coffee sent out by his wife. The boy then turned to watch the White Lady gliding across the harbor, as it blared its horn. He liked ships and wanted to someday become a ship's captain. A second later, he heard the coffee cup hit the tile floor. His first thought was that his mother was going to be very angry when she learned of the broken cup. His second, was why was there a large red spot in the chest area of his father's white robe?

CHAPTER 2

BLOOMINGTON, INDIANA

"I trust you all had a good spring break?" inquired Professor Karl Beck of his twelve graduate students. They were all seated around the long wooden table in one of the seminar rooms of Ballantine Hall on the campus of Indiana University. Like Beck, the table was old and showed signs of wear and tear, but still useful. He was "old-school" and always wore a coat and tie when teaching. This contrasted sharply to the varied attire of jeans, sweatshirts and surplus store Army jackets that his students wore. He'd been enlightening the youth of America on the joys of Pushkin and Tolstoy at I.U. for twenty years. Beck spoke English with the slightest indefinable foreign accent. The students were all working on Masters or Doctorates in the field of Slavic Literature. Not a area of study that would lead them to great personal wealth, but at least then, Beck knew they were seriously interested in the topic -- not just there at school to a get an advanced degree as a stepping stone to making big bucks out in the business world.

"Too short", replied Peter to the vacation question. Peter was the oldest of the students and closest to finishing the course work for his Ph.D., which made him the alpha leader of the student pack.

"And did you spend the break in the library or on some beach with beautiful girls?" inquired Beck, as he gave a wink to two female students seated to his right. The tall, blonde-headed Peter had a certain reputation as being quite popular with the ladies.

Peter gave the hint of a smile. "A little of both." Peter was accustomed to his professor's teasing inquiries about his social life. "And what about you, Professor? How did you spend the past ten days?"

"Oh, a little of this and that, visited a few friends, worked on my Ivy project." It was one of Beck's famously vague replies about himself. One never felt that he was being purposely evasive, but after a fifteen or twenty minute chat with him ended, a student didn't really know anything more about Beck's past, present or future activities than when the conversation had begun.

Professor Beck reached into his well-worn leather satchel and pulled out his lecture notes for the evening. His indicator that they were about to get down to work. The course was officially titled "The History of Soviet Crime Novels", but Beck generally lectured on whatever aspect of Russian literature happened to be on his mind each week. Beck's graduate seminars were always among the most popular and best subscribed in the Russian Language and Literatures Department. A slightly annoying point to a few of his colleagues, as he wasn't tenured and didn't even have a doctorate! Some anonymous donor had established a Chair of Russian Literature two decades earlier that had such specific requirements, it seemed no one but Beck qualified for the very well-paid position. At least, he'd been the first and only holder of the Chair to date. There had always been some speculation about the coincidence of the creation of the position and Beck's arrival in Bloomington the very same year. Explanations ranged from Beck being the illegitimate son of a wealthy New Yorker who wanted to keep him quietly hidden away, to Beck being an eccentric millionaire who had himself funded the Chair so he could have the fun of teaching at a university. A new version seemed to float around the campus each fall. Professor Short, one of Beck's few friends, suspected that Beck himself started some of the wilder stories, just for his own amusement. The true story of how he came to Bloomington was more unbelievable than any of the rumors.

For ninety minutes Professor Beck spoke about the impact of socialist realism on crime fiction written in the Soviet Union in the early 1930s. While the stories certainly hadn't been written as comedies, most of the students found a number of the them humorous. The idea that falsely accused people would willing accept punishment or even execution for the "good of the Revolution" in these stories struck the 21st century

American student as ridiculous and campy. There were no rich, amateur private detectives or brilliant individual policemen. Everything had to be achieved by the effort of the group, of the collective. And the butler never did it in these novels, as there were supposedly no more servants in the classless USSR. Beck focused towards the end of the evening on a mystery novel called "His Master's Voice" by Ivy Litvinova, published in 1930. It was actually a good story, which might explain why it had been published abroad, not within the Soviet Union itself.

Finally, Beck took out his plain medal pocket watch, with a picture of a young woman inside, to check the time. "I suspect your brains are tired and my, well, a slightly lower portion of my anatomy, is also numb. Let's call it an evening." He liked teaching graduate students. They reminded him of himself -- back when he was young and he too thought he knew everything.

As was the usual custom each Wednesday night, most of Beck's students reassembled shortly after the class, at a table in the back of Grazei's Italian Restaurant, down on the town square. Fortified with alcohol and tasty appetizers, they discussed the unreasonable reading assignments of Professor Finkleburg, the prospects for summer overseas study and the usual complaints of graduate students everywhere. After two rounds of drinks, the conversation turned to Beck.

"Where's he from originally? His accent is hard to place," asked the kid from New York, who had only arrived in Bloomington at the start of the spring semester.

"He mentioned to me once that he'd been born in San Francisco," offered the student from California.

"No, Nina Petrovka told me that he speaks Russian with an Odessa accent," added the plump, red-headed girl.

"He also speaks German quite well you know. I heard he'd escaped out of East Germany in the 1980s and that's why he has several bullet holes in his back."

"Sally, how would you know what a bullet wound looks like? And when did you see his unclothed back?" asked Peter.

They all looked at Sally. "He was swimming at the YMCA one day in January. I saw him in the pool. Honest."

There were a few lingering stares at Sally. The skeptical looks were because of certain stories about Professor Beck. No one in the group personally knew any female who claimed to have slept with him, but there were lots of rumors about the charming, widowed professor in connection with beautiful women of the university faculty and the town. Even if he was sixty, a guy that good looking, in that good of physical shape and who flirted so with his female colleagues -- some of those stories had to be true! If they weren't, the general consensus of the five females and two openly gay guys at the table was that it was a darn shame.

"Never mind who he's sleeping with," said Peter. "Where the hell does he disappear to over school breaks and in the summertime? You never get a specific answer from him."

His question started a new round of discussion about Beck's travels out of Bloomington, which, like the ones about his origins and his social life, was mostly speculation. Beck created some of the misdirection himself, as he delighted in giving contradictory "hints" if people tried to blatantly elicit personal information about him.

While his students were debating his origins and his sex life, Beck was relaxing in a comfortable chair with his feet up on the coffee table in the home of Dr. Cathleen Spenser. She was a first year Assistant Professor in the History Department, who specialized in Russian history. He had his shoes off, a glass of 12-year-old single malt in his right hand and a half-smoked cigar in the other. The cigar was part of why he liked spending time with her. She was one of the few people in the health-obsessed town who would let him smoke in their home. Her rented house was furnished with a combination of her left-over graduate school book shelves and used furniture she'd picked up once she arrived in Bloomington. Enjoying a steady and good salary for the first time in several years, she had splurged on a decent living room set and a good quality bed mattress. A couple of nice water color paintings done by local artists had helped her turn at least her living room into a pleasant oasis in the house. The potted plants and ferns added a nice tranquil touch to the room where she spent most of her time when at home. Nobody to date, but her, had had the pleasure of experiencing the quality mattress. Her excellent cooking also appealed to Beck. He appreciated good food, but had somehow never gotten around to learning how to cook. He considered the microwave oven one of the top five inventions of the 20th century. Most importantly of their relationship, he simply felt comfortable when around her.

Cathleen was thirty-two, an attractive, slim woman with jet black hair which she wore shoulder length. Her green eyes and a hint of freckles revealed her Irish ancestry. She also had the cutest ass on campus -- per the unofficial survey conducted by graduate student Peter, who'd taken a class from her the previous semester. Beck also greatly valued her keen sense of humor, her intelligence and the fact that she didn't suffer fools gladly. He had also independently come to the same opinion as Peter about her shapely "*zhopa*."

Her mother had been born in Belfast, Northern Ireland. Cathleen, in South Boston, where she'd grown up. Her college had all been private, East Coast institutions on full academic scholarships, albeit with a three-year break after her undergraduate degree for a failed marriage, before she started graduate school. She'd been in Bloomington about ten months. This was her first full-time teaching position after completing her doctorate and her first experience with the American Midwest. Professionally, coming to Bloomington had been a good move, but her social life left a lot to be desired in the quaint, southern Indiana town. All her male faculty colleagues she'd met to date were married, gay or so effeminate, they might as well have been. That may have been one minor reason she was having a late, mid-week dinner with a guy several decades older than herself. The main reason, however, was that she really enjoyed his company. He was like the best buddy, brother and father all rolled into one. Her father had died when she was still a young child and no doubt Freudian psychologists would claim that was part of her attraction to the much older Beck. Her own self-analysis was that having had such a terrible three-year marriage to a contemporary, she was none too keen on men her own age. She'd stopped her own education to work, to help put her husband through medical school. The idea being that she would return to school later, once he was practicing medicine. It had been a great plan, except for his announcement when it was time to begin his residency that he wanted a divorce, so as to marry one of his medical school classmates.

She'd tried to stay away from picturing Karl as a lover, though recently her mind had occasionally been drifting in that direction, in the early hours of the morning, her arms and legs wrapped around her full-body pillow. For the present, she was just glad to have such a good friend to spend time with and to go to concerts and shows.

Dr. Spenser was also a closet-Conservative. She had to keep her personal politics hidden on the politically correct campus if she ever wanted to get tenure, but with Karl, she could express her true opinions on any topic. It wasn't that he was such a Conservative in his own political views, but he had reached an age where he wasn't so conceited to believe that he was right about everything. He allowed that other views, such as hers, might be equally valid. That was intellectually refreshing in a town so arrogantly liberal that even the local town council sat around passing resolutions about being a nuclear free zone and other such worldly causes instead of worrying about fixing the potholes.

"What did you cover tonight in class," she asked.

"The writings of Ivy Litvinova. She wasn't a great writer, but she had an interesting perspective on life. She'd been born and raised in England, but then spent decades in Soviet Russia as part of the elite." He took another sip of his smooth whiskey.

"She was the wife of the Foreign Minister in the 1930s?"

"Right, Maxim Litvinov. He was the Foreign Minister, who then fell out of favor during the Purges, but luckily wasn't shot. Stalin later found him useful to send to America as Ambassador during the war. He died in the early 1950s and Ivy moved back to England late in life. I've been looking into her writings and history -- might make for an interesting book."

"I thought they'd split up in the late 1930s?" She leaned forward and poured Karl another touch of whiskey. "A wee drop for the road, as my grandpa would say."

"I don't know if they split up officially, but she did move out to Sverdlovsk in 1936 to teach English and stayed there till the war started. Perhaps Maxim thought it was safer for her to be out of Moscow during the Purges or maybe he thought it made him safer if his English-born wife was out of sight. When he was "rehabilitated" after the Nazis invaded and sent to Washington, she did go with him. In any case, I'm more interested in her fictional writings than her real life."

"Strange place to choose to go teach English! The only thing Sverdlovsk was ever known for is that it was where the czar and his family were murdered in 1918." She poured herself more coffee from the Irish porcelain pot.

"Even Anastasia?" asked Karl. "There was that woman who appeared years later, claiming to be the daughter. Did Anastasia die or not in that basement in 1918?"

"She probably died as well. There were DNA tests in 2008 that seemed conclusive."

"Ah, well, such tests can prove anything that the testers want," replied Karl with a little smile on his face. He couldn't explain to Cathleen, but he was grinning from recalling how DNA tests had "proved" that he had died some twenty years earlier. Both the US Government and the almighty NY Times reported his death, so it must be true.

"You think she survived?" asked Cathleen.

"Well, there's an Anastasia working at the Russian food store on the south side of town, but she seems a little young to be the daughter of Nikolai and Alexandra, as her highness would now be about 110 years old," he replied with a deadpan face.

She threw a sofa pillow at him. "That would make her almost your age then wouldn't it! Get out of here and go home."

He put on his shoes and rose. Her gave her a long hug and a quick peck on the forehead by the front door. "Goodnight my little dove."

"Goodnight ancient one." Maybe it was just her imagination, after all the wine with dinner, but she would have sworn that his hand slid ever so gently over her butt as he broke from their hug. She found it a pleasant sensation, imaginary or real.

When the slightly inebriated Beck arrived home, he found a voice message on his machine. "Professor Beck, I'm calling to see if you would like to take out a subscription to Today's Australia magazine. We're having a special discount offer right now for members of the academic community. I'll phone again in the morning." The message immediately sobered him. He checked that the windows and doors were all locked. After showering and preparing for bed, he took an old Makarov handgun from behind the books on the top shelf of the bookshelf in his second floor bedroom and placed it beneath his pillow. He bolted his bedroom door, which had a steel core, secured by hinges and the dead bolt attached to four-by-four studs in the wall. The interior walls of the room had one-inch OSB board from floor to ceiling between the studs, so that no one could even punch through what appeared to be standard drywall, to get around the door. Having those unusual construction specs used when he'd remolded the house had taken some explaining to his carpenter, but Beck had paid top dollar for the work and the worker figured everyone was entitled to his own eccentricities in Bloomington. With that door secured, his bedroom served nicely as a safe haven. He then went soundly to sleep, as if he didn't have a care in the world.

Beck's phone rang a little after 9:00 a.m. "It's Mr. Jones. I left you a message last night about our special magazine offer this week for academics. If you're interested, I could swing by at say 11:00 and show you some samples and explain the details."

"I appreciate the offer, but I'm really not interested. Goodbye." Beck put down the receiver and checked his pocket watch for the time. He subtracted one hour from the time mentioned on the phone, which meant that the meeting was for 10:00 a.m. He had about 50 minutes to get to the pre-arranged meeting spot to rendezvous with Mr. Jones. While a bit disconcerting, a phone offer for Today's Australia wasn't too bad a message to receive. It simply meant that there was something important that needed discussing ASAP in person and not at his home. A phone offer for a discount cruise to Bermuda, would have been a lot worse. It meant to get the hell out of his house and out of town immediately.

He doubted that anyone was following him in Bloomington, but as a matter of professional habit, he first made a brief stop at a drug store to buy some aspirins. He then proceed to a gas station and finally to a greeting card store to buy a needed birthday card. This gave him an opportunity to see if the same car or same person showed up at two or more of those three "cover" stops. There was no such thing as a coincidence in the intelligence world and seeing someone multiple times, at locations miles apart, would have been evidence that he was being followed. He was not, that day. He eventually parked his modest Buick on a side street, a block away from the small coffee shop on the west side of town, and walked the rest of the way to the pre-arranged meeting location.

Nell's Diner was on the "townie" side of Bloomington versus the college-oriented portion. On its walls hung photos of local high school basketball stars from past decades, not university players. Nor was there a single item on the menu described as "trans fat free" or "heart healthy." People came from miles away for Nell's sausage gravy and biscuits. This was not a place where Beck was likely to run into anyone from the university. He opened the door promptly at ten, his eyes darting quickly around the room to assess who all was there. Before 8:00 a.m., it would have been full of electricians and plumbers before their first call of the day. Now it was almost empty and had only one young waitress working the mid-morning shift. He saw a couple of good ol' boys in one booth, probably unemployed and killing time over endless cups of coffee. There was an elderly couple to his right sharing pancakes and in a back booth, Mr. Jones. He headed for the balding, freckled Jones as his brain flashed back twenty years to the first time that he had met the short, feisty Irishman in a similar place. Almost the same, except that coffee shop was in a working-class neighborhood of Prague and he had to determine which person in the shop was Jones from the rolled up newspaper he was holding in his left hand on the table.

He sat down across from Bob. The two men at the table were both much older and grayer now than at that first encounter, but just as skillful. "Bob, how are you? What brings you to Bloomington?"

"Have to do damage assessments on a couple of houses from those recent storms. You know how it is in the insurance business," replied Jones for the benefit of the waitress who'd approached to take Beck's order.

He ordered coffee and a giant cinnamon roll laden with icing and when it arrived a minute later, added real butter and jam to the top of it as Bob shook his head in disbelief.

"Hey, if a couple of bullets couldn't kill me, why should I fear a little cholesterol!"

The young waitress refreshed their coffees and went back behind the counter to read her fashion magazine and dream of a brighter future once her boyfriend finished his ninety days in the county jail. The two men's conversation then turned to their real business. Jones had not seen Beck since his return from Norway.

"So what's got the house on fire that forces you out here to the corn fields of Indiana on such a cold morning?" asked Beck as he poured real cream into his coffee.

"Looks like there might be some complications out of Bergen," answered Jones. "The police there could be a little more competent than they appear, or at least they got really lucky. They calculated the angle that the shot that killed Abdul must have come from and guessed it was made from a boat. Then they found this amateur film maker who was photographing the bay that afternoon -- a documentary about saving sea crabs or some such shit -- and bingo, the next thing you know, they have a lovely video of a gun barrel sticking out from the White Lady. That soon led them to grainy pictures from a security camera back on the dock of the people who boarded the ship that afternoon."

"Any sign that they've made a connection to Mr. Blackwell?"

"It doesn't look like it yet, but you never know. There couldn't have been more than a few hundred out-of-towners in Bergen that weekend and if they start investigating every single hotel guest..." He cocked his head and shrugged his shoulders. "Anyway, the boss instructed me to come out here to let you know the situation and tell you to lay low for the next few months here in Sticksville -- and for god's sake, don't appear on any TV programs so that one of those White Lady crewmen can see you and identify you!"

Beck smiled. "There isn't a lot of demand for Slavic Literature professors to appear on Letterman or Nightline. But I get the point. You think this might be the end of our beautiful friendship," borrowing one of his favorite lines from the movie Casablanca, "if they do come up with a decent photo of me?"

"Depends on how the investigation in Bergen turns out. Those cops have been so lucky to date, I hope they're all buying lottery tickets every day."

"Well, if it's the finish, it's been a good run. When you first showed up five years ago with your crazy story of government retirees from several countries who were going to 'privately' sort out some of the world's problems, I didn't think it would ever get off the ground, much less go on this long."

"We've done some good work, but maybe it's time for your second retirement. Get on with whatever you do in this godforsaken village." Jones was a native New Yorker and for him, anything west of the Hudson River was the middle of nowhere. "Seriously, I still have it on my conscience what happened to you and your family twenty years ago, and I'm taking no chances that you don't spend the rest of your days in peaceful retirement, reading Pushkin and looking at squirrels in the trees."

Beck had almost unconsciously taken out his pocket watch to check the time and caught himself staring at the fuzzy picture of his dead wife. "And what about you? You're not getting any younger yourself and you can't possibly still need the money."

"I don't, but my three ex-wives do."

Jones emptied his coffee cup and threw a twenty on the table. Beck pushed it back across the table and replaced it with a ten. "This isn't Manhattan, you dumb Irishman. You tip that much for a $7 check in Bloomington and the waitress will think you want a hand job in the back." They both laughed.

"I'll be in touch if we hear anything further. The boss has floated some rumors in Europe that it was a rival drug gang shooting, so maybe that will help kill the investigation. But she was emphatic that you're to stay right here in Mayberry till you hear further from me."

"Will do. But if this is in fact the last time we meet, I want to thank you for everything that you did for us in Prague and for me, after the... the shooting." He could say no more.

"Oh, shut up you dumb Russian."

Jones left first while Beck finished his coffee and reflected on the news. Just goes to show, he thought to himself, no matter how careful one is, dumb blind mother luck can still sometimes screw you. Well, at least now he knew that he would have his summer completely free and he could get on with his research into Ivy Litvinova. He would also have more time to spend with Cathleen. He knew he was too old for a "relationship", but she was very good company, for as long as it lasted. Other than a couple of weeks in Moscow in July for research, she too was planning on spending the summer in Bloomington, working on her new book. They could enjoy the summer together.

OSLO

Mustafa Mansour entered a Middle Eastern carpet store in the Arab ghetto of Oslo, greeted the clerk in Arabic and entered the backroom. Mansour, an Egyptian, had been residing for many years in Norway. The government asylum board had granted him political asylum fifteen years earlier, when the Egyptian government had requested his extradition -- on the basis that he faced possible torture and the death sentence were he to return to his native land. Norway would not extradite anyone to a country that had the death penalty. The board had considered as "irrelevant" to his application, the facts that Mansour had been a member of the outlawed, terrorist group, the Muslim Brotherhood and had blown up a police station in Cairo, killing twenty-two officers. His income came principally from his membership on a government-funded panel "to improve native Norwegian-Arabic relations" in the country and as the liaison contact point between the Egyptian community in Oslo and the police. He'd just come from a meeting with Deputy Police Commissioner Knudsen, where he'd been given an update about efforts to find the murderer of Mullah Abdul. The Norwegian Arab community had been in an uproar since the murder, complaining to the police and more importantly, to the press, about the blatant "anti-Islamic and anti-Arab" murder and lack of action to solve the crime. The government had responded so far by pledging to fund three new Arab community centers in Oslo and to hold day-long "sensitivity" courses for the nation's police officers. The latter to be organized by Mr. Mansour, for a tidy sum of money.

In the backroom, Mansour found three other Egyptians sitting in comfortable chairs, drinking strong, Middle Eastern coffee. The kind, if made correctly, in which the small stirring spoon could almost stand upright by itself. These three kept a much lower profile in the city than Mansour, for they were the leadership of an underground organization known as the United Jihad of Europe. It was headed by Mohammed the Elder, Karim and Mohammed the Younger. In the past year, they had organized successful suicide bombings in Paris, Madrid and Chechnya.

"What news do you bring us from the police?" asked Mohammed the Elder.

"They may have made real progress in finding Abdul's killer. They have a video tape of the shot being fired from a small tourist ship and a video tape from a security camera on the dock of everyone who'd been on the ship that afternoon."

"From this they can identify the killer?" asked Karim as he took a sip of his coffee.

"It's not a very good quality picture, but their technicians are trying to digitally enhance the faces of the people boarding and exiting the ship."

"Are they optimistic of finding the killer?"

"Maybe," replied Mansour. "But if there's no progress made in another week, I can probably get the promise of another community center out of the government."

All four laughed. That would certainly help the cause, as the government had also pledged that only Arabic firms would get the contracts to build these centers. The UJE would get about twenty percent of the building costs, either as a contribution or from extortion of the construction firms.

They had hated to lose Abdul. He'd been their best recruiter of young men for the jihad and had remarkable skills as an organizer. He'd personally put together the plans of the last three bombings, but his death would at least bring in tens of thousands of badly needed kroner to their organization.

"Well, I have to get over to the university. The 'Friends of Palestine' student group are having a vigil in honor of poor Mullah Abdul. There probably won't be many people who show up, but afterwards, Anna, the group's president, will take me back to her apartment for sex -- it makes her feel like she's part of the worldwide movement and she knows it really annoys her wealthy father when she tells him how she is fucking an Arab."

"May Allah be with you," replied Mohammed the Elder with a smile.

After Mansour left, the three returned to the topic that had dominated their conversations ever since Abdul's death -- who had been behind his murder and was it but the first strike against the UJE leadership? The three were taking no chances and had stayed out of public places since the day of his assassination. Only their most trusted aides were even allowed to know of their whereabouts and further terrorist attacks were suspended until they knew more about who had killed Abdul.

"We know it wasn't the Norwegians," offered Mohammed the Elder, "so I still think it was probably the French or Spanish services, in retaliation for our attacks in Paris and Madrid."

"More likely the Americans. They've protested the most about Abdul's presence in Norway," countered Karim.

"Nonsense," responded the other Mohammed. "The American Administration has no stomach for such attacks and their high-minded Congress would never allow it." And as final proof of his argument, he added, "It's been ten days since the assassination. Had the US government carried it out, that fact would have leaked out by now and been all over the front pages of their newspapers." Having done three years of college in America, he considered himself an expert on how America worked. "This attack on us only occurred after the Chechnya bombing. Most likely, it's the Russians behind the killing of Abdul."

Mohammed the Elder had the final word of the day. "If Mansour can get us the name of Abdul's assassin, we should be prepared to kill him ourselves -- regardless of for whom he works."

CHAPTER 3

With the news from Jones that the "Group", as it was simply called by its members, would have no further operational work for Beck for the foreseeable future, he went back to his usual routine in the college town. That consisted of teaching two days a week, examining Ivy Litvinova's writings and taking long walks around campus and the nearby downtown area. He'd also become a regular at Grazei's Italian restaurant on Tuesday nights, when they had a piano player in the bar area. Beck was friends with the owner, Vincenzo, about whom there were almost as many stories about his vague past as there were about Beck's. The middle-aged Vinny had simply arrived in town one day ten years earlier from New Jersey, "offered" the then current owner of the restaurant at that location a large sum of money – all cash according to some stories – and converted it into an Italian restaurant. He'd made Bloomington his new home, but hadn't completely abandoned his East Coast origins. Twice a year, a tailor flew in from New York and fitted him for a selection of new suits for the coming fall or spring season. He always wore a suit at the restaurant. Grazei's featured excellent Sicilian-style cuisine, good wines and only well-endowed women wearing low-cut blouses were hired to be bartenders. They were hired obviously for viewing pleasure, but Vinny also made it well known that these ladies were to be treated with complete respect. In the first year, a local businessman hadn't believed that that quaint rule applied to him and had made crude propositions to one of the attractive bartenders. The man had mysteriously been dumped outside the hospital emergency door later that night with a broken arm. He claimed to the police that he couldn't provide any description of the assailant. Since then, there hadn't been any further improper comments to any of Vinny's bartenders.

Vinny would always save a table near the piano for Beck on Tuesday nights. Beck was an unabashed Elvis fan, as that had been the first Western rock and roll music he'd been able to get his hands on as a teenager out in Siberia. Dave, the piano player, humored Beck's repeated requests for obscure Elvis tunes because he knew he was a friend of the owner and because he always left a generous tip in the jar on the piano. While listening to the music, Beck would often close his eyes and appear to drift off to his own little world. Different expressions would come to his face, as if he was reliving chapters of his life from days long past. Everyone would respect his privacy on piano night. A student or fellow professor known to him might nod as they passed by, but only a very good friend would ever be invited to join him – of whom Beck seemed to have few. Having been in Bloomington for twenty years, he knew lots of people, but rarely let anyone get too close.

The local city fathers had delusions of becoming a major city, but Bloomington was just a small, charming college town and always would be. Small enough to get to know people in it fairly quickly and Beck could walk from his home to almost anywhere. He lived close to campus and when he couldn't sleep at night, he would go out and walk, even in winter. Having grown up in Siberia, he was accustomed to the cold. The nightmares weren't as frequent or as bad as during his first few years in America, but he still occasionally had dreams about the shooting. He would always try in his dreams to pull his wife and son down beneath him so that the bullets didn't strike them, but even though he knew what would be coming, he was never fast enough -- and then he would wake up in a cold sweat. Walking alone at night was his best way to get over the nightmares of watching his family die before his eyes. During these strolls, he would often speak softly in Russian to Olga and Pavel, his dead wife and son, telling them of his day. It kept them alive in his heart and his Russian soul. He'd never been a deeply religious man like his grandmother, but he felt somehow, that wherever they were, they could still hear him. After a few years, the university and local police became accustomed to Beck's nocturnal wanderings. They would just wave from their patrol cars and move on. Sometimes, he would run into a few of his students coming home from the bars at two or three in the morning. His nighttime walks and his habit of talking to himself during such strolls only added to the stories of "Beck-the-charming eccentric" or "Beck-the-crazy", depending on whether being told by someone who liked or disliked him. And there were some who indeed didn't like him, generally over the blatantly independent streak he exhibited towards traditions of the Academy. He found much to like in the university world, but also a lot of mindless pomposity. He'd also seen a lot of petty personal backstabbing, especially when it came to the competition over which junior faculty would get tenure. As the years went by, except for his actual teaching, Beck spent less and less time involved with "university life." He read his books, listened to his music and enjoyed the company of a few friends. He floated through Bloomington society, but limited his participation in it.

As for his eccentricity, one well-known tale told of the time in which several students decided to wait outside his home and try to clandestinely follow him, to learn what the devil he did on these excursions in the middle of the night. Given his background, Beck spotted the amateurish surveillance in a matter of minutes. He led them through the old part of campus and then after turning the corner of one building, suddenly vanished. He actually had had 30 or 40 seconds before the first student reached the corner, but by the second or third year's retelling of the story, it was down to supposedly just a matter of seconds, when a student surveillant had reached the spot where Beck had "vanished." Beck had actually lifted a steam grate and simply lowered himself below ground level before any student reached the corner. He quietly remained there until the students had given up and gone home. He'd later considered revealing the truth of his disappearance, but after the detail was added of it supposedly having been a full moon the night he'd vanished, he saw no reason to ruin such a great myth.

His social outings with Cathleen grew to two or even three times a week that spring. Karl had no delusion that their time together signified anything more than that they enjoyed each other's company. His realistic side told him that as soon as she found a suitable man closer to her own age, her *"starik"* as she jokingly called him in Russian, the "ancient one", would be a past figure, like the history she studied. She'd cook them dinner. He'd get tickets to the symphony. On Sunday mornings, she'd come to his place where he would pretend to cook breakfast. They would then lounge around in his comfortable living room the rest of the morning, listening to Russian composers and reading the NY Times, often in silence, like an old married couple. One Saturday night, he'd gotten very drunk at her place and she suggested he just sleep in the guest room. He declined on the grounds of what would the neighbors think, if they saw him going out on Sunday morning.

Everything changed the last week of the semester after a Thursday night dinner at her place of pot roast, green beans and potatoes, washed down with two bottles of good Chilean red wine he'd brought. She was impressed with Beck's knowledge of wines from a variety of countries, generally based on his having been in that country. He was the most well-traveled academic she'd ever encountered. Before settling down to after-dinner coffee and Armenian cognac, Karl insisted on helping with the dishes.

"With you washing and me drying, we can have these done in no time." Inebriated people shouldn't do dishes together. He accidentally splashed water on her thin silk blouse. He grabbed a dry dishtowel.

"Here, let me help you." It started innocently enough, as he daubed at the material on her upper chest, but turned more interesting as the towel moved south and her nipples turned hard. She stared up into his face and they both froze for a long moment. Then he leaned over and softly kissed her. She put her arms around his neck and kissed him back.

They quickly moved their kissing and teenager-like groping to her living room couch, leaving a trail of clothes from the kitchen. After a break in the passionate action a short time later, she stated quite matter-of-factly, "I don't have any pajamas that will fit you."

"It's O.K. I don't wear anything to sleep in."

As they were crawling into bed, she commented "you were worried about the neighbors on a Sunday, what about on a Friday morning?" she asked with a mischievous little smile.

"On Fridays, all your neighbors will have already gone out by the time I'll leave," he stated quite calmly, as if giving a report to the faculty council. He then pulled the blanket completely over their heads like a little boy and started tickling her.

Thus began with little fanfare, their May-December romance. She slowly awoke in the morning to the pleasant sensation of a body behind her and an arm draped over her waist. He was still sound asleep, so she slipped quietly from the bed and prepared to go to campus to teach her class.

She came back into the bedroom just before she left. He was still laying in bed, only half awake and a big smile on his face.

"This is a very comfortable mattress," he commented.

"Here's a key to the front door." She laid it on the nightstand as she leaned over and gave him a kiss. "I know you don't have class on Friday, so I left you a list on the kitchen table, of things to buy at the store today that I'll need to fix us a nice dinner tonight."

She went off to campus to teach. He first went home to shower and change clothes and then headed on foot to the library. Along the way, he spoke to Olga. *"You know I still love you as much as ever, but perhaps it's time I rejoined the living for the few years I have left on this earth. She's very different than you, but very nice. You remember, I told you she's Irish, also a very passionate people like us Russians."*

When Cathleen came home around five, the requested food items were in her small kitchen and he was on the sofa, shoes off, reading a Russian literature journal. They had an unremarkable dinner conversation about classes and upcoming final exams, as if nothing special had happened between them the previous night. While Cathleen was in favor of not making a real big deal of their changed situation, she thought something probably should be mentioned by one or the other about what had happened. At least a little mumble from him of "I love you" would be nice. Shortly after dinner, she got her "real big deal" conversation.

Once they were snuggled up on the living room sofa, he began simply enough. "I love you."

"And I love you."

"There are, however, some things you need to know about me, if we are going to continue seeing each other... like this."

She turned her face to his, but stayed snuggled within his arms. "O.K.," was all that she managed to say. Internally, she bizarrely found herself thinking, "my god, I'm about to hear the secrets of the mysterious Professor Beck."

"My name is really Nikolai Parshenko, or at least it used to be. I was a Russian intelligence officer before defecting to the United States around the time that the Soviet Union was falling apart. My wife and child were killed by the KGB during our escape. I was wounded by several bullets, but survived. In return for the information I provided, and I suppose in part from a guilty conscience over the death of my family, the US Government provided me American citizenship, a new name and this teaching position. I was out of the spy business for many years, but then, five years ago, I was recontacted by a small group of private individuals. They asked me to assist in certain clandestine operations for the good of America and one might say, for the good of mankind in general. Such private work may also now have come to an end and I feel myself free to focus on other things, you in particular."

Cathleen found it hard to believe her ears. She kept waiting for Karl to break into a grin and tell her he'd been pulling her leg, but he didn't. After an awkwardly long silence, all she managed to mumble was, "So, you're not joking?"

"No, not joking."

"And just what sort of work have you been doing for this private group?"

"I'll tell you all that I can, but some details must remain secret. My tasks have varied from trip to trip. Sometimes, it would be to gather information about shady arms deals planned by certain European companies to third world dictators. That information would then be leaked to the world press. My first work for the Group was a trip to Indonesia. I posed as a Russian black market arms dealer and sold doctored weapons to an Islamic terrorist group in that country that would explode after a few uses. My last mission consisted of traveling to Norway to assassinate a radical Islamic mullah who had been actively organizing terrorist acts."

Cathleen let out a small laugh, which seemed an inappropriate response to his telling of murder. Karl gave her a quizzical look.

"I know you don't understand what's funny about that. It's just that I've been wondering how to let you know about my mother's and grandfather's past activities in the underground IRA, but my little family secret seems rather trivial to yours. And I will tell you about them shortly, but first, thank you for sharing with me the truth about your past -- and the present. I presume very few people know who you really are?"

"Other than the people who brought me to America twenty years ago and invented 'Karl Beck', no one knows. I've never told anyone until now, but I love you and you have the right to know. There should be no secrets between us."

"I have so many questions that I don't know where to even begin."

"We have all night to learn about each other and all summer to see what may become of us, but let me tell you one important thing now. I know this relationship between us, given our ages, is ridiculous and probably won't last, but believe me when I say that I've never felt this way about any other woman since my dear Olga died twenty years ago." A tear wandered slowly down his weathered face.

"Shut up, *starik,* and kiss me."

A little later, Karl poured them both glasses of cognac and settled himself at the end of the sofa. She put her legs across his and got comfortable. "So why did you want to defect? I mean the Cold War was over, communism was over, why leave when you did?"

Karl gave her a smile as he did when one of his undergraduates asked him a naive question. For someone having a doctorate in Russian history, Cathleen sometimes seemed to completely misunderstand Russia. "I could no longer stand the hypocrisy. The Soviet Union had collapsed, yes, but the same people that had run the country as true believers in communism, suddenly became true believers in capitalism -- as long as they still controlled everything. Little had truly changed. I didn't want my son growing up in such a country. Also, for all the outward smiling, nothing had really changed with our intelligence services either, except the names. The KGB was eventually split into two organizations. The new FSB took over all internal security matters and the new SVR ran most all of the overseas operations. I became part of the SVR. It was supposedly a new day in relations with the United States, yet we were still running a number of high-level political and military American agents. If the Cold War was really over, why did we need such agents?

"So you just packed up your family and left for America?"

"It wasn't quite that simple. I'd been the head of the American Department in the First Chief Directorate of the KGB. I knew many things that the new leaders of the Kremlin would not want told to their supposedly new best friends in Washington. Through my contacts, I was able to acquire Russian passports for us in other names -- at that chaotic time, everything was available for a price -- and we boarded a train on a Friday night for Prague. I phoned the American Embassy in Prague on Saturday morning and managed to get in touch with someone from the military attaché's office. We negotiated a deal."

"Negotiated a deal seems a rather strange way to phrase it." She took a sip of her drink and felt the liquid create a warm glow through her chest and down to her stomach.

. "Old KGB officers at that time wanting to come to America were like buckets for a ruble on market day. I had to show Bob -- the American Army captain I met from the embassy -- that I had something special to trade. I showed him some of the files I had stolen from my safe two days earlier, with the names of several senior American government officials and politicians who were on the KGB payroll. I told him I had even more names to give, once we were safely on American soil. So, yes, I basically bought our way to America."

"But something went wrong? I mean, if you don't mind talking about your wife and son?"

"I told Bob that the Kremlin would stop at nothing to prevent me from reaching America -- and that by Monday morning the alert would be out for me all over the world. There was no time to lose in getting us safely to America. He just smiled and assured me that the 'old days' were over and that all would be fine."

"He didn't take you seriously that there was a physical danger?" She reached out and took his hand in hers.

"Not really. We didn't leave Prague for three more days and by that time, god knows how many people within the USG had learned of my impending defection. Perhaps one of the Soviet moles I was going to reveal learned of my location and sent word to his KGB handler. Maybe some US official couldn't resist bragging and shot off his mouth to a journalist. You'd be shocked at how much intelligence we used to get through the journalists we had recruited in America. The journalists would get the most amazing information, just by flattering your politicians, who wanted to show off how important they were by revealing secrets. Wherever the leak, our car was attacked on the way to the airport. One American official was seriously wounded, my wife and son died immediately and I nearly died as well at the hospital. When told several days later of my wife and ..." Karl's voice wavered and his eyes welled with tears.

"Never mind. We can talk more in the morning. It's late, let's go to bed." She stood and headed to the bedroom without looking back. She sensed that he didn't like to be seen crying. There was no passionate love making that night. She simply put her head on his chest and fell asleep in his arms.

During the night, Karl rolled over onto his stomach and in the early morning light, she saw the scars of the two bullet wounds on his upper back that had almost killed him. She gently ran her fingers over them. They slept late that morning. Emotional strain can be as exhausting as physical exertion. Over cups of strong, freshly brewed coffee at her kitchen table, he continued the story of his journey to America and Bloomington. "Soon as I could be moved, the Americans smuggled me out of the Prague hospital in the middle of the night to an American military base near Frankfurt. I read a few days later in an article on page 3 of the International Herald Tribune that I had died without ever regaining consciousness. Several weeks later there was a small burial ceremony for me and my family in northern Virginia. This news was intentionally leaked to the press. This was the American government's way of trying to assure that the Russian government wouldn't continue searching for me. I laid low in California for almost two years, while the senior politicians and military leaders I had identified as moles were investigated to confirm my information. A few managed to flee the country, a few were arrested and a few from prestigious families were permitted to commit suicide, so as to save everyone the embarrassment of a trial. Then *'vot i tak'*, Karl Beck sprang to life and arrived in Bloomington to start teaching Russian literature. And the rest, well, you know already about the eccentric Professor Beck," he added with a smile. "It's much too nice to stay indoors. Let's take a walk over to the Farmer's Market."

"First, I need another cup of coffee and a shower." She rose from the table. "Pour me a cup and bring it to me in the shower", she said as she left the kitchen. She stopped at the doorway, turned and gave him her most seductive smile. "Perhaps you'd like to join me."

They strolled along Kirkwood Avenue, the town's main street of bars, restaurants and quaint little shops that ran from campus to the town square. Though almost eleven, not many people were out and about yet. Life starts late in a college town on the weekend. They made a quick stop at the Donut Shop to get Karl a cruller to satisfy his sweet tooth.

"So what's this about your family and the IRA?" he mumbled, stuffing the last of the donut in his mouth.

"My mom's side of the family is from Northern Ireland and both my mom and my grandfather were fairly active with the underground IRA. That may have had something to do with her divorce when I was six. In any case, my father died in a traffic accident about a year later and after that, I spent the next seven or eight summers back in Ireland with my grandparents. Even though I was born in America, she wanted me to know my Irish roots. It was during those summers that I became very close to grandpa."

"Your grandparents are still alive?"

"My grandpa is. I don't think mom and grandpa were ever directly involved in the killing of anybody, but grandpa has told me that they both did a lot of odd jobs for 'the boys' during the Time of the Troubles." She'd unconsciously slipped into an Irish accent. "They smuggled weapons, ran safe houses where people on the run could hide, that sort of support work. If grandpa is to be believed, he even served as the contact man between the IRA and some Russian spy, who arranged for Semtex plastic explosives to be sold to the IRA. You two might have mutual acquaintances," she teased.

"Not likely. It was our GRU, the Russian military intelligence service, that dealt with the IRA -- providing them weapons and explosives. But, I had no idea you came from such a dangerous family."

"That's right and just you keep that in mind. If grandpa were to hear that you were trifling with his little one's affections just for your physical pleasures." She held her hand like a gun and put it into his side. "Well, it wouldn't go well for you, *boyo*." They both laughed. He took her hand. They strolled along like a couple of young students in love.

They wandered around in the market for over an hour, which was the largest of its kind in the state. Cathleen bought some vegetables from local Amish farmers and they inspected a lot of the hand-made crafts that were also on display at various booths. There were wood carvings, jewelry, and even home-made floral soaps. Bloomington had been quite a magnet for hippies of the Midwest in the 1960s and ever since for that matter. A fair number had simply stayed on in the area after their college days, or returned after a few years of struggling out in the real world. "Alternative life style" had long since replaced the term "hippie", but a number of now balding men and grey-haired women came to town on Saturdays to sell their products -- so they could spend the majority of their days playing flutes, smoking weed and talking with God or Vishnu or long-dead Uncle Fred.

After shopping, they strolled back over to the town's traditional square, with an old limestone courthouse in the middle. They took an outdoor table at Grazei's Restaurant for an early lunch. Vincenzo came out to greet them.

"Hey, this about the third or fourth time you're in here with the same beautiful woman -- you must be getting serious," kidded the middle-aged, Italian-American owner. "You let me know when you two getting married. I'll fix you the most delicious wedding dinner you've ever eaten!"

"What! Come here and get food poisoning on my wedding night!" replied Karl as he slapped Vinny on the back.

"Excuse me a second." Vinny intercepted a waitress headed for a table where a young family of four were finishing lunch. The dad was wearing his Marine Corps ball cap and had a prosthetic leg from the left knee down. Vinny took the check, wrote a large zero on it and told his girl, "Tell the man thanks for his service and that there's no charge today."

"Will do," responded the girl, who didn't seem surprised or act like this was the first such occasion that Vinny had crossed out a check for a wounded vet.

He turned back to Karl and Cathleen. "O.K. I gotta go see what they're burning in my kitchen. You two have a nice day." He clearly wanted to be gone before the check arrived at the vet's table.

"Pretty nice gesture" commented Cathleen.

"Yeah, I've seen him do that a number of times. I don't think he was ever in the military himself, but he seems to have a real soft spot for vets."

"You know, you're the first spy I've ever known, Russian or American -- at least as far as I know," mused Cathleen.

"Well, technically, I was a *razvedchik*, an intelligence officer, not a spy. A *spion* is the person I would recruit to collect information for me. But is there something specifically you wanted to ask?"

"Oh, just tell me something I probably don't know about that world."

"Well, you Americans have unreasonable expectations about your intelligence services. You have a crisis like 9/11 or an intelligence failure, and you immediately think a bureaucratic reorganization will solve the problem. The fact of the matter is, no intelligence service in the world is always right or has a complete picture about any ongoing event in the world. An organization usually only has half the facts, and by making educated guesses, a service tells its political leaders what it thinks is the situation somewhere in the world and what may happen. Sometimes, you have incorrect information, but get lucky and predict correctly. Sometimes you have great information, but the political leader ignores it, because it doesn't fit his preconceived notions. Did you know that prior to Germany attacking Russia in June 1941, Stalin had received more than 80 intelligence reports about what Hitler was planning, but he ignored them all."

"Stalin didn't believe them?" she inquired, as she stuck a fork into her plate of delicious Mama's Meatballs.

"No, he believed all the reports were British disinformation -- trying to ruin good Russian-German relations. Stalin thought he knew better than all of his intelligence officers -- and he wasn't the kind of guy you disagreed with, if you wanted to stay alive -- so the Russian people got clobbered by a 'surprise' attack on June 21st."

"I've read of course about the horribly lopsided results in those opening days of the war, but hadn't heard about how Stalin had ignored all the warnings."

"Yes, a mistake by that megalomaniac that needlessly cost hundreds of thousands of Russian lives. But back to my point, most people of the world think there is something almost mystical about espionage work. During my time, our Soviet leaders could read in an American newspaper what the U.S. president planned on doing, but unless we in the KGB stole, or bribed someone to tell us, the exact same thing, they wouldn't believe it. I'm not sure today's Kremlin leaders are much better."

"I must say, you've totally ruined my illusions of espionage. It's like you've pulled open the curtain and there is no wizard back there."

He gave her a little smile. "Well, sometimes, there's wizardry. When we Russians stole all the atomic secrets out of America back in the 1940s -- that gave the Soviet Union the ability to build an atomic bomb three-four years sooner than developing one ourselves, and saved us billions of rubles. That was pretty close to magic."

"Stole our A-bomb did you! In that case, you have to pay for lunch today."

Eventually, the conversation returned to Beck's current work for the private group of retirees. Cathleen was quite curious about his part-time spying activities.

"This group you're involved with. I assume most of these people are Americans?"

"The majority are, I believe, but not all. Why?"

"I was curious whether you find it a bit odd to do such work not for a country, but a private group? Why does such a group have the right to decide if someone should live or die?"

"The Norway operation was an unusual one, in that someone died. Most often it's a matter of ruining a certain company's finances so it can no longer sell arms to bad people, or bringing to public attention certain facts about a person's or a company's activities. Call it obtaining information that confirms what people may already suspect."

"And the man you killed in Norway?" He'd told her earlier a few general facts about this mullah, but not any specifics.

"Why did he deserve to die or why did our group have the right to decide that?" asked Karl.

"Both."

"As for the first, the harm and deaths he was causing to others I think earned him a death sentence. If Abdul was so upset about American troops in Iraq or Afghanistan, then fine, he should have gone there and fought the American soldiers. But this man wanted to sit in Bergen and send out misguided young Arab men to blow up innocent civilians around Europe. There is no honor in that, there is no justification. As for why my group, and me specifically, had the right to make such a decision -- well, in a perfect world, organized governments and legal systems would take care of men like Abdul and his activities. But when you have a situation as in Norway, where its own government took the cowardly way out, preferring to look the other way as long as Abdul and his followers didn't carry out attacks within Norway, then somebody had to do something. Did we take the law into our own hands? Yes. Is the world a better place without him? Yes, again."

"And these actions are taken for whose benefit?"

"I suppose you might say it's for mankind's benefit. Rarely, is there an action taken that appears to be solely in one country's interest, but there would obviously be no universal consensus on this. It's the old story of how one man's terrorist is another man's freedom fighter. But from your questions, I take it you disapprove of such work by a group of private citizens?"

"As for assassinations, aside from any big picture, political objection, there's also a religious one. I was raised a Catholic you know. And though I haven't been to church in a long time, there is still that sixth Commandment, Thou Shall Not Kill, that sounded like a pretty good idea. As for other, less lethal activities, I don't know. In many ways, any spying now that the Cold War is long over seems a little pointless. When there were real ideological differences between "capitalist" and "communist" countries, maybe it was more justifiable putting people's lives on the line to engage in espionage. Why did you join the KGB anyway?"

"Oh, I was a true believer as a young man. The Soviet Union was leading the world to the workers' paradise and I was one of the protectors of that path to the happy future. Sure, there had been a few mistakes along the road, but all countries occasionally make mistakes. As the years went by, I started to see that it wasn't just mistakes made by a few individuals, but that the whole communist theory was flawed. There was corruption and hypocrisy by the entire Communist Party leadership. The Party wasn't leading the workers and peasants anywhere; it was just fooling and exploiting all those people. The average person existed practically in poverty, while the *Nomenklatura*, that privileged group of Party members and the elites of the scientific, artistic, and even the sporting world, lived comfortable lives off the backs of everyone else. And I was as much of a hypocrite as the others in those days. Having lived a number of years abroad, I tried convincing myself that I wasn't really aware of how life was within Russia, or at least I wasn't responsible for unpleasant actions by other parts of the KGB against our own people. However, the truth is, my family was given a very nice apartment. We shopped for food and clothing at special stores, accessible only to members of the KGB. I turned a blind eye to reality, until almost the very end, when I will say, that once Gorbachev came to power, I started to reflect on how we, the elite, lived, as opposed to ninety percent of the population. With the collapse, at first I thought the country was really going to change, but as I told you earlier, I soon came to see that only the names were changing."

"And why did this private group contact you? If I have my math correct, you'd been quietly living in Bloomington as Beck for almost fifteen years before this began."

"Correct. It was Bob Jones who made me the offer to become involved with the Group, and it was my choice to accept or decline. Bob was the American military officer in Prague who'd handled my defection and who'd checked in on me once or twice a year ever since, to make sure I was doing OK -- not professionally, but just as a concerned friend."

"I'd say you've been lucky to have such a good friend over all those years."

"Yes, it was comforting, especially in the first few years when I was quite an emotional wreck over my wife and son, to know that there was always somebody I could turn to, if I needed to talk or needed anything really."

"And Bob is the head of the Group?" asked a fascinated Cathleen. She still found it a little hard to believe that such a private espionage group existed on the scale that Karl had described. Some of her more radical-minded acquaintances in the university would regard the existence of this group, if they learned of it, as confirmation of all of their wildest conspiracy theories about the American political system.

"No, the head is a woman named Joan. I don't even know her last name. She had been a very senior government official, who got Bob involved once he retired from the Defense Intelligence Agency, and he in turn, me. They first contacted me when they needed someone who could pass himself off as a former KGB officer and now black market arms dealer. That was my Indonesia trip."

"It's a good thing I'm in love with you and trust you; otherwise, I might think you're the biggest liar in all of America!" She reached over and squeezed his hand. "I was only kidding. I believe you. No one could make up such a story as yours! But I'm still curious as to why you got back into the game, regardless of how well intentioned this group's motives?"

"I could tell you that I did so solely because of the desirable goals of the Group, or to atone for my years in the KGB, but to be completely honest, maybe I had missed not being a part of the game, as you called it. Some say spies are just little boys and girls at heart who refuse to grow up. That's an exaggeration, but there is something about the profession that gets into your blood -- the mental challenge, the excitement, sometimes the danger. Let's face it, pretending to be another person, traveling the globe and outwitting your opponent is fun. On top of what you feel about the value of your actions for your country or world peace or whatever, it's fun."

Cathleen could tell by his voice and facial animation how excited he'd gotten simply talking about the work. The same way a musician or painter would emotionally talk about a great performance or a painting. Abandoning his profession for fifteen years and becoming a mild-mannered professor of literature may have been almost as hard on him as spending those years without his Olga and Pavel. "I can tell how much you enjoy the work and I suspect you're very good at it."

He smiled. "I do O.K."

"I enjoy history, but I'm not sure I feel as passionate about it, or anything else, as you do about your espionage work."

"You're still young. Perhaps you simply haven't yet found your real calling in life."

"Maybe. I seem to have simply drifted into the field of history, more than really having had a passion for it, though I do like learning about the past and why things happened the way they did." She stared up at several large fluffy clouds floating by.

"While we're discussing our pasts, may I ask about your marriage? You mentioned once you'd been briefly married."

She smiled. "Ah, yes, the great disaster. Well, that's not true. It started well enough during my senior year. Jack and I were madly in love. We graduated on a Friday, got married on Saturday and he started medical school a few months later. I put off my plans to start studying for a Master's degree, so as to work and support us while he went to medical school. It was my noble sacrifice, so that he could become a great surgeon and save lives."

"Not the first time that a couple have staggered their educations and helped each other get through school," replied Karl.

"It was a fine plan, except at the end of med school, Jack announced that he'd fallen in love with his classmate, Brandy, and also that he'd decided to become a plastic surgeon. Last I heard, the jerk was in Los Angles, fixing the noses and sagging chins of the rich and famous -- so much for saving lives!"

"It's good you're not still bitter," teased Karl. They both laughed.

"Anyway, after the split, I went back to school and here I am in Bloomington, Dr. Spenser, Ph.D., historian extraordinaire."

"No romantic temptations since the divorce?"

"That debacle taught me that romantic attraction, or call it love, is not the only ingredient for a successful relationship. Finding a spouse is more like finding a good roommate. So, to answer your question, no, no romantic temptations since then. Although, recently I've met a guy who isn't too bad to spend time with."

"You mean I have competition?" he replied in feigned shock.

She reached under the table and gave his knee a squeeze and blew him a kiss. She glanced at her watch and sighed. "Well, I have several mundane errands to do today and I promised a group of my students I'd meet with them this afternoon for a review session."

"Ah, yes, this is Finals week coming up, isn't it. Say, that new spy movie's playing on the West side -- shall we take that in tonight?"

"You actually watch those Hollywood versions of you?"

"Never miss a one! They're really quite amusing."

Cathleen had barely gotten home when her mother phoned from Boston.

"Cathy, how are you?"

"I'm fine mom, how's everything in Boston." Soon as she started talking to her mom, Cathleen sank back into a perfect, South Boston accent, instead of her educated, upper-class English she'd perfected in college.

The official reason for her mom's call was to confirm that Cathleen would be home for her birthday in a couple of weeks. "I just spoke with your grandfather and he swears he'll be here on the Wednesday just before the big day. Said he already has his airplane ticket."

"That will be great, seeing both of you. It isn't every day that a gal turns fifty! I knew he wouldn't pass up your celebration and to see that many candles on fire." She loved kidding her mom about turning the big five, zero.

"Hush, there'll be no candles on my cake."

After ten minutes or so of planning for the "big visit", mom got around to her favorite topic. "So, have you met any nice fellas out there yet?"

Being in a mischievous mood, she decided to just go ahead and shock dear old mom. "I don't know if he's nice or not, but I've slept with this fellow professor the last two nights and the sex was great."

There was a long silence at the Boston end. "I never know when you're joking with me." Mom had had no problem with IRA bombings, but she was still a good old-fashioned, Irish Catholic girl when it came to sex, which meant prudish. If one was going to engage in it before marriage, you certainly shouldn't go talking about it and especially not to your mother!

"No joking, mom. His name is Karl and he teaches Slavic literature at the university."

"Oh, that's wonderful. Tell me all about him."

"He's very charming, about six feet tall and in good shape. I think he's good-looking. He's traveled all over the world and has a great sense of humor."

"Has he been married before?"

"Yes, he's a widower."

"Children?"

"No, his son died as well. A terrible car accident, it was," improvised Cathleen.

Mom's interrogation session continued for several more minutes. "Is he younger or older than you are?"

"Oh, he's a few years older."

Mom sensed something in her daughter's voice. "How much older?"

"I attended his 60th birthday party back in February."

Another long silence. "It's a sin, you know, to tell lies to your mother. I suppose you think this has been funny telling me all this nonsense about a mythical lover."

"He's not mythical mom."

"I'm hanging up now."

CHAPTER 4

The semester over, Beck and Cathleen settled into a daily summer routine of both doing their research work in the mornings and afternoons and reserving the evenings for relaxing – be it going to a movie or concert or just reading. Beck concentrated on the writings of Ivy Litvinova and her life. Cathleen liked to work up at the library in the heart of campus, while Beck preferred the solitude and quiet of his home. That morning, he brought a large mug of freshly-brewed coffee into his den and settled into his favorite Scandinavian leather chair. Back in 1960, Ivy had made audio recordings of a number of her literary works. The tapes had lain in a box gathering dust for over fifty years at a British university and had only recently been "discovered" and made available on CDs for researchers. He was likely the first person to have listened to them since she made them in London. Khrushchev had personally given her permission to go visit her home country of England for a year. Beck had learned from her personal papers that she had considered not returning to the USSR, but she still had family in Moscow and knew there would be unpleasant consequences for them if she defected. He followed her oral reading with the text propped in his lap. Ivy had a strong, firm voice, belying her age of 70 at the time she made the recordings.

He was listening that day to Ivy read the mystery novel she'd written in the late 1920s, "His Master's Voice." He'd already listened to her read several of her short stories from a collection titled, "She Knew She Was

Right." He wasn't certain exactly what he was looking for in these old recordings. He hoped it might give him a different perspective on the stories, if he heard the words coming from her own voice -- perhaps her intonation would give a different meaning to certain passages. At least it would be a new angle, as probably he was the first person to listen to them since she'd made them.

About four o'clock, Cathleen let herself into Beck's house and found Karl sound asleep in the chair, headphones around his ears and the CD still playing. She gently lifted the headphones and whispered to him, "so, this is what you call research?"

"I was just resting my eyes," he sleepily mumbled.

She switched off the CD player. "How are you and Ivy getting along?" she asked as she lowered herself down onto his lap and put her arms around his neck.

"Good. How was your day up at the library?"

"I suspect I got more done than you did, judging by what I found when I walked in. You want to go out somewhere for dinner tonight or shall I fix something for us here?"

"Let's stay in tonight," he suggested. "I'll help you fix up some salads."

While chopping veggies for the salad, Karl began discussing Ivy with her. "It must have been hard for her to move off to Russia in her mid-twenties when she married Maxim, leaving behind her homeland of England, and then fifty years later, she left Russia and moved back to England for good in her early 80s."

"Sounds like a courageous woman to me -- to take such dramatic steps when so young and again when so old in life."

"I certainly sympathize with her, having changed countries myself once. It's hard to leave behind what you know, even if you don't like it. It's the fear of the unknown."

Cathleen pulled the cork on a bottle of white wine she had taken from the fridge. "Was Ivy that much of an ideologue herself?"

"I don't think so. She came out of a very progressive family, and she was Jewish, but basically she moved to Russia because she was in love with Maxim. He was 39 and she only 25 when they married."

"Wow, 14 years difference. Let's see, you're how many years older than me?" she teased.

"Don't go there," he responded in a mock serious tone.

Diamonds and Deceit

The following morning, Beck was back to listening to Ivy read "His Master's Voice." He was about two-thirds of the way through the story. She had just finished describing the prosecutor's latest theory on who had murdered Pavlov, when she began talking about how Czar Nikolai II and Alexandra must have felt that night of July 16, 1918 at the Ipatiev House in Ekaterinburg. "What the hell?" he commented out loud. He went forward and backward several pages in the book, thinking he might have drifted off again for a minute and missed a page. Events in the written novel had been happening in Moscow. How did the story get to Sverdlovsk? He backed up the recording. He replayed this strange section of the recording several times. He'd not been daydreaming. In the middle of her reading chapter XV, there was a ninety second portion, totally unrelated to the published story. He played it repeatedly till he'd managed to copy down her exact words:

> Yakov Mikhailovich said that the 16th had been a very warm day. The telegram addressed to him personally had arrived the previous day. Telling him to eliminate the problem. He awoke the family after midnight and told them that there was fighting and shooting nearby and for their own safety they needed to dress and come down to the cellar of the Ipatiev House. Nikolai and Alexandra looked very frightened, as if they sensed what was coming. Yakov said that afterwards, there was blood everywhere and the smell of gunpowder filled the small, closed cellar. Even though it had been almost twenty years, the scene still haunted his memories. They found hundreds of jewels sewn into the clothing of the women, which was why it had been so hard to kill them just by shooting them. This gave him the idea to go alone and search the room of Nikolai immediately thereafter, while the others dealt with the bodies. He hid what he found initially in his own room, underneath a loose floor board. Later, he moved them to the place he told me of. He'd initially taken the jewels as sort of a protection, depending on how the Civil War turned out, but after a few years, he could think of no

way of turning in the jewels without getting himself shot, particularly once Stalin had taken complete control.

He said all the jewels were mine if Maxim and I could get his daughter out of the *gulag*. He obviously hadn't heard how precarious were our own positions. I told him I wasn't sure if I could do anything for his daughter, but he said he doubted if he had long to live and I was his only chance. Was this all a *provokatsia* to try to entrap me? A couple of months later, after hearing that Yurovsky had died, I took the chance and went to the place he had described. My God, there were dozens and dozens of diamonds and rubies and Yakov's note. I took them all to my one true friend, Pavel Ivanovich, and had him place them in my books. Books of historical facts, even if the facts have to change with the times. I tried to bring them with me, but they had to stay in Russia at a place that was a dancing girl's salvation. Unfortunately, I was never able to do anything for Yakov's daughter.

Maxim is gone and I have no one now to counsel me as what to do. I may not have long to live myself and needed to record these facts somewhere, so that someone, someday may know the truth and do what is right with the jewels.

Beck stared at the words for more than an hour, wondering what on earth all this really meant. He grabbed one of his history books off the shelf. First of all, who was Yurovsky? The name sounded vaguely familiar, but he remembered no details. When he finally found an entry for Yakov Mikhailovich Yurovsky, he said quite out loud, "*boge moi!*" "Yurovsky had been the head of the guard detail and lead assassin of Czar Nikolai II, his family and several personal servants in the very early hours of July 17, 1918 at Ekaterinburg. Yurovsky was rewarded for his bloody work by being given various cushy government jobs in Moscow, until he died of natural causes in August, 1938. However, his daughter, Rimma, who had become a senior official in the *Komsomol* youth organization, had fallen afoul of the system during the Purges in 1935 and had spent the next 20 years in Soviet labor camps. Yurovsky made a number of visits back to

Sverdlovsk, the new name for Ekaterinburg, in the mid-1930s for rather macabre reunions with those who had participated in the murders of the royal family. Beck checked his notes on Ivy. She'd spent most of 1936 through early 1941 teaching English in Sverdlovsk. Could the paths of Yurovsky and Ivy have crossed in Sverdlovsk in 1938? He glanced at the clock. He had to go retrieve Cathleen from the library, as they had planned to go to a movie that evening.

She gave him a quick kiss as she slid into his car. "How was your day?"

"It was an unbelievable day," he responded with a smile. "Do you mind if we skip the movie? I want to take you home and show you something and see what you think."

"Sure, we can go another evening. But what's so exciting at home?"

"It's better you read something first, then we can discuss it."

He poured both of them a glass of wine, then handed her the transcript he'd made of Ivy's comments in the middle of her mystery story and also his notes about Yurovsky.

She quickly read his hand-written notes. "Is she really referring to what I think she is? I mean, this sounds like the murder of the Russian royal family in 1918!"

"That's certainly my interpretation of it. Nikolai, Alexandra, Yurovsky, the date of July 17 -- the facts all seem to fit only one scenario. Of course, what she was trying to convey in that bit of recording done in 1960 and the historical truth of 1918 may not be one and the same."

"Meaning what exactly?"

"I mean, I see three distinct possibilities here, in descending order of possibility. First, Ivy might have been senile by the time she made the recordings and its all nonsense. Second, maybe Ivy was just having some fun, by telling such a tale on the tape. Third and least likely, it's all true and somewhere there's a hidden cache of Romanov jewels worth millions of dollars, first stolen by Yurovsky and then later offered to Ivy as a bribe."

"I like the part about the jewels," stated Cathleen, holding out her fingers as if modeling one of the precious rings. "But how can you possibly go about investigating her statements, some fifty years after she made them? She's long dead and even her children are probably also dead by now."

"Not an easy task, but if all true, the most critical challenge would be -- how to solve the riddle of where she hid the jewels? Who is Pavel Ivanovich and what books are Ivy talking about?"

"Let me see your sheet again. What exactly does she say? 'Books of historical facts, even if the facts have to change with the times.' And even if we determine what books she meant, god knows where they've gotten to since 1938? "

"Lots of questions, which need research, but first we need some food. I'll get started on dinner." Cathleen headed into the kitchen while Karl took several more books off their shelves and piled them on the floor around him. They'd settled into a routine where Cathleen would come cook dinner or they'd go out for dinner and then she'd spend the night, but only every other night. This was their slightly bizarre way of neither feeling like a major commitment had been made between them. They both felt strongly about the other, but the unspoken truth was that both were a little scared. She'd had her disastrous marriage. And while Beck had not lived the life of a monk for the past twenty years, he'd had no long-term relationship with any woman since the death of his wife.

They resumed their conversation over the scrambled eggs and hash brown potatoes she prepared. "Make any progress, Mr. Holmes?" He gave her a blank look. "You're Sherlock Holmes, I'm Dr. Watson." Another puzzled look. Despite his two decades in America, there were still serious holes in his cultural knowledge of the West. "Never mind. Just tell me if you've made any headway in your investigation."

"More progress on a plan of investigation than the actual investigation, but I've not just been sleeping in there. First, I've identified a grandson of Ivy's, who's still alive and residing in New York City. If he'll speak with me, perhaps he can shed some light on whether Ivy was senile by 1960 or what kind of sense of humor she had?"

"As good a place to start as any. By the way, just what do you plan to do with the jewels, if by chance, you do find where they're hidden?"

Beck's eyebrows raised, as they did when he was concentrating. "A good question. I'm sure they're long gone by now, if they ever did exist, but it's an interesting legal and moral question. The Russian government and descendents of the Romanovs would certainly both make a claim to them. Descendents of Yakov Yurovsky or Ivy Litvinova might even make a claim, given the financial value at stake. But let's not sell the skin till we shoot the bear."

Beck was a whirlwind of research for the next several days up in the stacks of the Wells Library. He tried learning as much as he could about those fateful days in July 1918 for the Romanov czar and about Yurovsky's life over the subsequent twenty years from when he supposedly stole the jewels. The downward spiral that finally brought the two men together on that tragic night began in February, 1917. The protests and riots, as much over the lack of food and antipathy towards the war as a dislike for a monarchy, grew and grew in the Russian capital. And unlike with previous protests, after two years of disastrous warfare and the deaths of hundreds of thousands of loyal soldiers and officers, there were no more dependable troops in St. Petersburg. When soldiers were called out from their barracks, they simply shot their officers and went over to the crowds in the streets. When Nikolai II abdicated on March 15, 1917, the Provisional Government, headed by Alexander Kerensky certainly made promises about the safety of the czar and his family. There were initial talks about England accepting the Romanov family, but they collapsed. The czar and entourage were located at first in the Alexander Palace at Tsarskoye Selo, just a few miles south of the capital. In April, supposedly for their own safety, they were moved hundreds of miles away to the Urals, to the Governor's Mansion in the small city of Tobolsk. They still had a large retinue of servants and enjoyed the best of food and drink available, even though most of the country was starving. The "October Revolution" brought Lenin and the Bolsheviks to power. Kerensky was gone. In April, 1918, the family was moved to Ekaterinburg, to the Ipatiev House. The family was allowed to retain only a few longtime personal servants and were placed on "soldier's rations." The Romanov family came to be treated more and more like simple prisoners, rather than royalty, and were finally executed that fateful July night. Their dead bodies were burned and hidden in an unmarked grave in the forest.

Yakov Yurovsky died in August, 1938, apparently of natural causes. A feat some ten million Russians did not achieve during those years of the Great Purge, directed by the paranoid Stalin. As an old intelligence officer of the KGB, who'd made his living assessing people's character and looking for their flaws, Beck tried to form an opinion about Yurovsky's. What would have been his motivation for stealing the jewels in the first place and then supposedly of using them to bargain for his daughter's freedom? At first, it seemed unlikely to Beck that a young man who'd joined the Bolsheviks in 1905 and who was, by all accounts, a dedicated revolutionary and member of the *Cheka*, the secret police, would have stolen the jewels in the first place. Here was a man who followed orders to kill the czar and his family without any hesitation, because it was for the good of the Revolution. But the more he read and analyzed the personality of the then 40-year old Yakov Mikhailovich Yurovsky, with a wife and three children, he began to see the character trait he always looked for in his own human targets -- call it greed, call it "looking out for number one." Beck developed a very different mental picture of Yurovsky. Here was a man who'd been the eighth of ten children in a poor, working class family and who wanted better for himself and his own family -- that's why he'd become a revolutionary. The outcome of the Russian Civil War was far from certain by that July and the White Russian Army was closing in on Ekaterinburg. Perhaps even a dedicated *Chekist* such as Yurovsky might have been tempted to take out a little personal insurance in such uncertain times -- all those jewels in the czar's room for the taking and no witnesses. Opportunist, that was the word that came foremost to Beck's mind to describe Yurovsky in 1918. Then over the next two decades, whatever loyalty he'd had to the revolution and the Party had slowly vanished as he watched Stalin murdering millions and especially after he saw his own daughter unjustly charged and sent off to a Siberian prison camp in 1935. Beck saw certain parallels between Yurovsky's actions with the Romanov jewels in 1918 and his own decision to steal sensitive documents and defect some seventy years later. They'd both been looking out for their families in chaotic times.

When he returned home at the end of one summer's day, he found Cathleen already there, waiting for him in the living room. She had a glass of single malt for him in one hand and in the other, a reply letter from Viktor Litvinov, the grandson of Ivy. "Which do you want first?"

"Both!"

Rather than phone, Beck had opted to write to Viktor, simply telling him that he was doing research on his grandmother's writings and would appreciate the opportunity to stop by one day soon and speak with him about her. That was the truth; it just wasn't the whole truth. Beck figured it best, at least initially, to avoid any mention of missing Romanov jewels. The grandson, a retired teacher of probably seventy years, had graciously replied that he would be happy to meet with Professor Beck and help him as best he could. He provided a home phone number so that Beck could call him when he had a precise date of his planned visit to New York City. He read the letter out loud to Cathleen.

"That certainly sounds promising," she responded. "Of course, it's hard to say how well he knew his grandmother, but certainly worth you flying to the coast to meet with him."

"Why don't we both fly to the Big Apple and make the trip a little vacation for us?"

"Sounds like a wonderful idea, but a bit expensive when you add up the airfare, hotel, restaurant bills and maybe a Broadway show."

"I think I can afford it, if you don't eat too much!"

She stuck out her tongue and gave him a dirty look. "Say, just how much money did the US government pay you for all of those stolen documents?"

He gave her a little smile and answered, "enough."

"Ah, handsome and rich! Look, I have this birthday thing with my mom and grandpa next week in Boston. How about I go there on Wednesday for the festivities, and then swing down to New York City on Saturday afternoon to meet you?"

"You sure you only want to spend three days with your family?"

"If you knew my mom, you'd know that three days is quite sufficient, which is why I'm also doing you the big favor of not inviting you to come meet her."

"I was going to be polite and offer to accompany you to Boston, but I can take a hint. I know you're ashamed to be seen with me in public." Beck put on his best dejected look -- just before he grabbed her and started tickling her sides.

By the time she broke free, she was in tears from laughing so hard. "OK, call Litvinov and see if he can meet you that Saturday and I'll fly down from Boston to meet you by the time you're done with him -- and then we'll do the whole Big Apple fancy dinner and show that night."

"Sounds like an excellent plan."

"Now that that's settled, did you find anything interesting at the library today about the players in the Romanov drama?"

"I learned that the Soviet government was convinced that many diamonds and other jewels that had belonged to the Romanovs had gone missing and there were numerous investigations up until about 1933 of former servants, priests and nuns -- anyone who'd had any contact with the captive royal family up until the day of their deaths. The NKVD, the successor to the *Cheka,* was very persistent and occasionally turned up a diamond hat pin or some small item, but never the large cache that they were convinced had been secreted away by some friend or servant of the royal family. Wouldn't it be ironic if the real thief had been one of their own!"

"Ironic is hardly a sufficient word. And what have you decided about Yurovsky? You were talking yesterday about his possible motives."

"Yes, I believe he could have done it, either out of simple greed or a sense of personal self-preservation. As the lead executioner of the royal family, he surely understood what a wanted man he would be if the White Army prevailed in the Civil War. Having a hidden nest egg could have come in handy, had it been necessary for him and his family to flee.

"What about historical circumstances? Have you found any evidence that he and Ivy ever met in Sverdlovsk?"

He poured himself a little more of the 12-year old single malt whiskey. "Well, she was certainly in the city in 1938. Yurovsky by that time had serious heart and ulcer problems and perhaps understood he was not long for this earth. Yurovsky could have made one more trip back out to Sverdlovsk before he died in August, 1938. One last sentimental journey to the scene of his great triumph, or crime, depending on how he viewed it by that time. All I can say for now is, that her story is plausible. I'll have a better idea if it's probable, after I talk to the grandson."

Further research was put on hold the following morning while Beck went to a long-scheduled breakfast with his friend of the Classical Studies Department, Horatio Short. Short had the stereotypical appearance of a man who'd devoted his life to studying ancient Rome and Athens -- grey hair, uncombed in years, a bow tie and slightly stooped shoulders. The two didn't seem at first glance to have that much in common, but for whatever reasons, they had gravitated towards each other and become friends over the passing years together in Ballantine Hall. Perhaps being of almost the same age had something to do with their friendship. Or maybe it was that both had realized, more than most people do by their ages, that there was nothing left that they needed to achieve to prove to others that they had been successful in life. How they now spent their time was decided by whether they enjoyed doing it or not -- not to garner any additional external accolades.

By the middle of their breakfast in the cafeteria of the Student Union Building, the conversation had turned to ancient Rome. Beck had a question. "Did the citizens of Rome see the decline of the Roman Empire coming? Or did the collapse take them by surprise?"

"Oh, they saw it happening for over a century or more and even had a rough idea of the causes for their problems. They just couldn't do anything to change the fundamental factors bringing about the decline," explained Short.

"I was curious because I've been thinking recently about America today or call it America and Western Europe lumped together? Is Western Civilization past its zenith and we just don't recognize the signs?"

"We don't like to think we're over the hill do we?" replied the Roman expert, as he attacked his breakfast sausage. "We look at economic statistics about the rise of India and China and proclaim loudly that we'll bounce back with the next generation of video game. We watch our politicians squabble and spend more effort on staying in office than at solving problems, but won't admit we have a domestic political problem. We tolerate every sort of perverted life style as acceptable "alternatives." We hold no one personally responsible for their actions because their father or society mistreated them as a youth, yet we don't think we've got a morality problem. And even the Romans never treated or paid their star gladiators what we pay sports figures in America today, but no one admits we've got a problem over priorities. As you can see, I'm in a cynical mood today, but let me ask you a question, with your European background. On the eve of the First World War, did the royal houses of Europe see that their entire world was about to come to an end? Did the czar of Russia understand that the whole house of cards was about to be swept away?"

"No, I don't think he and the other royal family members had a clue that their time had passed. The Romanovs were completely out of touch with real life in Russia, with all the suffering of the average person. I doubt if they grasped the level of hatred and despair in the land -- just waiting for a spark to set all of society ablaze. And the more desperate people are, the more radical the solutions they're willing to listen to, to solve their problems. In the case of Russia in 1917, it was Lenin and the Bolsheviks."

"Exactly! And that's what worries me about America today. We have politicians throwing multi-million dollar weddings for their child while an average man here in Monroe County can hardly find a job to feed his children. When you have fifty year old men filling out applications to work at fast food chains for minimum wage, we've got problems." Short finished the last bite of his breakfast.

"You're in a feisty mood today! This might be the day you'll actually write that letter to the editor you're always threatening to send," chided Karl.

Short looked at his watch. "Not today, I'm afraid. I have one of my doctoral students coming by my office in thirty minutes and I promised myself I would positively finish the third chapter of my new book on Cato today. Maybe if I'm still upset tomorrow, I'll write it. But before I go, mind if I ask about this new woman in your life? Suzanne of the Slavic Department told me that you and a young lady of the History Department are now an item. What's the story here?"

"Her name is Cathleen Spenser. This was her first year at I.U. Russian history is her field and yes, I'm quite fond of her despite the absurd age difference."

"Good for you. About time you found a good woman. Not good to be alone so much." Short was rising from the table. "Remind me to tell you next time I see you what Cato said about good women!"

"Goodbye." Beck thought to himself that his relationship with Cathleen must be quite publicly known, if it was now the subject of Ballantine hallway gossip. He walked out the front door and down the long steps into Dunn Meadow. There was a young man practicing juggling and a girl walking her rabbit on a leash -- pretty standard stuff in the large meadow where students gathered to pass the time.

Beck began talking to Olga as he strolled along the small stream that ran though the meadow. *"Perhaps Horatio is correct. Maybe I've spent too much time alone. I thought it was much too late in my life to again find a wonderful woman like you, to share it with, but perhaps there is still time for me. But is it Cathleen I'm in love with or just the idea of being in love with somebody? No, I can't be that wrong about my feelings towards her. Well, we'll see how our trip together to New York goes. I remember how much you liked Manhattan those couple of days we visited there ..."*

A student laying in the grass observed that the old guy strolling by must be in a good mood; he certainly had a big smile on his face as he stared off into the distance.

CHAPTER 5

BOSTON

Cathleen was the first up on Friday morning. Her mom's fiftieth birthday party the night before had been a late night, rousing affair, befitting an Irish family with Irish friends and neighbors. She made coffee and was sitting in her mom's small kitchen when her grandpa wandered into the room at about ten o'clock. Nearing seventy, Tommy wasn't the vigorous, powerful man he'd been as a youth, but he still had a quick step to his walk and a twinkle in his eye. And the mind under his permanently disheveled, grey hair was as sharp as ever.

"Good morning, darlin'. Any more of that coffee available?"

"Sure. You sit down and I'll pour you a cup. You want anything to eat? I can fix you up some eggs or whatever I can find in the fridge."

"Just some toast and jam would be grand. Your mother still sleeping?"

"Yes, and I doubt if we'll see her before noon."

"Good. It'll give you and me a chance to talk, like we used to when you'd come spend the summers with us. Tell me about this new man in your life that your mother keeps vaguely referring to. What's his name anyway?"

"Karl Beck." Cathleen proceeded to tell him how she'd met Karl on campus and that they had simply started spending more and more time together, because they enjoyed each other's company. "Then, a few weeks ago, it suddenly turned romantic, but we were good friends first. What has mom all worried is that Karl is 60 years old. He's a very well-preserved, athletic 60, but he is almost twice my age." She waited for his response while he slowly stirred his coffee.

"If you two love each other, that's all that matters. I've known men who were 25 chronologically, but acted like they were 70, and vice versa. But what is he, a German?"

She paused. She'd been dying to discuss with someone her relationship with Beck -- the real Beck. And she'd never felt comfortable lying to her grandpa, ever since she was a little girl around him. "Well, that name is Austrian, but ... If I tell you something, can you keep it just between you and me, not even mom?"

He gave her one of those big, grandfather smiles. "I've been known to keep a few secrets in my day."

"He's actually Russian. He was a defector in the early 1990s from the KGB. His wife and child were killed while they were escaping through Prague. The US government gave him a new name and resettled him in Bloomington."

Grandpa stared at her for a long moment. "And you're sure he's not just crazy? Because that's quite a story."

"I know, that's why I did some historical checking. He told me his real name is Nikolai Parshenko. I found newspaper articles from that time frame about him, including pictures. He's definitely Parshenko."

He reached over and took her hand. "Like I said, if you two love each other, that's all that matters. And I suppose no one is trying to kill him these days?" He gave her a little wink.

"No, after twenty years, he figures he's long been forgotten about by Moscow. Another piece of toast?"

NEW YORK CITY

Beck arrived at LaGuardia airport late Saturday morning. He grabbed a cab to his midtown hotel to check in and get rid of his suitcase. He still had a couple of hours to kill before meeting Viktor Litvinov. The weather was nice, so he decided to walk the fifteen blocks uptown to his appointment. He went by Rockefeller Center. He stopped for a minute to look at all the tourists. *"Ah, Olga, I remember how much you liked this spot when we visited here. In was wintertime and we went ice skating on the rink down there. I do love this city. It's so full of energy, with people from all over the world. Everyone comes here to prove they can make it in the Big Apple. That's what makes America so successful -- all that talent and energy flowing in from every continent."*

Beck arrived at Litvinov's residence promptly at two o'clock, as scheduled, and rang the buzzer.

A tall, thin and rather effeminate gentleman welcomed him warmly. Before settling down in the living room, he showed Professor Beck the many photos of his grandmother and various Russian aunts and uncles that adorned the walls of his upper Eastside brownstone home. There were also a number of fine paintings on the walls and the entire home was beautifully decorated. There was no evidence of a Mrs. Litvinov, at the present time or in the photos, so either Viktor had brought in a first class decorator, or mathematics wasn't his only talent. He'd prepared tea for Beck's visit. Beck judged Viktor to be near seventy years of age. His guess based on his host's wrinkled face and age spots on the backs of his hands, which made his obviously dyed, dark brown hair seem a rather futile gesture to appear youthful. There were also many photos from his nearly thirty years of teaching math at a private preparatory school. "Do you miss teaching?" inquired Beck.

"I miss the students, but I was ready to retire and I have other pursuits to keep me busy these days. So, are you writing a book just about Ivy or Ivy and Maxim?"

"Ivy's literary writings actually, but naturally her life and her family affected her writings, so I'll be looking a little bit at Maxim and her personal life."

"Of course. I hear a slight accent in your English. Where are you from originally Professor?"

"I was born in Austria, but moved with my family to California as a young boy." Beck told his lie as smoothly as if it were the truth.

About thirty minutes into the conversation, Beck eased into his real questions. "I take it you must have known your grandmother fairly well while you were growing up in Moscow? Before she moved permanently back to England."

"Oh yes, I would often be at her apartment as a teenager and she helped me with my English. Then after she returned from her one year visit to

England in 1961, I'd see her perhaps not as frequently, but we were still in regular contact."

Beck had a notebook with him to scribble down a few details. "Did Ivy have a good sense of humor about her, at that age? I mean, as she went into her seventies?"

"Well, she would laugh at a good joke and saw the ironies of life, but overall, I would say she was a fairly serious person. Why do you ask?"

"Oh, just something on one of the recordings that she made of her own stories. I was wondering if she'd the sense of humor to make a sort of insider's joke -- by adding something in the audio version that wasn't in the original, written version?"

"If you mean like a prank, no, that was not grandma Ivy. She particularly took her literary writings very seriously. Just what did she put on the tape?'

"It's nothing really, sorry I brought it up. I've taken up enough of your time, but just one last question if I may?

"Anything."

"Did Ivy ever talk about Czar Nikolai II and his family or about Yakov Yurovsky, the fellow in charge of the group that assassinated the royal family back in 1918 in Sverdlovsk, the city where she spent several years teaching English?"

"No, I don't recall her ever saying anything about the royal family or their deaths. Despite her husband's profession, grandma was not a political person."

"Did any of Ivy's personal books by chance end up with you?" Beck realized as soon as he asked the question and saw the puzzled expression on Viktor's face that he'd been too pushy. He quickly added, "I was just curious if she'd perhaps written any personal sentiments to you in some of them or she'd annotated any of them?"

"No, unfortunately, upon her death, except for her personal papers, most of her things were just passed out to friends there in London. She'd had to leave almost all of her books and other valuable possessions behind in Moscow when she was given permission to immigrate to England in 1972. Some items might have been left with my Aunt Tatiana in Moscow at that time, but god only knows where anything is now, because eventually, she also moved to England and died many years ago."

"Well, thank you for your time. This has been most helpful." He shook Viktor's soft hand and departed.

Soon as he closed the door, Viktor smiled. "Not as helpful as you were to me."

Beck hailed a cab and headed to the Shamrock, an Irish Pub on 2nd Avenue, where they'd agreed that Cathleen would go directly to from the airport and wait for him there. They thought that it was better if Karl met Viktor alone in any case.

He found her at the bar. "How was your flight?"

"Crowded, but on time. I only arrived here at the bar about ten minutes ago."

"Any of your old IRA friends here?" he jokingly asked as he gave her a quick kiss.

"Well, I wouldn't go making any toasts out loud to the English. You might be surprised just how many retired IRA members there are in here."

They'd talked several times on the phone while she was in Boston, so he already knew how the birthday party and the visit with her grandpa had gone. She had left out the part about revealing Beck's true background and name to him. She figured she would ask Karl's permission to tell grandpa about his past, when the two of them were about to actually meet someday.

So what did you find out from Litvinov?"

"Less than I'd hoped for, but he claims that Ivy wasn't senile, nor given to practical jokes." He filled her in on the details of his chat with Viktor.

"Well, it sounds like you got about as much out of him as you could reasonably expect. At least, he didn't tell you that Ivy had been crazy as a loon in her later years."

"True. But I was hoping my conversation with him would have generated some concrete ideas as to what to do next. Also, he's a rather odd fellow and I had a gut feeling that he was hiding something, but I'm not sure what."

"Slightly changing subjects, is this what you did as a KGB spy? I mean, posing as somebody you weren't and eliciting information out of people."

"At times, yes. But usually, I played my role as Soviet diplomat in my true name as I did my cover work as well as my espionage duties."

"Which was?"

"Trying to recruit you Americans." He gave her a smile.

"And how would you do that? I mean, did Americans spy for you for ideological reasons?"

"No, the last American who spied for us because he believed in Communism was about 1955! Sorry to tell you, but you Americans just love money."

"And what about with this private group? Do you travel around in the name of Karl Beck?"

"No, I use alias documents when I'm doing that work. There is no connection to Beck or even Bloomington."

"But if there's no connection to the US government, how do you get passports and credit cards in another name?"

"No, there is no government connection, at least as far as I know. As for the alias documentation, this is America. Everything is available in America, for a price." He rubbed his thumb and fingers together, and laughed. "Perhaps Bob could explain to you better than I can about the work of the group. And I'd like for him to meet you anyway. I could call him and maybe set up something for tomorrow, if he's in town?"

"OK, I'd enjoy meeting him."

"I saw a payphone back in the corridor by the men's room. I'll be just a minute."

"Don't you have your cell phone in your pocket?"

"Yes, but I don't want a record of a call to his home number on my cell phone account."

Cathleen was beginning to get a taste of Beck's secret world. Actually, it reminded her a bit of some of her mother's habits when Cathleen was still a teenager. She remembered that her mother was often going off to use public pay phones too! She humorously pictured someday introducing her mother and Karl -- the two could sit around and talk about the similarities of clandestine tradecraft by the IRA and the KGB!

Beck returned a few minutes later. "We're set for brunch with Bob for tomorrow at 11:00, further up on Second Avenue, at a place called Danny Boys. You should feel right at home there!"

A few hours later, Cathleen and Karl were headed out from their hotel for dinner and a Broadway show. At about the same time, Viktor was taking a taxi to a bar out in the Brighton Beach area, home to thousands of

Russian émigrés. A bar, according to the FBI Organized Crime Squad of New York, which was owned by a senior member of the Mogilevich crime family of Russia.

Two large men in ill-fitting suits stopped Viktor and patted him down before he was admitted to a private room in the back where "Nick" was enjoying the company of two recently arrived teenage girls from Russia. For the moment they were his personal property. In a few weeks, they would be passed along into his profitable prostitution ring. Nick and his older brother, Arkady, had an arrangement with a senior general in the Russian Military Intelligence Service, the GRU. The general's people would find young girls out in the small towns of rural Russia, who had no real futures and who wanted to move to America, London or Paris. Nick's girls thought they had signed up for a program to study English in America and learn secretarial skills. They would arrive in New York City on a Russian military plane, carrying passports showing them to be dependents of Russian military personnel on holiday. Nick took their passports once they were through American Immigration control -- that was one hold over them. They would then be lodged in his "special houses", where they could enjoy all the food and liquor that they wanted, and even try drugs. They were told that their classes would start in a few weeks. But in the meantime, in order to pay off their "housing bill" to Nick, they needed to be nice to a few businessmen friends of his -- and so it began. On occasions, Nick would perform a few other little favors for Gennady, the GRU general, favors that usually involved industrial theft of new technological gadgets. The pay to Nick was good and it never hurt to have such a high-level friend, as Gennady Klemenko.

"Ah, my old friend Viktor," shouted Nikolai Nikolaiovich in Russian. "Nick" to his American partners, friends and clients. "Hey, you want a blow job? Olga here is getting pretty good." He let out a loud, alcohol-fueled laugh at his own private joke. A joke, because he suspected that Viktor was *"golyboi."*

The refined, educated Viktor stopped in front of the table and stared for a moment at Nick in silence, as he thought to himself how much he truly loathed the man. Hollywood couldn't have found an actor who looked and acted more like a Russian Mafioso thug than this genuine abuser of the human race. Nick was about fifty and broad-shouldered, but with a spreading middle. He had a mean face with a few small scars from many street fights as a youth.

"No thanks, I've come here on business," he replied with almost a sneer. The sophisticated Viktor hated dealing with the crude Nick. He wondered to himself, why was it that *"nekultyrni"* asses, such as Nick, always had all the money?

"Business? You've come here to pay me the $20,000 you owe me?" Nick switched to English and sent the girls over to another table. He didn't like to be distracted while talking business.

"Well, not directly, but it does concern money," replied Viktor as he took a seat.

"Not about money and horse racing I hope. You don't seem to have much luck when it comes to the combination of those two subjects." Nick was referring to Viktor's penchant for betting on horses -- horses that unfortunately liked to run behind other horses.

"No, not horses -- diamonds. The Romanov diamonds to be precise." That got Nick's attention. Most every Russian criminal for decades had heard the stories of the missing Romanov diamonds, probably worth hundreds of millions of dollars at today's prices. No Russian Mafioso had ever actually seen any of the diamonds, but many claimed to have had a fellow prisoner who had a grandfather who had told them a story about the jewels. The closest any of them had actually come to such famous diamonds was confidence games they had run against naive foreigners that had visited Mother Russia since the collapse of the Soviet Union. Occasionally, those were quite lucrative scams, but a chance to actually get one's hands on the Romanov diamonds -- that would be a real score.

"So, you've found the diamonds?" sarcastically asked Nick.

"If I had the diamonds, I wouldn't need you would I, but someone came to see me today that makes me wonder if he isn't on a good trail. You know who my grandmother was?"

"*Da, da,* you've told me a dozen times what big shots your ancestors were. What do they have to do with the Romanov diamonds?"

"When I was a small child, my grandmother would tell me stories about beautiful diamonds of the czar and czarina. It was all rather fantasy like and I always assumed they were just bedtime stories she'd made up. But then when she was in her late eighties and I had gone to visit her in England a few months before she died, she would ramble on when half asleep about the diamonds of the czar and how Yakov Mikhailovich had

Diamonds and Deceit

given them to her. Stories similar to what I remembered her telling me as a small child, except for the new part about Yakov. I still didn't take the stories seriously at the time."

"Let's get to the point of this meeting, Viktor. I have other things to do," he added, as he looked over at the two intoxicated teenagers and blew them a kiss.

"This afternoon, a professor from Indiana University came to see me, said he's writing a book about my grandmother and her writings. Claimed his ancestry is Austrian. If he's Austrian, I'm a Mexican. Anyway, he had a number of questions about whether Ivy ever talked about the royal family or about Yakov Yurovsky, their assassin. Wanted to know if my grandmother was senile late in life and whether I had in my possession any of her books."

"Did he say anything about diamonds?" asked an impatient Nick.

"Of course not, he wouldn't be that stupid if he's onto a lead to their location. But, I'm telling you, he's looking for those diamonds and thinks my grandmother left some clue as to their location. Seeing the skepticism on Nick's face, Viktor added, "You know, if you were to find those diamonds, you wouldn't have to take orders from your older brother, or from anybody for that matter, ever again." Viktor understood well Nick's pathological mind. He knew that working for Arkady, who he hated, was a particularly sore point with Nick.

"And you're certain that he isn't just some dotty old professor?"

"No way. I don't know what he is, but a simple, old, Austrian professor he isn't!"

"What exactly do you want from me? And more importantly, what's in it for me?"

"You have 'capabilities' that I obviously don't. You can investigate this man. Perhaps persuade him, shall we say, to tell you what he knows. As for what you get out of it, we split 60-40 to you, of whatever is eventually found."

"Let's say 90-10, plus I'll forget what you owe me now and if this turns out to be looking for the wind in a field, I won't have your legs broken. Is that agreeable?"

"A very generous offer on your part and I assure you this is no wild goose chase."

"You know where he's staying in Manhattan?"

"Unfortunately, not. I only know he lives out in Bloomington, Indiana and teaches at the university there." Viktor then gave Nick all the details he knew about Professor Beck, except he left out the part of the story about the audio versions of Ivy's stories. Come Monday morning, Viktor would look into getting his own audio copy of Ivy's readings of her novels. Perhaps he could figure out for himself why the professor had inquired about Ivy's sense of humor in doing those readings back in 1960 and then he might not need Nick at all. A split of 100-0 sounded a much better deal than the one he'd just made with the gangster.

Cathleen and Karl both enjoyed the Broadway musical comedy show, but it had been a full day and they headed straight for their hotel afterwards. It might be the city that never sleeps, but they needed theirs. They were exhausted and within minutes of locking their room door they were in bed. Cathleen fell quickly asleep. He laid there in that half-asleep state, his mind churning about Ivy's cryptic message: *"Books of historical facts, even if the facts have to change with the times."* Strangely, his mind drifted back to Bergen and what a lovely day it had been. Something kept clawing at his memory as he drifted in and out of a dream of that Sunday in Norway. What was it? He was back in Bergen, killing time by shopping in little stores by the bay. There was the young Russian girl in a small store selling Russian *matriochka* dolls, icons and old Soviet-era books. All part of the Russian nostalgia for the "old days." Suddenly, he sat up, wide awake, as if cold water had been thrown on him. "Of course!" he shouted out loud, scaring the heck out of Cathleen and waking her.

"What is it?" she sleepily asked?

"That's it, it has to be."

"Has to be what? What are you shouting about?"

Beck turned on the nightstand lamp. "What books of historical facts had to change with the times in the Soviet Union? The Great Soviet Encyclopedia! As people fell out of favor, especially during Stalin's years, articles about those people would be replaced and even photographs retouched so as to remove "non-persons" from them. It wouldn't do to have a disgraced person appear in a photo with the great Stalin in the official encyclopedia!"

Cathleen knew of this Soviet practice of conveniently rewriting history to fit whatever was the current dogma or to enhance the image of whoever was in power. She remembered the famous story of how the article about the secret police Chief Lavrentiy Beria had to be cut out of every encyclopedia in the country, once he'd lost out in the power struggle after Stalin's death in 1953. That page was replaced with a new one, containing an expanded article about the Bering Sea. "It does seem to fit her cryptic statement, doesn't it?"

"Yes, and the set had fifty or sixty volumes to it, as I recall, so there would have been room for many diamonds."

"What exactly did she say in her audio message? That her true friend Pavel Ivanovich put them in the books? Did she mean he simply cut out spaces in the pages for the jewels?"

"Hard to believe they would have remained undiscovered for very long if that was the case. Could he have somehow put them in the book spines?"

"Maybe. Do you know anything about this Pavel Ivanovich?"

"Not yet."

They discussed their exciting theory for a little while longer, then crawled back under the covers. Any research into Pavel would have to wait till their return to Bloomington. She fell asleep with her head on his chest. She felt very safe in his arms.

The Bloody Mary's at Danny Boys on Sunday morning were well made, with just enough Tobasco sauce in them to wake up the taste buds. The decor of the bar was pretty much the same as at all the Irish establishments in South Boston where Cathleen had grown up. They'd cleared away enough of the sports banners on one wall to have a tribute to all the firemen and policemen who'd died on September 11th. Otherwise, one Irish pub looked about like any other, anywhere in the world. The waitresses and bartenders were all authentic Irish -- maybe they had work permits, maybe they didn't and nobody who drank there cared.

Karl and Cathleen had secured a booth before Bob arrived and ordered a round of Bloody Mary's for the three of them. The tune "Four Green Fields" was playing on the music system. Cathleen guessed which one was Bob while he was still half way across the room, heading in their direction. His face remained pointed towards Karl, but his eyes kept darting around the room to check out who else was in the bar. She'd watched her grandfather do the same thing when he entered a room. Bob was about five foot six, thinning, fair hair and lots of freckles. He appeared to be a few years older than Karl, but still in good physical shape. He had the walk of a man who'd spent many years in the military. The blue blazer, tie and gray slacks seemed a bit much for this particular bar.

"Bob, this is Cathleen."

"A pleasure to meet you," he replied with a sincere smile and a firm handshake.

"I'm glad to meet you and see that you really do exist. I'm never sure whether to believe everything Karl tells me or not," she said with a wide grin.

He knew instantly he was going to like Cathleen. "Oh, you can't believe hardly anything this dumb Russian says," replied Bob while loosening his tie. "Sorry for being overdressed, but had to look respectable for mass at St. Patrick's you know."

They ordered their food and went through the typical introductory conversation, about where she'd grown up in Boston, gone to school and how she'd met Karl. Towards the end of the brunch, Bob himself brought up the subject for the real purpose of the meeting. "Karl told me that you're intrigued by the Group. What would you like to know?"

Cathleen was taken a bit by surprise at his directness, about a presumably very secret enterprise. "Well, who started this group and when?"

"About six years ago, a handful of retired, senior officials from different U.S. government organizations that had well-known, three-letter names were at a funeral for a friend who had died during a covert operation. The consensus among them was that the person had needlessly died because of the general lack of testosterone at the top of those organizations, and also over at the White House, to act quickly enough to save him -- diplomatic niceties be damned. After enough rounds of alcohol, this group decided that if the government bureaucracy had grown so sclerotic, it was time for a small, professional group of private citizens to give attention to delicate problems of the world. It started with these few Americans, but has expanded to include a few likeminded foreigners as well."

"And how is this group financed? From the few things Karl has told me, his trips and operations are very well funded. Retiree pensions can't be that good."

"No, they're not. The money comes in from a small number of wealthy, private contributors and not just right-wing fanatics either. You'd be surprised at some of the names across the political spectrum that see the value of such a non-governmental entity. They don't know the specifics and they have no say in what actions are taken. They simply trust the word of the leadership of the group that the right things are being done."

Cathleen figured if Bob was being so frank, she'd ask her hardest question. "I can see doing some of the espionage missions, but what gives your group the right to kill someone? We have a pretty strong tradition in America, in fact in most civilized countries, of trial by jury, one's right to confront witnesses, etc. I don't see France or England going around assassinating people."

Bob gave Karl a quick glance and a little smile. "Well, Cathleen, you might be surprised at what "civilized countries" do when they think their vital interests are at stake. But to your specific question about our group and assassination, this option has only been used in a very few situations. There are five people who serve as the 'leadership' of the group and the decision to kill someone has to be a unanimous vote by them. Then, participation by any individual in carrying out any aspect of the planned operation is on a voluntary basis. There were actually several people besides Karl involved in the Bergen operation, all of whom knew exactly what was the end goal of the plan. One person did the initial casing of the target. Another smuggled the rifle into Norway and a third passed it to Karl. You know, I've heard rumors that on occasion, the IRA would kill any member of their own that they believed to be working for the British -- without there being a trial by jury."

"Touché, about the IRA. So this fellow in Norway was that much of a threat?"

"Yes, he was quite a bad guy and for whom there appeared to be no other solution. His gathering of funds for terrorism, recruiting young men to be suicide bombers and the planning of attacks was deemed unacceptable to be allowed to continue. And these were attacks on innocent civilian targets, not military ones." He pulled five photos from his side coat pocket. "I thought this might come up, so I brought along a few pictures of Abdul's work. Sorry, the ones of the school are a bit graphic. Thirty-two children died in that bombing."

Given her family connection to Northern Ireland, Cathleen had seen pictures of dead bodies before, but the picture of numerous body parts in a school playground got to her. She handed them back to Bob and stared down at her plate for a minute.

"Pressure on the Norwegian government to act had failed several times. Trying to generate public pressure for something to be done within Norway, and around Europe, by publicizing facts about his work, had also failed. So, the decision was taken to solve the problem unilaterally and unofficially. You also need to understand that by killing Abdul, we not only stopped his activities, but it sent a message throughout similar radical Muslim underground groups. The message that there would be a penalty for their activities, even if they could manage to avoid legal punishment from their gutless, host countries."

Cathleen still wasn't totally convinced, but finally replied that, "I'm always telling my students that the world is one of grays, rarely easy black and white political situations. The question of assassination of really bad people is obviously one of the murkier situations. Naturally, it's a whole lot easier to discuss the hypothetical assassination of a Hitler or a Pol Pot, than to hear about a real, current-day case."

"True, the real world is a very messy place," added Karl.

"Well, thank you for your frankness in discussing this with me," concluded Cathleen.

"Changing to a more pleasant topic, what brought you two to New York? Surely, it wasn't just to visit me!"

Karl answered that one. "I had to come here for some research on this book on Russian literature I'm writing and we just decided to turn the trip into a Big Apple weekend -- Broadway show, good dining and a little shopping."

"I've been telling you for twenty years my old friend, there's nothing like this city anywhere else in the world. But if you're happy out there in the cornfields of Indiana... Although, I may raise my opinion of Bloomington, now that I see what charming women you're hiding out there -- and Irish women at that!"

The waitress came by to check if anyone wanted another drink. The two gentlemen passed, but Cathleen ordered a cocktail.

"I'd like a vodka martini, shaken not stirred."

"Yes, m' am. Be right up."

After the waitress had walked away, Cathleen leaned forward and told her two old spy companions. "I've always wanted to say that line." All three laughed.

CHAPTER 6

BLOOMINGTON

On Monday morning, Cathleen and Karl took the morning flight back to Indianapolis, retrieved his car and an hour later, were home in Bloomington. They were both a bit tired from all the running around as tourists, but in very good moods. They'd made progress on the search for the Romanov jewels, had several excellent meals and seen a good musical comedy on Broadway. Most importantly for Cathleen, by meeting with Bob, she felt better about Karl's occasional work with this private organization. She wasn't completely convinced about the wisdom of their full range of "options for action", as Bob called them, i.e. murder, but was glad to have learned that the man she loved was involved with a well-intentioned and professional group. These weren't just some right-wing crazies, who liked to run around in the woods of Michigan shooting paint guns.

On Monday evening, three twenty-something Russian émigrés working for Nick Tsimbal also flew from New York to the Indianapolis airport, rented a Cadillac and headed south through the cornfields of Indiana. Alerted of their travel by the New York field office, four local FBI special agents watched their arrival and in two black Crown Victorias, followed the Caddy south, down Route 37. They wondered where in the hell, three big city, Russian Mafia thugs were headed to in southern Indiana. The FBI men were still scratching their heads an hour later when the Russians took rooms at the most expensive downtown hotel that

Bloomington had to offer. The Feds left the most junior special agent in one car, to sit and keep an eye on the rented Cadillac all night, while the other three registered at a much more modest chain motel out near the 37 bypass. To get the US government discount rate, they showed their FBI credentials during registration. This freaked out the college-student, night clerk, who had a bag of weed stashed under the counter to help him pass the boring night. Soon as they left the lobby, he flushed it all down the manager's office toilet.

The three Brighton Beach Russians found no one in their hotel bar, so they ventured out onto the streets of Bloomington. The first place they came to was Grazei's Italian restaurant. They found a table in the fairly empty bar area and all ordered beers. They chatted in Russian.

"So, what exactly are we looking for here?" asked Alex of Oleg, the twenty-five year old leader of the trio. Oleg had moved up into "management", after having killed a couple of troublesome Colombians for Nick earlier in the year. "Like I already told you, we're to find out everything we can about the research work this Professor Beck is doing on Ivy Litvinova. Grab his papers at his house maybe, ask him directly, maybe. That's all you need to know." The fact was, that's all he knew himself. Nick had been rather vague when ordering Oleg to make the trip to Indiana. "I got a home address of the professor. We'll get started tomorrow morning on him." While answering his colleague's question, Oleg's attention had really been on a nearby table of five college girls, obviously celebrating something. He decided to go introduce himself.

"Ladies, what are you celebrating tonight?" asked Oleg in his heavily accented English.

"It's my birthday," shouted out one of the drunken young ladies, who then put down another tequila shot.

"Birthday party. That's great, but you know what you're missing for real party? Me and my friends. I'm Oleg. You should invite us over to join you."

The leader of the five look-alike, dyed blondes turned to take a careful look at Oleg. She eyed his gold chain and gaudy-colored sport coat. "Auditions for "Guys and Dolls" ended last week." The girls all laughed at Suzy's brilliant one-liner and turned away from him.

Oleg was not accustomed to having his approaches turned down. The women in Brighton Beach bars knew who he was, and thus knew better than to offend him. "What, you all lesbians?" he angrily asked.

Suzy was about to respond, when Vincenzo appeared behind Oleg and said to him very quietly, "I think it's time for you to leave."

Oleg turned around to face a well-dressed, middle-aged Italian. He wasn't any bigger than he was, but Oleg recognized a look on Vinny's face that he'd seen on Nick's on a few occasions. It wasn't a friendly look. His two friends started to rise from their table when two very large guys from the kitchen appeared; one carrying a meat cleaver. Vincenzo often gave members of the football team summer jobs, so that they could stay in town and work out in the off-season. Two defensive linemen had secured jobs in the kitchen that summer.

"Don't worry about your check. Just leave, now," added Vincenzo.

Oleg didn't like the odds, particularly since he hadn't been able to bring a gun with him on the plane. And he knew that Nick would be very unhappy if the three of them wound up in the local jail, instead of doing what they'd been sent to town to do.

"You come visit me sometime in New York old man," was the best retort that Oleg could think of on short notice. He nodded to his two colleagues that they were leaving. Out on the sidewalk, Oleg decided that he might have to put up with being humiliated by an old Italian, because of the circumstances, but he was certainly going to take out his anger on this stupid professor who'd brought them to town in the first place. The original plan had been to first, ask nicely. Now, Oleg decided, they'd beat the hell out of Beck just for fun before asking him anything. They headed for their hotel, where the young FBI agent still had the red Cadillac under close observation.

As the three Russians withdrew from the restaurant, Vinny turned back to the girls and said, "I'm terribly sorry for the disturbance." He nodded to their waitress, standing nearby. "Bring the ladies another round, on me." The girls started slapping their hands in unison on the table and shouting "Vinny, Vinny." He bowed slightly at the waist and returned to the bar.

On Tuesday morning, Cathleen and Karl headed off very early on foot from his house to campus. She went to her office, and he to the Wells library for more research. His main task was to try to find out who had been Ivy's great friend, Pavel Ivanovich? Millions of Russian males had this common first name and patronymic, so he needed to come up with a last name, or something to narrow down his search based on Pavel's profession or location. This person was probably also in Sverdlovsk in 1938 and perhaps he'd been a bookbinder, but both of those assumptions were only educated guesses. Fortunately, the IU Library had one of the best Russian-Studies collections in the country. The graduate student assistant of the Slavic section found for him a Sverdlovsk city phone directory for 1938, which listed an antiquarian book and repair shop. There were no personal names listed with the store, but there was an address. At least it was a starting point. After three more hours of digging, Beck needed a break and headed home for lunch. A gentle, but steady, summer rain shower began to fall when he was only half way across campus and naturally, he had no umbrella with him. The morning weather forecast had said nothing about a chance of rain. He actually enjoyed listening to the rain hit the leaves as he tried as best he could to stay under the tree canopy, but running from tree to tree was not an effective way to stay dry. As a soaked Beck turned the corner onto 1st street, about fifty yards from his house, he noticed a young man standing across the street from his home, also trying to stay dry under a tree. He too had forgotten to bring an umbrella. He was smoking a cigarette and doing nothing. Even at that distance, he looked Russian to Beck. Though officially retired from the business for twenty years, Beck knew surveillance when he saw it. He kept his head down as he walked right on past his own home. At the start of the next block, he saw two more, young, Russian-looking men in a bright red Cadillac. The two had nice tans, cold chains and open neck shirts under their sport coats. They, too, were doing nothing. He'd never seen that car before in his neighborhood, nor any of the young men. Further down the block was a black Crown Vic with two very clean-cut, all-American-looking young men in suits and ties, doing nothing. "Christ", he thought to himself, "what is this, a surveillance convention on my street!"

He immediately phoned Cathleen on his cell phone as he headed back to campus. "How about joining me for lunch at the Tudor Room in the Student Union?"

"Sure, I was going to take a break in an hour or so. How about one o'clock?"

His voice remained calm, but turned a bit authoritative. "I'm starving now. Can you meet me there, in say, ten minutes?"

Call it woman's intuition or just her imagination, but she sensed that there was something more afoot than just his hunger. "Sure, I'll leave now."

The soaked Beck stopped briefly at his office in Ballantine Hall where he kept a spare shirt and dress coat, for emergencies when he had to look respectable. This qualified as an emergency. Suzanne, the Slavic Department secretary, also took pity on him when she saw him and loaned him an umbrella.

The Tudor Room in the large Student Union building was aptly named, with its limestone walls, dark wood paneling and chandeliers hanging from wooden beams in its 75 foot high ceiling. There were massive, antique tapestries on several walls, which gave the place the look of a medieval Great Hall. For summertime, it was unusually packed. Beck then remembered that Mini-University was underway. This was an annual gathering of some 500 elderly alumni who came back to campus for a week each summer to hear lectures and pretend they were nineteen again. Beck in fact was scheduled to give a lecture the very next day to part of the group about Dostoevsky's famous novel, "Crime and Punishment." Beck was a regular at the dining room and had befriended the young man who played noontime manager, while working on his doctorate. When he saw Professor Beck and Cathleen at the back of the waiting line, he waved to them and nodded for Beck to drift on into the dining area. He gave them a nice table under a window.

"You do have friends in lots of places don't you," teased Cathleen.

"Always nice to have friends." Beck was a firm believer in equality and democracy, but he'd observed that even in the great democracy that America was, certain groups enjoyed certain perks. Doctors held their professional conferences in lovely resorts, businessmen wrote off golf games as business expenses on their tax filings and politicians - well, they had so many perks and privileges that one couldn't count them all. As a lowly college professor with few such perks, Beck figured that getting to jump ahead of a long line at his favorite campus restaurant didn't make him too much of a hypocrite as a supporter of equality.

They started down the self-serve buffet line. "Professor Beck, how are you?"

Karl turned around to see Professor Short of the Classical Studies Department. "I'm fine. Did you already give your talk for Mini-U?"

"I spoke this morning, on gambling in ancient Rome. I think it went over reasonably well. I'm lunching with some of the attendees now. When is your presentation?"

"Tomorrow -- on "Crime and Punishment"."

"Will you make poker night this Thursday?"

"Not, this week, I'm going out of town for a few days. Perhaps the following week. By the way, this is Cathleen Spenser of the History Department."

"Ah, very nice to meet you." He reached over and shook her hand. "Well, I'll let you two get on with your lunch. Oh, yes, Karl, do remind me to tell you what Cato had to say." He have Karl a little wink and moved off.

"Interesting fellow," commented Cathleen as they moved on down the food line.

"Yes he is. He cites Roman poetry while playing poker. I think he does that to annoy the other players and distract their thinking."

Cathleen and Karl returned to their table with their food and then he began to explain the reason for his sudden desire for lunch. "I don't want to worry you, but some people are watching my house. They look Russian, but not professionals like I was. I don't know who they are, but one was standing in the rain across from my house and two more were nearby, in a flash car that only some big city pimp would drive. And in the next block, two young men in suits and ties in your standard US government-issue car are watching the pimp car."

Had it been anyone else telling her this, she would have started laughing, but given his background, she remained open minded. "What makes you think these 'Russians' are staking out something on your street or your house in particular?"

He gave her a little smile. "I do have some practice at this. I know when a man is doing surveillance, but all these guys are such amateurs. Nor did the Russians seem to even know me on sight, as I walked right by all three and they showed no reaction."

"Don't you have an emergency phone number or something for this sort of situation?"

"Twenty, even ten years ago, yes, I did. But after so many years have passed without incident, I doubt the old number even still works. Besides, if the Russian Intelligence Service was watching me, it would be much more professional."

"So, who else have you pissed off?" she asked with a smile.

"Perhaps a better question is, who have I spoken to recently that might have triggered an interest in me by Russian-looking thugs?"

"Viktor Litvinov. But why?"

"I tried being subtle, but maybe he guessed that I have some other interest in his grandmother besides her writings. If that's it, then he probably knows more about Ivy and the jewels than he let on, though Viktor sure didn't come across as the kind of guy who had these types of friends to call on for a favor."

"So, should we go kidnap one of them and make him talk or just shoot all three?" she asked with a perfectly straight face.

"Just how much time did you spend with your IRA grandfather while growing up?"

"Sorry, I got excited. Well, what's your plan?"

"I gave this a little thought while walking here. First, let's take your car and go spend the night over at the little town of Nashville in a private B&B -- it's twenty minutes away and there'd be no computer credit card record to trace of our being there. Then, after I give my talk tomorrow afternoon, we'll fly to Moscow and start searching for the jewels. Whoever these guys are, they can then sit here and watch my house and each other for the rest of the summer for all I care. If Viktor is now in pursuit of the diamonds as well, we may not have much time to spare, if we want to get there first. As soon as he listens to the audio recording of Ivy reading "His Master's Voice", which I'm sure he'll be doing in a matter of days, he'll be working with the same clues as we have. The race is on."

"Well, I'm glad to see that you don't make snap decisions! But I do see a few flaws in your plan. First, a few days ago you were skeptical that Ivy's story could be true. Now, we're going to fly off to Russia to pursue this. What exactly is it that we're going to do there? All we have now is a nice theory about the Great Soviet Encyclopedia."

Beck pulled from his leather satchel a Russian book he'd found that morning at the library about Soviet foreign policy, published in 1936 in Moscow. It had several photos of the then Soviet Foreign Minister, Maxim Litvinov. One of them, a happy family picture with Ivy by his side, in his den at home in Moscow. "What do you see on the book shelf just to the right of Maxim's head?"

She squinted at the small photo. "My god, it's a set of the Great Soviet Encyclopedia!"

"Right, so we know that as of 1936, they had a set of the encyclopedias.

I also found an address for a book repair shop in Sverdlovsk in 1938, so we have a place to start looking for Pavel Ivanovich."

"OK, but what about reservations, visas, clothes for you and oh, yes, the little detail of the Russian Government once tried to kill you?"

"You already have a visa for your upcoming trip in July, which is valid now. I have an alias credit card and passport, which has a valid multiple entry business visa for Russia. I can slip into my house tonight and get those documents and some clothes. As for airline tickets and hotel reservations, all that takes is money. Once there, you just tell the State Library in Moscow that you've arrived a few weeks early. You can do your research while I go look for the jewels."

She hated to admit it, but he did have answers to every objection she could think of at the moment, except for one. "But is it safe for you go back to Russia, in whatever name?"

"It's been twenty years, I doubt if my whereabouts is at the top of anybody's to-do list today, even if they think I'm still alive. Besides, I don't exactly look the same now, with white hair and a wrinkled face. I made a brief trip to southern Russia last fall in this name without incident, so I think it's safe to go to Moscow."

"Would it be easier if you travelled alone? This is an intriguing historical scavenger hunt I'd like to be part of, but how does this alias persona of yours explain traveling with me? Am I going to make your trip more complicated than it already will be?"

"I think this is an adventure we'll enjoy sharing and until we know who these guys are, I don't feel comfortable leaving you alone here in Bloomington anyway. Too many people around here know of our close association, and if they can't locate me, they could turn to you for information on my location." He didn't want to alarm Cathleen, but the fate of Olga was on his mind. He would take no chances of any harm coming to her while he was away. "As for you traveling with Mr. Blackwell, if asked, our story will simply be that I met you in the JFK airport cocktail lounge."

"Great, first you tell me I may be in danger here and then that I have to play the role of a cheap slut who let an old, rich guy pick me up in an airport bar! This just gets better and better."

"It will get you up into business class." He put money on the table for the check.

She gave him a big smile as they rose from the table and she took his arm. "Well, in that case, let's go sugar daddy!"

They went first to her place so that she could pack, get her passport and her car. Next, to Beck's bank where he withdrew $20,000 in hundreds, and then they stopped at a small travel office on the edge of town to check on possible flights and hotel reservations in Moscow for the day after tomorrow. As Beck couldn't get to his alias documents till late that night, he explained that he was still thinking about going or not. Cathleen went ahead and provided her credit card information for a business class plane ticket and to reserve a hotel room in Moscow, if one was available on such short notice in the summertime.

They left the travel agent to do her research and headed east for Nashville. "Why didn't we just wait till tomorrow and book the flights together?" asked Cathleen.

"This way, there will be separate flight records on separate credit charges, so we won't obviously appear linked, if anybody checks the airline computer travel records. You'll start in Indianapolis, me from Cincinnati or Chicago. We'll link up at JFK."

"You are a devious man. I'm glad you're on my side!"

They made a quick stop on the way to Nashville at a discount store to buy a few items for Beck, including some black jeans, black long-sleeve shirt and a sock cap to cover his white hair. He also bought a miniature flash light and a thin sheet of flexible red plastic, which he later attached over the lens of the light with a rubber band to create for himself a "safe" light. It wouldn't be visible from outside his house, but would provide sufficient illumination to allow him to maneuver around the furniture. It being a week night, they easily found a small B&B near Nashville that had a room available. The host happily took cash and didn't even smile when they registered as Mr. and Mrs. Smith. Over a great dinner of country cooking at the Hob Nob restaurant on the main street in the little town, the couple discussed again the possibilities of who might be watching Beck's house. They still came up with no better suspect than Viktor.

Beck looked at the clock on the wall. "We should head back to the B&B and go to bed soon."

She looked at her watch. It was barely eight o'clock. "And just why do we need to go to bed so early?" she inquired with a mischievous grin.

"Because, we'll be getting up at 4 a.m. and driving back to Bloomington.

If anyone is watching my house all night, by 5 a.m. he'll be really bored, if not asleep, yet it will still be dark."

"You're quite knowledgeable about the night time habits of people. Does this come from sneaking out of women's homes before sunrise?"

"That's it exactly."

He would have preferred not involving her in his little nighttime operation, but decided he needed her as a lookout and getaway driver, if a hasty exit might be needed. Fortunately, one could easily walk from the next street over through his neighbor's yard and into his own backyard. There was then a line of thick bushes almost the entire way up to his house, so he would have good cover right up to the rear doorway. Anybody staking out the front of his house would never see him approach. If, however, someone was waiting inside for him, that would be a different problem altogether. As he lay snuggled up behind Cathleen that night, his arm over her waist, he thought about how much she meant to him. He realized that he was becoming very attached to her, which scared him a little. He'd dated a few women and had sex with a few, over the last fifteen or so years, but he'd never let himself get as emotionally attached to anyone as he was already with Cathleen. He'd lost one woman he loved and would do everything he could to protect Cathleen. He didn't like possibly putting her in harm's way, but Cathleen struck him as a woman who could take care of herself pretty well.

The B&B had a separate entrance for guests and the car park was a fair distance from the house, so their middle-of-the night departure didn't wake the host. In twenty minutes, they were back in Bloomington and nearing Beck's neighborhood. As they approached the place to park the car on 2nd Street, he reviewed with Cathleen her instructions. "You give two short honks if you see something suspicious out here, then drive away, but don't speed. You go to the all-night Waffle House and wait there. There are almost always cops in there at this time of the morning having breakfast. Same destination if you hear shots. Otherwise, sit here and wait till I return and be ready to drive like the wind if you see me running." He gave her a quick kiss and then he was gone.

Beck moved slowly along the line of bushes, stopping every twenty yards where he waited a minute or two to see if he saw or heard anything. Unfortunately, his handgun was up in his bedroom, so he stopped first in his garage and armed himself with a 15 inch pipe wrench. Not much use against a 9 mm at a distance, but for close-up fighting, it would make an impression on any opponent's skull. He reached the back door and unlocked it as quietly as possible. After a quick search, he decided he was alone in the house, but he hadn't been the first person to make a nighttime visit. He found his den ransacked, as well as the drawers of his bedroom. A number of his notebooks filled with notes about Ivy were missing, but the thieves had paid no attention to the box of CDs with the audio versions of Ivy's readings. Obviously, they hadn't known exactly what they were looking for. Luckily for Beck, he'd had the most important part of his research in his satchel that he'd taken to the library the previous morning. He retrieved his Makarov gun and then quickly packed a suitcase of clothes. He returned to the garage and opened the concealed trap door in the wall beneath his work bench to retrieve his alias documents and "Mr. Blackwell's" cell phone.

He was back at the car in fifteen minutes, but it had seemed like an eternity to Cathleen. He laid down on the backseat and told her to drive slowly away from the area. At the edge of town, he joined her in the front seat.

"Somebody had been there before me and searched the place, taking some of my Ivy notebooks, but it doesn't appear that they really knew what they were looking for."

"That would definitely seem to point back to your friend Viktor. Unless competition in the field of Russian literature is so fierce that you guys burgle each other's research in the dead of night."

"No, that's only done in the Classics department. I think that Viktor already had some clue that his grandmother was somehow connected to the missing Romanov jewels, but he doesn't have the specifics I recently found on those audio recordings. I told you I felt he was hiding something, during my talk with him. My visit and questions confirmed for him what he already suspected and he sent these guys to find out what I know."

By 6 a.m., they were back in bed in Nashville and slept till almost ten. After a hearty breakfast of freshly made waffles with blueberries at the B&B, they drove back to Bloomington. Their first stop was the travel agency. The helpful, middle-aged lady had good news for them.

"Your airline reservations are set. Finding a hotel room was a little harder, but I finally found you a nice room at the Hotel *Metropol,* in downtown Moscow. I booked you a room with a King bed." She looked at Beck and gave him a knowing smile. This wasn't the first time she'd booked travel for an elderly professor and a much younger person to some city away from Bloomington, though generally not so far away. For heterosexual couples it was usually New York or Miami, for the gays, it always seemed to be to San Francisco.

"And have you decided to accompany the young lady?"

"No, I'm afraid I have to stay behind and work."

The woman looked positively crestfallen. Not only at the loss of the anticipated commission on another business class air ticket, but her romantic fantasies of what was going on between the two were shattered as well.

Once back in her car, Beck used the cell phone he'd retrieved during the night to call the travel agent in Chicago that Mr. Blackwell used regularly and booked his similar reservations, but starting in Cincinnati.

"OK. We're on the same flights from New York onward. After my lecture this afternoon at Mini-University, we'll drive to Cincinnati and spend the night there. Tomorrow, I'll sit around at the airport till my flight departs from there, while you drive back up I-74 and begin from the Indianapolis airport. There'll be no link between Blackwell and Spenser at all, till we happen to meet at JFK."

She dropped Beck near the Student Union Building. He would just hang out there till his one o'clock presentation. Cathleen kept their suitcases and his research and drove to Grazei's to have a leisurely lunch. Beck directed her there as he knew she'd be safe under the watchful eye of Vincenzo.

"Ladies and gentlemen, it's good to see so many of you back again at Mini-University." Beck was a perennial favorite and always drew around 200 people to his talks, no matter what his topic. The ladies found him charming and everyone loved his sense of humor. He told great stories. No one cared if all of them were true or not.

"The tragic villain of our famous story is Raskolnikov, who -- and I hate to spoil the ending for those of you who haven't yet finished all 576 pages of the assigned reading -- ends up in prison in Siberia." After the laughter subsided, Beck proceeded to explain the basic plot of the story and most importantly, why it was still considered today to be one of the great works of Russian literature. About two-thirds of the way through his ninety-minute presentation, Beck noticed two of the young Russian surveillants from the day before on his street come into the back of the Whittenberger Auditorium. He guessed that not having found him, or even much of his research about Ivy Litvinova, during their midnight visit to his house, they'd decided to try to track him down on campus. Unfortunately, there were no side or backstage doors to the auditorium. He would need a distraction.

"Folks, I have a special treat for you today. Two up-and-coming young Russian authors are here and have agreed to answer questions about crime fiction today in Russia and give autographs." He pointed at the two men standing at the back right corner of the auditorium. "Thank you for coming today." Amidst the applause, at least fifty of the attendees rushed towards and encircled the two bewildered Russians. Beck moved quickly up the left-hand side aisle and out one of the doors, claiming to people that wanted to speak to him along the way that he really had to get to the bathroom, but would be right back. Out in the large hallway before the auditorium, he also spotted the two "government men" he'd seen in the Crown Vic on his street the day the Russians showed up. They didn't appear to recognize him. Their final report would note the peculiar fact that two of the Mafioso visitors to Bloomington had taken in a lecture on Tolstoy.

Beck turned left and headed into the hotel portion of the building, then down a back staircase. Instead of exiting through one of the main level doors, he used the basement to reverse course, back to the other far end of the massive building and out a service door. A freshman orientation tour group was passing by. He joined into the middle of the hundred or so new students and their parents, having a guided tour of the campus. He stayed with them until they stopped at the Sample Gates at the western edge of the campus, for a talk by one of the student volunteers. Beck separated from them and headed down Kirkwood Avenue on his own. He covered the six blocks to reach the square and Grazei's in record time.

He found Cathleen sitting at a table in the back of the restaurant. She'd just started on her dessert that Vinny had insisted on her trying. She looked at her watch. "You're done early."

"It was a tough audience, especially the two young Russian guys I saw yesterday near my house who showed up at my lecture. So, I cut my talk short and got out of there when I saw an opportunity. I don't think any of the Russians saw me walk down here, but it's hard to say if there are only three of them in town. Soon as you finish that, let's hit the road for Cincinnati."

At that point, Vinny brought over another piece of his famous cheesecake and a fork for Beck. "No sense you letting her eat alone."

Beck knew that you never turned down a piece of his cheesecake, which he had flown in special from a little shop in Newark. "Thanks, looks delicious." He picked up the fork and began to eat. Vinny walked away satisfied and took up his traditional spot at the end of the long bar, resplendent in his black silk sport coat, white shirt and a black tie.

A minute later, Alex of the Russian trio, approached Karl and Cathleen at their table. He was one of the Russians who'd been in the auditorium. Once he'd escaped from the throng of alumni and got outside, he got lucky and had seen Beck hurrying down Kirkwood and followed. He had his right hand in his coat pocket. Perhaps he was bluffing. Perhaps he'd acquired a gun since the embarrassing incident in Grazei's on Monday night. "Let's go some place where we can talk, privately." He motioned for the two of them to rise and to walk in front of him towards the front door of the restaurant. They did so. Vinny noticed that they hadn't finished their desserts.

As they approached Vincenzo, he asked Beck, "Will we see you next Tuesday night?"

Beck responded, "Not if that piano player of yours keeps playing all of those horrible, old Elvis tunes."

Vincenzo got the subtle hint. He also recognized the young man walking behind Beck from Monday night. After the Russian passed by, Vinny snapped his fingers to the buxom, raven-haired girl behind the bar that day. She quickly handed him a fifteen-inch long piece of lead pipe, half of it covered with golf club grip material. Alex never felt a thing as he crumpled to the ground after the blow to the back of his neck.

"Thanks," said Beck.

"Perhaps you two might want to use my back exit?" suggested Vinny. He asked no questions of Beck as to why some young Russian tough had tried kidnapping him.

"Will you have trouble over this?" asked Beck.

"No, I've dealt with this Russian bum before."

As the two exited out the back door, the waitress handed Vinny a short rubber hose connected to a funnel and a bottle of vodka. He sat Alex up against the bar, put the hose down his throat and poured vodka into him. When he would be found later by the police in an alley, his blood alcohol content would test at 1.6 and the conclusion drawn that he had fallen while drunk and injured himself.

All was going well, except that Cathleen's car was parked out on the square. They quickly got in it and drove away. Unfortunately, Oleg was sitting out on the square, waiting for the return of Alex. He noticed the couple and wrote down her license plate number. Another one of those dumb, blind bad luck instances, like in Bergen.

The Indianapolis FBI final report back to New York noted that the three Russians appeared to have had a run-in with one Vincenzo Lorenzo, formerly of Newark, New Jersey, while in Bloomington. They asked Bureau Headquarters in Washington DC for any information on Mr. Lorenzo. The field report concluded that it wasn't clear, exactly what was the purpose of the Russians' visit to Bloomington. The New York FBI office dutifully filed the report and moved on with their other investigations.

CHAPTER 7

MOSCOW

The following evening, Cathleen was sitting in the Business Class Lounge at New York's JFK International Airport when Mr. Robert Blackwell, a businessman of Chicago, sat down next to her.

"Hi, I'm Robbie."

"I'm Cathleen." She was relieved to see him. She'd had a horrible feeling that his plane out of Cincinnati would be delayed and then she wouldn't know whether to continue on to Moscow without him or not. "How long are we supposed to pretend that we've just met?"

"That story is more for once we land in Moscow."

"Too bad. I thought you were going to buy me a drink, tell me how your wife back in Chicago doesn't understand you and offer to show me the nightspots of Moscow." She nodded towards the bar. "There's a guy up at the bar who's been eyeing me up and down. I bet he'd buy me a drink."

Robbie leaned over to her and kissed her neck. "Now he won't." They both laughed. Not much had happened since she'd dropped him at the Cincinnati airport that morning, so soon they both lapsed into reading magazines. When the first announcement was made that their flight was ready to board, Blackwell told Cathleen he'd be right back and went over to a courtesy phone on a table in the corner.

"Hey, Bob. It's Blackwell. I'm at JFK waiting for my flight."

"Robbie, I wasn't expecting to hear from you. Aren't you supposed to be convalescing out in Indiana?" replied Bob Jones.

"I need to make a quick little trip to Moscow with my young friend. Just thought I should let someone know, so that the bills will get paid while I'm traveling."

"How did you get a visa for Russia?" asked the clearly surprised Jones.

"Had a multiple entry visa from my trip last fall to Odessa for Joan. You were off in Asia for several months when I traveled. I guess you never heard about it."

"What the hell are you up to? Does Joan know about this?"

"Need to know and all that old friend. I'll be checking my email regularly, so do let me know if anything develops further on that Norway situation."

"Where in Moscow will you be staying?"

"They just called my flight. Have to run. I'll phone you when I get back." Blackwell hung up and returned to Cathleen. "Shall we board?"

"Who did you call? Another of your many girlfriends?"

"I had to inform Bob that I was using these documents, so that the bills would for sure be paid while I'm traveling. He wasn't happy at all. I knew he wouldn't be. That's why I waited till the last minute to inform him, so it would be too late for him to do anything."

"Will you get in trouble with the Group, for using their documents for personal reasons?"

"Oh, nothing real serious. I also wanted him to know this passport was in play, in case anything more develops in Norway that he thinks I should immediately know about."

They boarded, took their comfortable seats and enjoyed a glass of champagne before takeoff. It had been a stressful and tiring 48 hours and shortly after dinner, both were sound asleep.

"Good morning ladies and gentlemen," announced the pilot over the PA system of the 747 aircraft. We're about ninety minutes from landing at Moscow's Sheremetyevo International airport. It will be sunny today, with an expected high of 30 degrees Celsius. Thanks for flying with us and have a nice day."

Businessman Blackwell of Chicago and his "new" acquaintance were finishing their excellent breakfasts, served on real china with real silverware.

She leaned closer to Robbie. "You know, I could easily get use to traveling in Business Class."

"I told you at the lounge in New York it would be good for us to become acquainted." He gave her a wink.

"OK. So, what's our first move once we get out of the Moscow airport?" she inquired.

"We both make our own way to the Hotel *Metropol* and check in. I believe the *Evropeisky* restaurant is still there on the second floor." He looked quickly at his pocket watch and did a little mental calculating. "Let's meet there at two o'clock. I'm not too worried about us being seen together in the coming days, but avoid calling my room if possible. Try not to leave any phone/computer records of our association. If asked by anyone, we simply met on the flight. And be careful of what you say in either of our rooms. Every room in that hotel was wired long ago by the KGB and I doubt if they tore out the microphones in the recent renovations."

"Got it. But what's our first research move?"

"Well, one theory we have is that when Ivy permanently moved to England, she might have left the set of encyclopedias in Moscow with her daughter, Tatiana. I have Tatiana's last address in Moscow. She's been gone for thirty plus years, but if I get lucky there will still be a few *babushkas* around who will remember her and may know what became of her belongings once she moved to England."

"Ah, the secret weapons of Russia -- the little old grandmothers -- who see all, know all and really run the country!"

"You got it! If that doesn't lead anywhere, then I'll catch a flight out to Sverdlovsk in a day or two."

"And how do you explain to Tatiana's old neighbors why you're asking?"

"My aunt lived near Tatiana in Lowe, England and they were good friends. I promised her before she died that if I ever got to Moscow, I would find Tatiana's last home and any friends still around. That I would try to track down Ludmila Ivanova -- to give her something dear auntie had bequeathed to her.

"Who the devil are your aunt and this Ludmila Ivanova?"

"Both are figments of my imagination, but it justifies asking my questions and I can guarantee that one of the old *babushkas* will claim to remember a Ludmila!"

"You, Sir, are a devious man."

"Thank you." He leaned back, put the ear buds back in place and returned to listening to Prokofiev's Lt. Kije Suite on his digital music player.

Two hours later, Mr. Blackwell stepped up to the Passport Control window and handed his passport over to the very serious-looking young man on the other side of the counter. The name of the country had changed and a lot of things were much more open, but the Border Security guards still acted like everyone wanting to enter the country was a spy, a terrorist or enemy of some description. He knew intellectually that there shouldn't be any problem with his alias passport, but emotionally, passing through Russian control was still stressful.

"What is purpose your visit?" the young official asked in halting English without a hint of a smile.

"Tourism," replied Blackwell with an equally stern face.

"Where you are staying?"

"At the Hotel *Metropol*."

"What exactly type tourism you make?"

"I came to see if Russian girls are as beautiful in person as they are on their websites."

That was an answer the Border Guard understood. Another old, Western male coming to Russia to sleep with young Russian girls. He stamped the passport. "Russian Federation welcome you." Still no smile.

Thirty minutes later, with baggage finally in hand, Blackwell entered a taxi. The driver fought heavy traffic all the way to reach the hotel in the heart of Moscow. He couldn't believe how much worse traffic had gotten in twenty years. It was close to an hour before he reached the *Metropol*, where the cabbie demanded twice the amount of what it showed on the meter. Not wishing to display his Russian language skills or appear different than all the other foreign suckers who were robbed by such drivers, he simply paid.

Check-in at the opulent, hundred-year old hotel went smoothly. The desk clerks were all beautiful Russian women, each fluent in several languages. Within a matter of minutes, he was in his room and he finally relaxed a little. He'd safely made it into Moscow. Hopefully, departing, in a few days would go as smoothly. Though he had one of the more modest rooms, he still had a great view of the famous Bolshoi Theater. Lots of memories came rushing back to him.

"Quite a nice view isn't it, Olga. I remember how much you loved going to the ballet at the Bolshoi. It's been a long time since we were back in Moscow. So many changes in the city. We had many happy times here didn't we."

He stood at the window for several minutes, remembering activities with his wife and son around Moscow, while tears rolled down his face.

He walked into the hotel restaurant promptly at two. Cathleen arrived a minute later and they were given a table by a window. It being past the peak lunch hour, the restaurant was two-thirds empty and the service was prompt. She ordered a salad and he tried the Chicken Kiev.

"You did notice what a room costs here a night!" she half whispered across the table to her new friend, Robbie.

"Yes, but as you can see, it's worth every kopek." He casually pointed at the unbelievable Art Nouveau decorations of the dining room, most of which were original and dating back to 1903 when the hotel had been built. "How's your room?"

"It's spectacular as well, but a little out of the price range of a poor college professor, isn't it?"

"Nonsense, Russians know that all of us Americans are filthy rich, even professors." He gave her a wink.

"They can think what they want, but in about five days, my credit card is going to max out staying here!"

"Not a problem." He quite openly took out a large roll of American hundreds, counted off 20 bills and handed them across the table to Cathleen while several waiters observed the transaction. "Here, make a down payment on your room bill with these."

She took the stack of bills and after putting them in her purse, nodded towards the watching waiters. "I presume you did that on purpose, so they would 'understand' our relationship?"

"Yes."

"Should we have sex right here on the table or wait till we get back to my room?"

"Let's wait. Our food is coming."

An hour later, Blackwell left the hotel alone and entered the nearby Metro station. The Moscow subway system had been built several hundred feet below the earth, so that it could withstand air attacks, and thus had some of the longest escalators in the world. The older stations in the heart of the city had beautiful statues and chandeliers in them as well -- a sort of art for the masses idea by Stalin. He traveled quickly to the Lenin Hills neighborhood, where Tatiana had last lived in one of the better state-owned apartment buildings of the 1970s. He was truly amazed at all the changes that had come to the city he used to call home. He'd seen TV coverage and movies of the "new" Moscow, but one had to walk the streets and look in the store windows to really feel the changes that had come to his old city. Everyone was dressed better and the variety of products in stores, albeit at high prices, took his breath away. There were certainly more cars on the streets, and not just little Ladas or *Zhigulis*. There were BMWs, Mercedes and even Hummers. Obviously, lots of people had money. Mafioso criminals and corrupt government officials couldn't be the only ones living a better life. He was glad to see that some of his former citizens had made real progress over the past twenty years. Capitalism hadn't come smoothly, nor evenly, but it seemed to be working for many.

He found the apartment complex easily enough and strolled into an inner courtyard of the tall brick buildings. Each ten story structure had the exact same architecture and each looked just a little tired and worn. Maintenance work was clearly not a high priority. As for their similarity in looks, there were many old Russian anecdotes, based on a drunk coming home and mistakenly wandering into the wrong building. As he'd hoped, there were three *bashbukas* on a bench in the courtyard, minding several grandchildren at play and gossiping. The clothing of the children was very Western, but the attire of these three grandmothers in their long colorful skirts and headscarves could have been from a century earlier. They stood for tradition. He spoke in Russian to them.

"Oh, what beautiful, happy children," he began. He knew how to get on the good side with any grandmother in the world. After several minutes of such harmless banter, the oldest of the ladies asked, "You don't live in our complex do you?" *Babushkas* had always been known for being direct.

"No, I'm a visitor from America, looking for any friends of someone who used to live here about 35 years ago, but you ladies are much too young to have known her."

They knew he was flirting with them. They loved it. "Nonsense, young man, I've lived here since 1962 and have known everyone who ever lived here," giggled the eldest.

"That's right. That's right," chimed in her two companions. "Who are you looking for?"

"Her name was Tatiana Litvinova. She moved to England in the late 1970s or so, to join her mother, Ivy Litvinova."

It was not the eldest, but the youngest who responded first. "I remember Tatiana Maximovicha. She was older than me, but she lived right next door to our apartment."

Blackwell proceeded with his prepared story of being on a sacred mission for his dear departed aunt and of his search for Ludmila Ivanova. As predicted, one of the grandmothers claimed to remember a Ludmila, but was having trouble recalling exactly which apartment she lived in with her husband and daughter.

"My aunt and Tatiana were very close in England, the last few years of Tatiana's life, and my aunt repeated so many of her stories to me, I feel as if I already know this complex."

He finally brought the conversation around to his questions of whether anyone else who had been close to Tatiana was still living there and the subject of how poor Tatiana had had to leave so many of her possessions behind when she emigrated.

"Yes, that's true," agreed the former next-door neighbor. She lowered her voice and looked around. The habit of a lifetime learned in a society that had been full of informants. "It was a different time of course. For those who could emigrate, they had to leave with just practically what they had on their backs. She sold all her furniture at that time I remember, because my papa bought a lamp from her."

"What about her books and things like that?"

"She didn't have many books. I always thought that odd, for a woman who made her living doing translations and working with literature. I don't think I ever saw more than five or six books on a tiny shelf in her apartment."

Blackwell just happened to have several American chocolate bars in his pocket, which he eventually gave to the *babushkas,* to distribute later to their grandchildren. He promised to return about the same time in two days, to see if anyone could remember more about Ludmila Ivanova. He walked back to the Metro station and made his way back to his hotel.

He'd not been doing a serious check for surveillance, but he didn't sense that anybody had followed him that afternoon.

He knocked on Cathleen's hotel room door. "Care to take a walk around Red Square before dinner?"

"I'd love to. Other than making a brief visit to the Main State Library, I've just been napping all afternoon -- trying to get my body adjusted to Moscow time." Moscow was eight hours ahead of Indiana time, so it would take a few days to get one's body clock in synch with the local time.

They headed for the most famous of tourist spots in Moscow -- Red Square and the Kremlin. The square was full of tourists, armed with every brand of digital camera known to man, photographing the buildings and each other. Once they reached the beautiful St. Basil's Cathedral, he began to relate to her his experience with the three grandmothers.

"You really have a way with old ladies. Too bad your charm doesn't work on younger women." She gave him a quick kiss. "So, what's your conclusion about Tatiana?"

"The gal who had been a neighbor could have been wrong about whether it was 5 or 10 or even 20 books, but I think she would have remembered if there had been a 65 volume set of the Great Soviet Encyclopedia in Tatiana's apartment."

"So you don't think Ivy gave the set to Tatiana when Ivy left for England in 1972?"

"Doesn't look like it, though that had been just one possibility as to what Ivy might have done with the encyclopedias when she left Russia. She might have left them with a friend, in hope of getting them out later. For all we know she might have managed to take them with her when she and Maxim went to Washington DC in 1941, when he was appointed ambassador to the United States."

"I guess it's a possibility," mused Cathleen. "It's been the same building for their embassy since then till this day. I'd hate to think the set might be sitting in the library of the Russian Embassy, gathering dust! So, what's our next move?"

"Tomorrow, I'll see about a flight out to Ekaterinburg, the old Sverdlovsk, to see what I might find out there. How'd you do at the library today?"

"I talked with the Director for Foreign Research. Apparently, showing up several weeks early just isn't done. He thought it might be two or three days before he could have a desk ready for me."

"Well, it will give you a few days to go play tourist. You said you hadn't been here in three years."

"True, or I could go with you to Sverdlovsk, or I guess we should call it Ekaterinburg these days. I might be useful you know. Unless you're sticking with the friend-of-your-aunt story, having a history professor with you could justify the asking of lots of questions about events of the 1930s."

Blackwell raised his eyebrows in thought. "True. The downside is the much greater risk to you, if you become directly involved and things go wrong. Let's think about it over dinner."

"OK. Where are you taking me to dinner anyway? I'll need time to clean up and dress."

"You look fine and we're almost there." He pointed at the golden arches straight ahead.

"You've got to be kidding. You brought me half way around the world to eat a double cheeseburger!"

"I can't resist. The Old Bolsheviks must be turning in their graves to have a Mickey Ds right outside the Kremlin walls!"

"Alright, this one time, but if they do really call them Lenin Fries, I'm walking out. Some Sugar Daddy you're turning out to be!"

When they returned to the *Metropol*, Cathleen went to the Front Desk to see if the State Library Director had sent over the registration forms she needed to fill out so that she could use the library. He'd promised her that someone from his staff would drop them off that very afternoon.

"There is no envelope, Miss Spenser, but someone delivered a bouquet of flowers for you a little bit ago. They're in our flower cooler. One moment and the boy will bring them out to you."

Cathleen walked back over to Robbie, who was waiting at the newspaper stand, reading the headlines of the various Western papers available. She took his arm. "You romantic devil."

"What?"

"That was quite sweet of you, having flowers waiting here for me this evening." She felt his arm muscles tighten and his eyes began darting around the lobby.

"I didn't send you flowers. We need to leave the lobby immediately."

He quickly led her down a side corridor of expensive shops. "It's an old trick to help someone identify their target. You leave a package or flowers at the front desk. Whoever picks up the item and walks away with it, is your man, or woman." They went back out onto the street to walk and consider the new situation.

"But who would need to identify me?" She didn't want to admit to him she was scared, but when Robbie spoke in his cold, professional voice, it was hard not to be a little worried.

"It can't be the Russian FSB. They wouldn't have to play around with such ploys to recognize you. This smells like Viktor again. They couldn't know the name Blackwell, under which I'm traveling, but it looks as though they have somehow gotten hold of yours and have tracked you to Moscow."

"How?"

"Maybe they asked around in Bloomington and learned we were a couple. Or, I was in your car several times after those thugs arrived in town. Maybe one of them spotted you and me together and got your license plate number. It would be a simple task after that to get your name and then to hack into the airline reservation system."

"You brought me along to Moscow to protect me and now I've simply led them directly to you."

"Just a small obstacle to overcome, but that does settle the question of whether you go with me to Ekaterinburg. You can't stay alone in Moscow. I saw a travel office still open in the last block. "Let's stop there now and see if we can get a couple of tickets for tomorrow."

They were in luck. There were still a few seats left on the 7 a.m. direct flight the next day. Blackwell then stopped at a street kiosk selling vinyl rain jackets and dumb-looking hats. He outfitted Cathleen with both and for himself, he bought a ball cap labeled "KGB."

"Oh, very attractive!" she commented.

"We'll go up separately to your room and you can pack what you'll need for a few days in your small bag. Leave some items and try to make the room look like you're still staying there. Then we'll spend the night in my room and be out the door in the morning at 4:30 a.m."

"What is it with you and pre-dawn departures!" While she was a little panicked by all this, she was impressed at watching him in action, under pressure. She suspected he had been a formidable opponent when running the KGB's American Department.

While Cathleen was packing, two local members of the Mogilevich crime family continued their vigil in the lobby, waiting for a Cathleen Spenser to pick up her bouquet. They were young, had tough-looking faces and wore the unofficial uniform of the Russian Mafia -- short black leather jackets. Blackwell was right. Her license plate had given them a name and in today's computerized world, it hadn't been difficult to learn of her airline ticket to Moscow and a reservation at that hotel. "Nick" in New York had only managed to send them a photo of Dr. Spenser from when she had given a paper at a conference some five years earlier. It was not a very flattering, nor accurate photo of her now. They'd been told to keep a low profile and only tail her to find one Karl Beck. The two had confirmed with a phone call that a Dr. Spenser was registered at the hotel, but no one by the name of Beck -- the person they were really looking to find, so as to have a "chat" with him. The two knew only that their New York colleagues were really annoyed at this Beck, as he had given them the slip in Bloomington and that one fellow Russian had been blackjacked and dumped in an alley. Beck was clearly a man trying to hide something. Something he should share with Nick, if he wanted to stay healthy.

"This is crap, sitting here all evening. I have a date at ten." He waved off his partner's gesture to be patient. Andrei strode across the plush carpet to the Front Desk and pulled a hundred dollar bill from his pocket. He laid it on the counter. "I have a date with Cathleen Spenser, but seem to have forgotten her room number. Why don't you give it to me."

The Receptionist gave him an icy stare. "It's against our policy to give out room numbers. You can use a house phone over there to have the operator phone her, if she is staying here."

Andrei added another Ben Franklin to the one already on the counter. The receptionist discretely pushed a buzzer under the counter and within a matter of seconds two large, former members of the Russian Army's equivalent to US Army Special Forces appeared at the counter. Their expensive suits actually fit them well, except for bulges under their left arms.

"Good evening, Maria. Is there a problem?"

"This gentleman is having trouble finding the exit. Please show him where it is."

The larger of the two hotel guards picked up the hundreds and stuffed them in Andrei's shirt pocket. "Walk!"

"I'll be back bitch," was all he got out of his mouth before the blackjack of the second hotel employee hit the back of Andrei's neck. The two grabbed him as he started to crumple and carried him out a nearby service door. It's not that the Russian Mafia couldn't exert influence upon the hotel management, but "requests" were expected to be made in a dignified manner -- not by young thugs in cheap leather jackets, and certainly not for two hundred dollars.

His companion went back to reading his newspaper. Nothing he could do now for Andrei was his philosophy. A minute later he left the lobby, to go find where the hotel security men tossed his partner.

About 4:15 a.m., Cathleen walked up to the Front Desk and asked for a taxi to take her to the airport. "I'm going up to St. Petersburg for a day or so, but I wish to keep my room while I'm away."

"Certainly," replied Maria. "Your name and room number?"

"Cathleen Spenser, room 109."

She made a quick call to the Bell captain to request a taxi be sent around immediately. Normally, Maria's personal policy, as well as the hotel's, was not to get involved in individual guest's problems, but she liked Miss Spenser. She liked the fact that she spoke Russian with her, just as a matter of courtesy, seeing as how they were in Russia. Lowering her voice a little, she said, "Miss Spenser, you should know that a very unpleasant young man was here last evening trying to get your room number. Naturally, it was not given to him and hotel security escorted him out the door. He appeared to be the type who has friends, if you understand what I mean."

"Thank you. Sounds like a good time to go see the sights of St. Petersburg." She gave Maria a big smile. A bellhop took her bag to the front door. Blackwell was waiting just outside for her, with his suitcase beside him. She quickly passed along Maria's information to him as they waited for the taxi to arrive. He simply nodded. As the taxi pulled up, he confirmed with the Bell Captain that Domodedovo Airport was the one they wanted for a flight to St. Petersburg. He wanted to leave as many false leads as possible, since clearly someone was on Cathleen's trail.

CHAPTER 8

EKATERINBURG, RUSSIA

There was no business class on their S7 Airline morning flight to Ekaterinburg. The breakfast food offered was horrible, the coffee tasteless and the service rude. Blackwell was amused to see that despite the Western appearance of Moscow, domestic air travel was still the same as during the days of the Soviet Union -- something to endure, not enjoy. The plane touched down almost on time at the city's airport, which was actually a fair distance from the city of that name. The Soviets had always built their airports far away from their cities, so that in the next war, the bombing of airports by the enemy would cause minimal damage and casualties in the nearby city. That made sense back in the 1940s. The theory was already flawed by the Cold War era, when the bombs would be nuclear and absolutely pointless in the 21st century, when no one would be bombing Russia with anything. Today, the airport was just inconveniently a long way from the city.

Given their sudden, and hopefully discreet departure from Moscow, they'd made no hotel reservations at their destination. While waiting in line for a taxi at the airport, Blackwell saw a billboard advertisement for a "five star" Regency Hotel in the center of the city and told the taxi driver to head there. The flight had only taken two hours and change, so it was still early morning. Forty minutes later, as the taxi approached the Regency, they saw that the hotel was quite new and modern, with lots of chrome and glass. It was situated on a large plot of land and surrounded by well-manicured lawns and gardens. It was located near the bank of the Islet River, which ran through the middle of this long time industrial and political center of the Urals. One couldn't say it was a beautiful city, but it looked quite clean. Cathleen had recently read an article that said that the mayor was fairly honest, by Russian standards, and quite efficient.

Blackwell had traveled in what he liked to call "expensive business casual" attire. He approached the young man at the Reception Desk and in his best upper-management tone, explained that his plans had suddenly required him to stop in the city -- and naturally, he would like to stay at the best hotel in Ekaterinburg, if they might have a suite available?

"Let me check," the clerk replied, in surprisingly good, British-accented English. "Yes, we do have a suite available until this coming Monday. I have a conference beginning that day that will take up every room in the hotel, but until then... Will your business be finished by Monday?"

"Yes, it will. You've been most kind." He slid his passport and credit card across the polished marble counter, accompanied by a crisp new hundred dollar bill.

"That isn't necessary, Sir," stammered the young man, probably on his first job and used to five dollar tips if that.

"Of course, it isn't necessary, but you have been friendly and most helpful. I like to show my appreciation to my friends." He glanced at the man's coat pocket name tag. "Yes, Pavel, you have been most helpful."

"Thank you," he replied, while practically beaming. "It might be a half hour or so before the suite is ready. I'll tell Housekeeping to start on that room immediately."

"Excellent." He saw that a restaurant off to the right was serving breakfast. "My, uh, secretary, and I will go have a little breakfast while we're waiting for the suite. Pavel, you can register the suite under just my name, can't you? Wives can so easily misinterpret perfectly innocent situations, can't they?"

Pavel returned Blackwell's "we're all men of the world, aren't we?" smile. "No problem at all, Mr. Blackwell." He indicated to the bell hop to put their bags in the storage room for the moment. "I'll come personally let you know when your suite is ready. Enjoy your breakfast."

"Thank you. I'm sure it will be excellent."

Cathleen had remained standing about ten feet back while all this transpired. He took her arm and proceeded to the restaurant.

"You are amazing," she said quite admiringly. "But aren't we trying to lay low here?"

"Sometimes, the best place to be out of sight is at the best hotel in town. And you're not even registered, so no one can track you. Let's get some breakfast."

The scrambled eggs were a bit underdone, but the Scottish scones were excellent as was the freshly squeezed orange juice.

"Shall we go ahead and get started with our search, or wait till we have our room and can change clothes?" she asked, as she finished the last of her OJ.

"I know you think I enjoy getting up in the middle of the night, but actually, I'd like to have a shower and a nap before we do anything else."

"To be honest, I could use both as well. I just didn't want to appear weak, compared to you, *starik*."

They lingered over their coffee, until Pavel came to inform them that the suite was ready and escorted them to their room on the top floor.

"I hope you're happy with the suite."

"Beautiful view. One last thing Pavel, could you arrange a private car to be available for me at say, two o'clock with a driver who knows the city well?"

"Certainly. We have cars here at the hotel, but speaking frankly, my uncle has a very comfortable car and has lived here for almost seventy years. If Uncle Yuri doesn't know a street, it doesn't exist!"

"Perfect, please ring the room at 1:30 and we'll meet your uncle out front at 2:00. Thank you Pavel."

Both Cathleen and Robbie were sound asleep within fifteen minutes.

Blackwell brought Cathleen along with him on the afternoon excursion. Not only did he feel more comfortable having her with him for safety reasons, but it might indeed prove useful having her along, to play the historian card if necessary.

Once in the car, Blackwell gave Yuri the old address for the Pushkin Antiquarian Book Cooperative, from the 1938 phone book. Yuri was pleasantly surprised at how well both Blackwell and the young woman spoke Russian, as his English consisted mostly of the names of tourist spots and the phrase, "good picture place."

Yuri took a glance at the address. "I know this street, but I don't think there's been a bookstore there for almost twenty years." They proceeded to the desired street, but true to Yuri's memory, there was now a children's clothing store at that address. From the items on display in the window, it was clear that Western fashion designs for children had not yet made their way to the Urals, or at least not to this store.

"So much for that angle," sighed Cathleen.

"One moment, Sir, let me ask at the bread shop on the opposite corner. It's been there forever and perhaps someone there knows if the bookstore moved elsewhere."

Ten minutes later, he returned smiling, with a sheet of paper in one hand and three loaves of bread under his other arm. "The old gal running the bread store remembers the man who'd managed the store in the 1970s and 1980s. His son took it over for a few years after the collapse of the Soviet Union, but couldn't make a living at it. He now has a shoe store a few kilometers from here. Shall we go there?"

"Yes, let's try that."

Ten minutes later they pulled up to a rather run-down brick building, probably built in the early 1950s. It housed on the ground level a shoe store, with apartments on the three upper floors.

"Perhaps you should come in with us and explain to the owner how we learned of him from the woman at the bread store."

"Gladly," replied Yuri, who was clearly enjoying this mystery game and hoped that his extra service would raise his tip as well. His nephew had told him how the rich American businessman had given him a hundred dollars just for getting him a suite!

After a few minutes of introductions and explanations, the elderly shoe store owner, Ivan Ivanovich, suggested they all move into his office for tea. He seemed quite taken with Cathleen, so Blackwell whispered to her that she should take the lead in asking about Pavel Ivanovich.

"Sir, we're trying to find what happened to someone who lived here in Ekaterinburg long ago, or Sverdlovsk, as it was called back in the 1930s. The person's name was Pavel Ivanovich and we think he was a bookbinder or possibly ran an antiquarian book shop around 1938. We don't have a family name for him. Does that first name and patronymic ring a bell with you?"

Ivan rubbed his chin a bit and then let out a loud, "Of course."
"My god, I've not thought of him in decades, but yes, there was a Pavel

Ivanovich who was a friend of my father. He was a little older than father. Papa said he was the best book repairman in all of the Urals!"

"That's probably the man I'm searching for," Cathleen responded in an excited voice. "Do you recall his family name or any other details about him?"

"His family name was Ledvedev. He lived somewhere not too far from the bookstore, as I recall, but I'm sure he's been dead for thirty years or more."

"Did he have any family?" asked Blackwell.

More chin rubbing before Ivan Ivanovich answered. "No, as I recall, it was one of those sad cases during Stalin's rule where his brothers and even his wife 'disappeared' one night in 1938, even though he'd been a Communist Party member himself. Unfortunately, that was a rather common occurrence in those years! Some people returned from the *gulags* around 1955, but not any of Ledvedev's relatives. I suppose they'd all perished."

"That is very sad. Were you ever by chance in his home? Did he have a large library of personal books?"

"No, I don't believe I ever was, but it's hard to believe that he was a great collector of books. My father told me once that he was a good man and very talented in his profession, but a very poor one."

Just on a whim, Cathleen decided to ask about Ivy. "While we're on the subject of the 1930s, I read recently that Ivy Litvinova, the wife of the Foreign Minister in the mid-1930s, had been in your city for four or five years teaching English. Did you ever hear of her special English language program?"

"Hear of it! My god, it was the high point of my father's life to hear him tell it. You'd have thought he'd met the Queen of England. He kept his certificate of graduation hanging in the bookstore the rest of his life."

"Amazing," she replied, while looking at Blackwell for a hint as to whether she should continue this line of questioning. He gave her a little nod. "Did he continue his English studies?"

"No, that was it." Ivan laughed. "I think he cared more about the certificate and having met Mrs. Litvinova than he did about actually speaking the language. I have a few old photos of him with her, if you'd like to see them?"

"I'd love to."

Ivan rummaged around in a four-drawer filing cabinet for a minute, then came back with an old photo album. He found the page with several photos of his father and a few other young language students in Ivy's apartment, during a New Year's Day celebration for both 1938 and 1939. "Here he is with Mrs. Litvinova." He pointed at his father in each picture.

"They certainly seemed to be having a good time," commented Blackwell.

After another ten minutes of tea and conversation about how Ivan decided to give up the book trade and move into shoes, Cathleen thanked him profusely for his time and the three departed. She managed to never really explain why they were inquiring about Pavel Ivanovich.

On the ride back to the hotel, having seen that history interested the couple, Yuri pointed out a few historical sites of the city. "Unfortunately, so much of the old city was torn down as we greatly expanded in the decades after the Great Patriotic War." They were passing the Yeltsin Federal University of the Urals. "There's one of the few places that's been untouched. A lot of new buildings have been added, but they've kept all the beautiful, old structures from when it was simply the Polytechnic Institute back in the 1920s and 30s."

"Yes, it's an impressive campus", responded Cathleen, quite truthfully.

"You two must be the only Americans who've ever come to our city and not wanted to see where the Ipatiev House stood."

Cathleen started to speak, but Blackwell touched her leg and he responded. "What's the Ipatiev House?"

"It's where our last czar and his family were all murdered in 1918," explained Yuri as he crossed himself. "The house was torn down years ago, but people still like to go see the spot where it stood."

"Oh, yes, I'd forgotten that the Romanovs had been killed in this city. Perhaps tomorrow, if we have time." Upon arrival at the hotel, Blackwell gave Yuri two of the beloved Ben Franklins. "Thank you for all your assistance."

"Goodnight. If you need me again, just let Pavel know."

"Goodnight."

"I'm starving," commented Cathleen as they entered the hotel.

"First, I need to stop in the Business Center for a moment and check my emails."

He logged in at one of the public email services as "LittleBlackBear69." Cathleen said, "I don't even want to know what that's all about." There was one email message for him from "LonelyCorvetteGirl" in which she spoke of how much she missed LBB69 and hoped to hear his voice soon.

Blackwell mumbled half to himself, "that's not good."

"I get worried when you say something's not good!" She took hold of his arm and gave it a squeeze. Why do I have the feeling that LonelyCorvetteGirl isn't simply some playful college girl in America?

" No, that was a message from the boss of the Group, Joan, letting me know that she needs to talk to me via phone. Let's have some dinner and then I need to take a little stroll in the city."

"I know this isn't the days of the Soviet Union, but how can you make a call to America from here without being worried about having your conversation monitored?"

"I won't call from the hotel." He gave her a smile. "What looks good to you on the menu?"

Once their food had been served, Blackwell returned to business. "Did you notice anything special in those two photos taken in Ivy's apartment at the beginning of 1938 and 1939?"

"Well, two students appeared in both years. One of them being Ivan Ivanovich's father, but there were several different people in each photo as well, if that's what you mean?"

"No, I mean that in the first photo, at the beginning of 1938, there was a set of encyclopedias on the shelf in the background, but not in the one taken a year later."

"I can't believe I didn't notice that detail."

"You were busy chatting with Ivan Ivanovich. Makes you wonder what she did with her Great Soviet Encyclopedia set sometime in 1938!"

"She might have taken it back to their apartment in Moscow and left it with her husband, but I don't see why she would have thought that any safer than being here -- if the books were stuffed with Romanov jewels. With the Great Purges still underway, Maxim might have been hauled off to the Gulag at any moment. And book repairman extraordinaire, Pavel Ivanovich, was here in Sverdlovsk."

"Yes, she could have put them in a number of places back in Moscow, but if it was me, given those uncertain times, I think I would have preferred to put them somewhere I considered safe, right here in Sverdlovsk."

They came to the conclusion that Ivy most likely would have kept the jewel-filled encyclopedias in Sverdlovsk, but where or with whom?

A few hours later, Blackwell changed clothes and prepared to go out for his "stroll." He slipped his digital music player in his coat pocket.

"You brought your copy of 'His Master's Voice' with you, didn't you?" inquired Cathleen, as she gave him a good-luck kiss at the door.

"Yes, it's there in my bag."

"I may give it a read while you're out."

An hour into his excursion, Blackwell found the sort of bar he'd been looking for. It was a plain place, for locals. There was no fancy decor, no sports banners or even TVs. This was a dive, where one came to get drunk for as few a rubles as possible. Blackwell found an open space at the bar. He ordered loudly, in English, and pulled out a wad of bills with which to pay for his drink. A few minutes later, he headed to the men's room, staggering a bit, as old men who've drunk too much will do. A tough looking local in his early twenties followed Blackwell into the men's room, contemplating just how much money the drunken foreigner had on him. A minute later, Blackwell walked out of the bar, apparently much more sober now and with one of the newest model cell phones in his pocket. The young hoodlum lay unconscious in one of the toilet stalls.

Blackwell sat down at a deserted bus stop several blocks away. He took out his digital music player, entered a special code, then connected it to the phone's data port. He dialed Joan's "work" number in northern Virginia, but spoke into his music player. Once the connection was made, all that any human or computer monitoring the call heard was a hip hop music tune. Digitally interlaced into the music was Blackwell's voice. "Hey, I got your message. What's up?" is what Joan heard.

"You on your phone?"

"No, I borrowed a local's."

"I was not thrilled to hear about you making your trip at this time, but you must have the luck of the Irish. A name unexpectedly came to our attention yesterday and I wanted to pass it along to you since you're there. I hope that you'll just forget about the past, but you have the right to know and to decide for yourself what to do." She paused for a moment. "We have the name of the man who killed your wife and son."

There was a long silence from Blackwell's end. "Who is it?" He took out a pen and small notebook.

"Valerie Ivanovich Verchagin. Did you know him?"

"No, he would have been in a totally separate department than mine. The 'wet-work' guys were kept isolated from the rest of the KGB. Do you have an address for him or any other details?"

"He is retired now, of course. Widowed. Last known address was 87 *Leninsky Prospekt, Korpus* II, apartment 22, in Moscow. That's all we have. It was a fluke that we learned this at all. It's second-hand information from an old friend of mine with a foreign intelligence service, but I'd say it's ninety percent certain that it's accurate."

"Thanks."

"I gave you the information, but here's my advice as well. Let it go Karl. You've a good life going now and I understand, a great new woman in it. Don't put that all at risk for revenge. Olga wouldn't want you to either."

"I appreciate your concern. I'll think about it."

"One more thing, Norway is still bubbling. Make sure you check your email every day, in case we need to get hold of you ASAP."

"Goodbye." Blackwell disconnected the phone and wiped his fingerprints from it. He left it on the bench, put his music player back in his pocket and walked off into the night. He could see the top floors of his hotel in the distance and headed in that general direction. He thought of Cathleen, waiting there for him. A woman in love with him and he with her, but he couldn't get Olga and Pavel out of his mind. He had promised them ten thousand times since that horrible day in Prague that he would someday avenge their deaths.

He walked and began to talk to Olga. *"Well, isn't this quite an unexpected turn of events. After all these years, I've learned who shot at us that day in Prague. And I'm here in Russia, where I can do something directly with the information. A person whose opinion I respect tells me to just let it go, after all this time, but I don't think I can do that. He stole from us all our years together and the bastard needs to pay. My friend says I'd be putting at risk my new life with Cathleen -- maybe, but that isn't how I calculate the situation. I'll think about it more, but Valerie Ivanovich has a real surprise coming in a few days."*

Cathleen was still up when he arrived back at the suite and was quite excited.

"You look like the proverbial cat who swallowed the crow," he commented, as he sat down beside her on the sofa that faced the large glass window. They had a spectacular view of the city, especially at night, with street lights and apartment windows shining far off into the distant.

"Canary, cat who swallowed a canary! How long have you been in America?"

She gave him a kiss, then went over and turned the radio up much louder to mask their conversation. He didn't have the heart to tell her that with modern technologies, a security service could easily filter out such background noises and hear their conversation perfectly clear if they wanted. Instead, he just pulled her close beside him, and whispered to her, "Speak very softly."

"I do have something, but first tell me, how was your walk?"

"It went well and I learned something very important to me, but let me think about it a little more and I'll tell you the details in the morning. But what's sitting on the tip of your tongue?"

"I started reading Ivy's mystery story and found something interesting. You remember that in her hidden vocal message, when talking of the books, she said, 'I tried to bring them with me, but they had to stay in Russia at a place that was a dancing girl's salvation.' I think I now know what she meant." She paused for dramatic effect.

"Well, what is your great discovery?"

She picked up the book and turned to a page she had marked. "I think the character Tamara, the young ballerina in Ivy's story, who is charged with murder, is the referred to 'dancing girl' and a library was her 'salvation' -- and that's the location of the encyclopedias with the diamonds."

"And your evidence for this conclusion?"

"Listen to these lines about the character, Tamara: 'She was reported to be in a highly nervous condition, eating badly and hardly sleeping at all. Whenever the regulations allowed it she devoured books, of which she received a new one from the prison library almost every day, but otherwise she was listless and apathetic...' And then on the next page it says: '... and I asked for a book from the library and by chance hit upon Tolstoi's *Forged Coupon*, and then everything was blindingly clear -- like a flash of lightning.' That sentence was in the letter Tamara wrote to the prosecutor.

That letter is what convinced him she was innocent." She handed him the book.

Blackwell read the pertinent pages. "OK, but what exactly is her salvation? The prosecutor Itkin, Tolstoi or his book, a prison library?" There seem to be a number of possibilities, even if Tamara is the dancing girl in question."

"There are of course several possible interpretations of the passages, but remember, it was 1938 in Sverdlovsk, when she did whatever she did with the encyclopedias. Would she have put them in a prosecutor's office or a prison library? I don't think so. Would she have taken them to Tolstoi's home at *Yasnaya Poliana*? Doubtful. I think she used a regular library. One that she figured she would have access to at a later date and one that was presumably still there in 1960 when she made the recording."

Blackwell nodded in silence, thinking. "You're right. She might well have taken them back to Moscow to a library, but she was here, so the most likely library was a local one. We need to find what local libraries existed in Sverdlovsk in 1938, ideally, substantial ones that she could have reasonably counted on would still be here in the future."

They stared out at the city in silence for several minutes, then looked back at each other and said simultaneously, "the Polytechnic Institute!" The large white colonnades of its main building, lit by floodlights, stood out boldly in the view from their hotel room. "We can make inquiries tomorrow about other old libraries as well, but the university library seems a logical choice," observed Blackwell. "I see more use of that noted historian, Dr. Spenser, as she makes a call at the university library!" He leaned even closer and gave her a kiss.

As he lay in bed that night thinking, Blackwell assessed their situation. Their search for the jewels appeared to be making progress. If they could keep Viktor Litvinov's people from finding them and avoid the Russian government from finding out that he and Parshenko were one and the same, all might turn out well. Those were two serious "ifs." Also by now, Viktor may have listened to Ivy's recordings and come to the same conclusions as he and Cathleen. What do they do if they run into Viktor in Ekaterinburg? And Blackwell still had to decide what to do about the assassin of his wife and child.

CHAPTER 9

After breakfast the next morning, Blackwell suggested they take a stroll down along the river, where they could talk without fear of microphones. A small park, with trees, benches and a walking path, had been created next to the river. It was still early, so there was little traffic noise yet and a cooling breeze was coming off the water. There were several elderly fishermen spaced along the banks, lines in the water, stoically staring into the Islet River. They settled on a stone bench as a good place for him to share with her what he'd learned from his phone call the previous night with Joan.

"Amazingly, after all these years, this private organization I do work with has stumbled across the name of the KGB assassin who murdered my family. He's retired, but still living in Moscow. Joan recommended that I forget the past and enjoy the present. However, I swore the day I woke up in the hospital and learned my wife and son were dead that I would someday have my revenge on whoever killed them. That hatred is what kept me going those first few rough years in America. Perhaps my desire for revenge does not burn as brightly now, as it did then, but it's still within my soul. I don't know if I can be this close and just walk away."

Cathleen instinctively knew that the decision had to be his alone. "I love you and don't want to risk losing you, but I understand your feelings. You'll have my support for whatever you decide to do." She took his hand

and held it tightly. They sat in silence for several minutes, both staring out at the currents of the river.

"This requires no decision right now," he finally said softly. "First, we'll deal with our problem of the library. I think this morning is a good time for a certain Indiana University Russian History professor to make a call on the Yeltsin University Library. Let's find out if the library has an old copy of the Great Soviet Encyclopedia on its shelves."

A taxi dropped them at the front of the University library, which was housed in a large, but modest-looking brick building. The foundation stone read 1926. There appeared to be a much more modern, concrete addition attached off to one side, which probably held most of the books. The Administration Section would no doubt be in this older, main building. Contrary to Moscow, where visiting Western scholars were always coming to do research, Ekaterinburg was a bit off the beaten path. The Deputy-Director, Ludmila Chervonayya, was positively effusive in welcoming a scholar from such a distinguished Western center of Academia as Indiana University -- well known for its Russian Studies. Blackwell was introduced simply as an acquaintance, who thought it might be nice to come along to visit the university.

"I came to Moscow to do research in my field of specialty -- local government -- but the Main State Library wasn't ready for me, so we decided to come visit Ekaterinburg for a few days. I couldn't pass up a chance of being so close without stopping by your well-known library and see if there might be any original materials that could be helpful to the book I'm writing."

The fiftyish-year old Dr. Chervonayya ordered her assistant to bring tea into her office for the three to enjoy and insisted that afterwards, she herself would give the two visitors a complete tour of their "modest" facilities. She related how many volumes they had at the library and what periodicals they subscribed to in fifteen different languages. Blackwell found the matronly-shaped grandmother of two as boring as he'd found every librarian he'd ever encountered in any country, but bravely kept smiling and looking fascinated. All those years of intelligence work still proved useful. Finally, they began the tour. The library had been built at the height of socialist realism. The attractive wood carvings and plaster reliefs all showed smiling workers and happy peasants. Fifteen minutes later they entered the main Reference Room and there on a shelf sat the

Holy Grail -- a complete set of the Great Soviet Encyclopedia. There were in fact several sets, appearing to be of different ages. Last on the right was the current Great Russian Encyclopedia, as it was now titled.

"Dr. Chervonayya. I find my old right knee bothering me a bit this morning. I wonder if I might just sit and wait here in your lovely Reference Room, while you show Dr. Spenser the rest of the library?"

"I understand perfectly, Mr. Blackwell. My knees on certain days give me difficulties as well. It's the changing weather you know. I could have Tatiana here escort you back to my office, if you'd prefer?"

"No, that won't be necessary. I might even think of something I'd like to look up in one of your reference books." He gave her his best ingratiating smile.

"Certainly, certainly. We'll only be a half hour or so."

The two ladies continued on their way. Once through the next door, she enquired of Cathleen, "How long has Mr. Blackwell been a widower?"

"Oh, I think it's been sometime. I don't know him well, but he seems a little lonely to me." Chervonayya checked to make sure all the strands of her hair were in their proper place.

Blackwell made his way quickly over to Tatiana at the Reference Desk. "Might I have a look at your Great Soviet Encyclopedia -- that old one there on the left?"

"Certainly, Sir," responded the young girl, probably early in her career as a librarian. "Which volume do you need?"

"What edition is it?"

"That one is an original 1926 edition. We of course have a more current one," she added, pointing at the one on the far right.

"I think it would be interesting to see some articles from the original version. May I have the volumes that would have Sverdlovsk, Marx and Stalin please?"

"I can only check out one at a time to you."

"Fine, let's start with the one that covers Stalin."

He was lucky the Deputy Director had escorted him through or he couldn't have used any of the materials without an official university user's card. He took the first volume to a table in a far corner, underneath a window. He explained to Tatiana that he needed good light for his old eyes. She gave him a look of "like I should care" as a response. A large portrait of a stern Lenin stared down at him from the far wall. He opened the volume to Stalin and started reading the multi-page entry covering the life of that megalomaniac. He waited till Tatiana got bored watching him from her desk and went back to other duties. Blackwell then pulled the large book towards him, so that it was half off the table and he could run his fingers along the spine. He felt nothing unusual, but if Pavel Ivanovich had been the master bookbinder the shoe store owner's father had claimed he was, nothing should have seemed out of order.

He took the volume back and asked for the next one. His examination of it also produced nothing. He soon returned it to the Desk as well and asked for the first volume of the set, letter "A", and returned to his seat with it. He opened the cover to read the title page. At the bottom left-hand corner, in small, neat Russian handwriting was the short sentence "For my darling Ivinchka." Ivinchka -- the diminutive of Ivy. That clinched it in his mind. This was all too much of a coincidence for there not to be jewels hidden in some or all of these volumes. Unfortunately, to prove his conclusion, he couldn't go ripping apart the books right there in the library, under the watchful eyes of Tatiana. How to get them out of the library? His intelligence-officer mind ran through various options. Deputy Director Chervonayya did not strike him as the type who would take a bribe, no matter how large, for letting him purchase the set. Tatiana would probably take such a bribe, but she would also crack in about two minutes under the withering glare of Ludmila the very next day.

He stood up, as if enjoying the view from the window behind him. The brick ledge of the window was only about 6 feet from the ground. The large old-fashioned, wooden framed window had only a simple latch at the middle point, where the upper and lower windows joined. He looked for evidence of an alarm. He saw an old contact point for an alarm on the outer frame of the window, but also noticed that the wire running from it had been cut. It looked as if it had been that way for years. When no one was looking, he reached up and flipped open the window lock. Typical Russian concept of security, he thought to himself. They had a massive front door, with several locks in it, and three layers of people checking your user ID to get inside, but there was a back window with a lock that any twelve-year old, or a sixty-year old, could open. It was all show and no substance. He gave the window a little tug, just to make sure it could move. Success. He took out his handkerchief and discreetly wiped everywhere his fingers had touched the window or frame. In a small attempt to make it look as though his attention had not been solely on the encyclopedias, he then asked to see several other books. He also started giving typical male sighs and looking frequently at his pocket watch -- the "how long must I sit and wait for that woman" look. He finally asked Tatiana to escort him back to the Deputy Director's office, so he could wait in a more comfortable chair.

MOSCOW

While Blackwell was cooling his heels in Chervonayya's sparse office, being fussed over by her secretary to make sure he didn't need more tea, Brighton Beach "Nick" was beginning a meeting in Moscow with four young members of the local Mogilevich crime family. He'd arrived on the morning flight from New York's JFK. Once Nick had gotten the name of Cathleen Spenser through a license plate check, done by a New York state trooper on his payroll, he went to another person who owed him money. This fellow worked in an airline reservation office and was able to inform Nick that Spenser had flown to Moscow, but there were no similar reservations for Karl Beck. Once Nick learned that the woman who helped Professor Beck slip away from his men in Bloomington had flown to Moscow, he was convinced there really was something to Viktor's story of Romanov jewels. Nick didn't believe in coincidences, and with potentially millions of dollars on the line, he'd decided to come supervise the search himself. Plus, he'd taken it as a personal insult how Beck had made fools of his three men in Bloomington. As to why there were no flight reservations for Beck, Nick wasn't sure, but suspected the guy might have used alias documents. If that was true, this was no simple professor.

Andrei had just finished telling Nick of his unsuccessful attempts at getting direct access to Miss Spenser, given there was no Beck registered at the hotel. Nick didn't look pleased after hearing of Andrei's crude attempt to bribe the desk clerk and it confirmed in his mind that he'd made the right decision to come himself to Moscow.

"And since your sloppy attempt to get her room number, she hasn't been seen in the hotel, nor answered her room phone, even though she didn't check out?"

"Right, but the Bell Captain remembered a cab being ordered up, real early the next morning for Miss Spenser -- and that she and an old guy with white hair took it together to the airport, to fly to St. Petersburg," added the Russian who'd stayed in his chair while Andrei was being tossed out of the hotel. "We've phoned several dozen hotels in St. Petersburg, but no luck for either a Spenser or a Beck."

Nick wasn't happy. He checked his watch. "OK, keep phoning hotels in St. Petersburg until I get back. I have an appointment." He left, without giving any clue as to where he was headed.

EKATERINBURG

Blackwell and Cathleen returned from the university library to their hotel about one o'clock. As they were passing through the lobby, guests were entering into one of the small banquet rooms for a luncheon hosted by the American Consulate's Cultural Affairs Attaché, Terrence Powell. Desk clerk Pavel was speaking to Attaché Powell as the couple passed by. Thinking he was doing him a favor, Pavel stopped Blackwell to introduce him.

"Mr. Powell, let me introduce you to one of your fellow countrymen, Mr. Blackwell, a prominent businessman staying here for a few days."

Being trapped, Blackwell made the best of the situation. Fortunately, Pavel was immediately needed back at the Desk, so Blackwell didn't have to introduce Cathleen as his secretary or mistress. Powell's comments about the area immediately showed that he hated being stuck in what he regarded as a backwater post of Russia and was thrilled at meeting anyone from home.

"And what do you do, Miss Spenser?"

Not knowing what else to say, she told the truth. "I teach history at Indiana University."

"Oh marvelous. Are you staying long in Ekaterinburg?"

"Only a few days, then back to Moscow for some research work."

"Too bad, I would have loved to arrange for you to speak at one of our weekly functions. Everyone wants to come over on cultural and educational tours to St. Petersburg and Moscow, but it's a bit harder to get them to venture out here I'm afraid."

After five minutes of polite banter, Blackwell finally managed to excuse himself and Cathleen from the lonely diplomat's company.

"You're both welcome to join our luncheon, if you have time."

"Thank you, but we have people waiting for us now," explained Blackwell with a shrug of his shoulders and a smile.

"Oh, of course, it was nice to meet you both. Dr. Spenser, if there's any assistance you need while in town, well, that's what my office does as well, help visiting academics." He gave her his card.

"That's very kind of you. I'll be sure to phone if I run into any problems. Goodbye."

When they were alone in the elevator, Blackwell observed, "You certainly made a conquest. Another ten minutes and he would have asked you to marry him this very afternoon."

She laughed as the doors opened to their floor. "Jealous?"

"Terribly." He opened the door of their suite and immediately suggested, "Let's take a shower."

"My, I'll have to get you jealous more often!" She gave him a seductive grin and started to undress. He headed straight for the bathroom and turned on the taps.

She joined him a minute later in the large shower stall. He leaned over to her ear so she could hear him without shouting. "This is actually how you counter the effectiveness of microphones. The sound of the rushing water keeps changing, so a computer can't filter out the background noise."

"You mean you brought me in here just so we could talk without fear of being overheard on a microphone?"

"Well, that was one of two reasons. I thought you might like to hear what I discovered in the Reference Room."

"I'm all ears."

"I found Ivy Litvinova's set of encyclopedias." She didn't reply, so he thought perhaps she hadn't heard him, so he repeated himself.

"I heard you. I just can't believe it." She gave out a scream of joy. "Don't worry; the microphone will only think that it was a cry of sexual pleasure." They both laughed.

"That's the good news. The bad news is that you can only check out one volume at a time and it has to be used right there in the Reference Room. No doubt they'd notice if I started cutting open the spines of the books, so I think we're going to have to steal them -- all sixty five volumes."

"And how do you propose doing that Mr. Willie Sutton?"

"Willie who?"

"Never mind. Just tell me how we rob a library."

He explained in detail the lock on the window and his plan of a midnight entry. In the end, she agreed that it was probably the only practical way of getting them.

"You said there were two reasons you brought me in here?" she asked with a big smile.

"Well, yes there was ..."

It was almost three o'clock when Cathleen phoned down to room service and ordered a couple of sandwiches and two Cokes. Despite what he'd told her about the shower being the only truly safe way to mask a conversation, she again turned up the volume of the radio, and turned on the TV as well, for masking. "When do you have in mind this little book hunting trip of yours? Tonight?"

"I'm thinking tomorrow night. I want to let at least a day pass after our visit, before the books disappear. We also need to figure out how to get 150 pounds of books back to Bloomington, without anyone X-raying them at an airport security check point. If we cut them open here, we'd still be stuck with smuggling the jewels, which would probably be harder than if we just left them in the books."

I guess there's Fed Ex or something like that, although the idea of trusting all those little "baubles" to an air express company worries me."

"Well, we can think about it over the next 24 hours. As soon as we have our sandwiches, I should go down and check my email."

MOSCOW

A uniformed, military guard stopped Nick's Mercedes immediately after he turned onto an unnamed road on the outskirts of Moscow. It was a well-paved road, going off into a pine forest. It ran about a kilometer into the woods, where there was a large, lovely *dacha* belonging to General Gennady Klemenko of the military's intelligence service, the GRU. There were a number of such anonymous roads and compounds in the area. It held the summer homes of the politically important and the new rich of Russia. The guard in the hut checked to see that Tsimbal's name was on the list as an expected visitor, while the other guard continued to hold a machine gun on the car. The driver's passport matched the name on the list and so he was admitted.

A few minutes later, Gennady warmly greeted his guest at the front door of his *dacha*, which had once belonged to Marshall Zhukov, of WW II fame.

"Nikolai, you look so pale. It's good that you've come home for a few days of Russian sunshine!"

He led his business partner to a back deck area where a table with delicious *zakuski*, including caviar, and a bottle of chilled vodka, were waiting for them. The general was never one for subtlety. His first toast was, "To our mutual profitability!" They both downed their glass of Russian mother's milk in one gulp. "So, what brings you to my home today, Nikolai Nikolaievich?"

"I need a little help in finding two Americans who've come to Moscow and are trying to avoid having a conversation with me." He proceeded to give the basic background to the story and the names of Spenser and Beck, but was vague as to exactly why he wanted to find them.

"Nikolai, you seem to have forgotten to mention why this is so urgent. You didn't travel 10,000 kilometers to find two university professors, because they owe you a hundred dollars. Why are these two so important?"

Nikolai had no intention of sharing millions of diamonds, even with his good partner, so he'd given careful thought to his explanation. "The man does owe me over a hundred thousand dollars in gambling debts, but it's a matter of honor and appearance. This Beck made a fool of my men I sent to Indiana to collect my money, and thus he made a fool of me. I want everyone to know back in New York that no matter how far he runs, I will find him. If one person gets away with this, it sets a very bad example for others."

"I understand," replied Gennady. "One's honor and image are important." He didn't believe a word of Nick's explanation, but realized he would get nothing more at the moment. He poured them both another round of vodka. "I will do what I can to assist you, old friend. To friendship," was his toast. Gennady pressed a little buzzer attached to the table and there immediately appeared an Army major in uniform. "Alex, my friend here needs to find two Americans who have come to Moscow. Take his information and send a few of my people to the Hotel *Metropol* first thing in the morning to make inquiries."

"Yes, General." The major indicated with his arm, that Nikolai should return to the house with him to take care of this matter.

General Klemenko leaned backed in his chair and closed his eyes. "It's been good seeing you Nikolai."

EKATERINBURG

Cathleen calculated that Attaché Powell's luncheon should have ended and he would have left the hotel by now, so she thought it safe to accompany Blackwell down to the Business Center while he checked his email. As soon as he retrieved and read his one message, which had been vaguely worded to disguise the true content, she could tell by the look on his face that it wasn't good news he'd received.

"Let's take a stroll out to the patio cafe for a coffee." They passed through a crowd of 25-30 Japanese businessmen in the lobby, who had apparently finished their meetings for the day and were headed for the bar.

Once Blackwell had ordered two coffees, he explained the bad news to Cathleen. "Bob's email cryptically informed me that the Norwegians are likely to put out an Interpol warrant within the next 24 hours for this name I'm using. If I get on a plane right now, I might just make it back to the U.S. before the international warrant goes out to all airlines."

"Then let's head for the airport right now."

"First, we have unfinished business here in Ekaterinburg and then I have something to do in Moscow. Plus, that email was sent five hours ago and the 24 hours was only a guesstimate. It may already be too late to get all the way home."

"Can your friends get a new passport to you here in Russia?"

"It might be possible, but it would take time and the boss would have to decide whether to put the whole organization at risk to help someone who'd been told not to use this name again and got himself into this mess. If I were in her shoes, I might not do anything either."

There was silence while the waiter delivered their coffees. A wide smile suddenly came across Cathleen's face, as she watched the Japanese drinking in the nearby bar. "I may have a solution for you. Keep drinking your coffee till I come back."

She returned to the lobby and then entered the bar area. Blackwell could see her through the large glass windows, as she went up to the bar to order a drink.

"Excuse me," she said in English to several of the Japanese gentleman. "I need to get to the bar. I definitely need something cold to drink on such a hot day." Her voice had dropped an octave as she did her best imitation of Blanche DuBois.

"Please, allow me to buy you a drink," offered one of the Japanese.

"Why, thank you." She smiled. He smiled. His colleagues all smiled and a conversation began.

She explained that she was recently divorced and had decided to take a trip through Europe and a part of Russia, to help forget the whole nasty affair. Her new Japanese friend sympathized with her and bought her another drink.

Fifteen minutes or so later, she told her benefactor, "I have to go up to my room now and make a call to Ireland."

"Can't it wait till later?" He indicated to the bartender for two more drinks to be brought, without waiting for her to answer.

"Well, my five year old son is expecting to hear from me at this time. He's staying with my parents while I'm traveling. I really do need to go call. Perhaps I'll see you later."

Mr. Nokamura had not become a multi-millionaire by age 40 by letting good opportunities of any kind slip away. He took his cell phone from his coat pocket. "Here, just use my phone to call your son. Now, you won't have to make that long trip upstairs."

She squeezed his arm. "You are such a gentleman. I'll just sit over there at that table, where it's a little quieter, while I talk to him. I'll only be a few minutes."

"Hi, grandpa, it's your favorite little colleen. I only have a minute. I'm in Russia and need a big favor."

Five minutes later, she returned the phone to her new friend at the bar.

"Is your son well?"

"Yes, he's fine. Now, where is that drink you ordered me?"

Two drinks later, she finally managed to excuse herself from Nokamura, with a promise that she'd meet him back there at the bar around ten that night. She headed for her room. Blackwell saw her move and a minute later joined her upstairs.

"I see you've been improving Japanese-American relations -- and I saw you borrow his phone. Very clever."

"Well, I didn't want you to have to go out and beat up another young man for a phone!" She stuck her tongue out at him. The four drinks in the space of an hour had put her in a very good mood. She lay down on the bed.

"So, who did you phone?"

"I phoned my grandpa. In three days, one of his old IRA pals will have an Irish passport waiting for you in Moscow at a place called Paddy's Pub. I think we'll dye your hair red for the photo. You'll look like a giant leprechaun." Those were her last words before she fell asleep with a smile on her face.

Blackwell was happy to see that she was as imaginative and cool under pressure as he'd thought she would be. He let her sleep till almost nine. He gave her a gentle nudge. "You feel hungry?"

Her head hurt and her mouth felt like cotton. "The things I do for you", were her first intelligible words. He brought her a glass of water and two aspirins.

"Shall I order us some food for here in the room or did you make other plans with your Oriental friends?" He enjoyed teasing her.

"I don't know what all is in a 'Siberian Sling', but I'll never drink another one the rest of my life. I did tell you what I'd arranged, didn't I, before I passed out?"

"Yes, you told me. Your grandpa is a handy man to know in a crisis. Now all we have to do is get back to Moscow."

"Can we risk flying, since it's only a domestic flight?"

"We might make it, but the new Russia is a lot like the old Russia when it comes to keeping track of people's movements. I wouldn't be surprised if all flight reservations, domestic or otherwise aren't matched against a centralized data base kept by the FSB. In theory, Russia honors Interpol warrants on non-Russians. In practice, who knows how quickly they respond to such warrants being posted. I'd prefer not to take the risk if we can avoid it."

"How about a train or bus?"

"Maybe, or perhaps a private car."

"Your thinking of Pavel's uncle?"

"Yes, good old Yuri. But we'll have to come up with a semi-plausible story of why we want to ride in a car for 900 miles over bad roads, instead of just flying two hours."

Cathleen decided to try sitting upright. "You're right, I'm hungry. I can probably think better once I have some food. Call down and order us something, while I take a shower."

With the benefit of the aspirins and the hot shower, she was soon back among the living. "Oh, grandpa said don't worry about it now, but when we get back to the States, we need to send him $6,000 for his 'assistance.' He's old buddies with the provider of the fake passport, so they know he's good for it, but he'll need the cash pretty quickly after we get out of Russia."

"Just what does your grandpa do these days?"

"Not much of anything. Grandma died several years ago and with mom and me over in America, I think he spends most of his days down at the Dove and Whistle pub, near his little flat there in Belfast. He sits around talking of days gone by with the other old fellows. I think my request for help will be the most fun he's had in years! He has a bit of a pension and the owner of the pub is another old IRA man, who I suspect writes off at least half of what grandpa puts on the slate."

"He doesn't want to come live with your mom or you?"

"No, he says his roots are there and he'll die where he was born."

"Sounds like my kind of man. I look forward to meeting him one day."

There was a knock on the door. "Room service."

Over two orders of Chicken Kiev, they spent the next hour working out rough plans of how to rob the library, get the books safely to America, travel to Moscow via car, pick-up the Irish passport and fly back to America -- and possibly kill Valerie Ivanovich.

"My brain's tired," she commented as she finished off a bowl of berries for dessert. "No wonder you defected, if this was the kind of stuff you had to sit around and figure out every day as a spy! Can I go to bed now?"

"Not quite yet. First, we need to go back to the university and take a look around. We need to check if there's a night watchman at the library and how deserted the campus is after midnight. A couple, strolling around arm-in-arm, looks a lot less suspicious than a single man walking around in the dark."

"OK, but I want a really good back rub when we get back to the room!"

They took a taxi to a street full of bars and restaurants near the university, then walked the rest of the way to the library. They strolled around the building for an hour or so and all was quiet, both inside the library and in the surrounding area. There didn't appear to be a night watchman for the library, nor any police presence on campus at nighttime. Being the summertime recess, there were very few students around anywhere. Blackwell was finally satisfied and whispered to Cathleen, "If it's this quiet tomorrow night, stealing the books should be easy. Let's call it a night." Unfortunately, there wasn't a taxi in sight anywhere and they had to walk the two miles back to the hotel.

"This spy stuff takes a lot more work than I thought," she grumbled. "I've never seen any movie or TV spy have to walk all the way home!"

CHAPTER 10

TUESDAY

Having been out quite late casing the university library, the two slept in the next morning. There were a few minor details yet to arrange, but it was mostly just a day of waiting, so there was no rush to get out of bed. Cathleen finally got her backrub. Blackwell had strong hands and knew where all the tension points were on her body. She fell back asleep and only awoke when she heard room service knocking on the door with coffee.

Around eleven, Blackwell went down and found Pavel. "Can you arrange for your uncle to come around in the next hour or two for me to chat with him -- about hiring him and his car for a special trip?"

"Certainly, let me try to phone him on his mobile right now." After a few sentences with Yuri, Pavel turned back to Blackwell. "He can meet you here in the lobby in thirty minutes. Is that good for you?"

"That's great, thank you." He went to the newsstand, bought a day-old London Times and sat down in a deep-cushioned, floral print chair in the spacious lobby to wait. After reading a few articles, he closed his eyes and leaned back in the comfortable chair to reflect on the incredible events of the past few days. It was hard to believe that he'd probably found a stash of Romanov jewels missing for almost 100 years. He'd know for sure within the next twelve hours. This necessitated his having to seriously think about the question of what to do with the jewels. By law, the jewels might still technically belong to some descendent of Czar Nikolai II or to the Russian government, the successor to the Soviet government, which had claimed all properties of the czar. The problem with laws is that they required lawyers and courts to sort out which law would take precedence and a case as complicated as this could drag on for decades. No, Blackwell decided, this was a situation where he would just make a decision, based on what to his mind was fair, regardless of whether it was strictly legal or not.

True to his word, Yuri walked into the lobby precisely thirty minutes after the phone call to him. "Good afternoon, Mr. Blackwell."

"Good afternoon, Yuri. Have a seat. Would you like something cool to drink?"

"No, thank you. I only have a few minutes to spare today. Pavel said you wanted to arrange a special car trip?"

"Would you consider driving me and Miss Cathleen back to Moscow?"

Yuri let out a low whistle and pulled on his left earlobe. "It must be almost 1500 kilometers to Moscow and the roads are not that good in many parts. It would take several days." Yuri then cocked his head a little and gave Blackwell a look of "are you crazy, or is something illegal going on here?"

"You're wondering why we'd want to go by road instead of flying back?"

"Yes."

"Well, it's a bit embarrassing at my age, but Cathleen is in a very unhappy marriage. Her husband is a wealthy and powerful man who treats her badly, but doesn't want a divorce for appearances sake. A friend of hers called her this morning and warned her that he's in Moscow now with several detectives. He is flying out here tomorrow, but his detectives are watching the Moscow airport and given his influence, I suspect he can check all flight reservations as well. I just don't want to create a big scandal for her sake. If I can just get her back to Moscow, without there being an unpleasant scene at the airport, it will be much better for her."

Blackwell could see he'd struck a sympathetic chord with the old gentleman. He tugged again a little on his left ear, clearly thinking about something. He finally spoke. "You really don't want to make that horrible trip by road back to Moscow. What if I could get you on a cargo plane to Moscow, with there being no record of you being onboard?"

"And how could you arrange that?" asked an intrigued Blackwell.

"That's where I worked for 40 years, before I got too old and got into this taxi business. I still have lots of friends at the cargo airline. It will cost you maybe US$ 700 for each of you."

"That's a fair price and another $700 for you for setting this up."

"Well, I'm in no position to turn it down, but that isn't why I'll help you. When we were out the other day, I noticed how that young lady looks at you. She's definitely in love with you. I hope you two can work things out when you get back to America."

"How early tomorrow can we leave Ekaterinburg?"

"There's a 2:00 p.m. daily cargo flight. I'll pick you up here at noon sharp and take you where you need to be. It would help if I could have $700 now, so I can show my friends that this is for real. You give them the other $700 when you take off."

Blackwell reached across the small table and shook Yuri's hand. "You're a good man." As the two stood up, he discreetly slipped him the $1400. We'll see you tomorrow at noon."

MOSCOW

Five men in civilian clothing, but with military bearing and haircuts walked into the lobby of the Hotel *Metropol* and headed directly for the manager's office suite. The leader of the group, Captain Borodin, showed his GRU credentials to the attractive, young secretary in the outer office and explained that he needed to speak immediately with the manager. Whether the old Russia or the new Russia, Russian citizens knew you did what a Russian security service official told you to do. She buzzed the manager and told him who was waiting. He was immediately at his door. "Come in gentlemen. How may I be of assistance to you today? Do you have time for a coffee while we talk?"

They didn't. Five minutes later, the hotel records for Miss Cathleen Spenser and everyone else who had checked in on the same day were on the manager's desk for the review of the captain. One of his subordinates began reviewing recent security tapes of the lobby, restaurant and entrances. The other three spread out to interview hotel staff, to see who remembered the attractive *Amerikanka* who spoke excellent Russian. At the end of two hours of diligent work, the GRU team had narrowed the list of possible suspects of who might be the white-haired Karl Beck down to one white-haired Robert Blackwell, a businessman from Chicago. They'd checked in at almost the same time and several employees remembered seeing the two of them together. Both Spenser and Blackwell still had rooms at the hotel and personal possessions in them, but they had not been seen since they allegedly took a cab to *Domodedovo* Airport, to catch a plane to St. Petersburg. A tech officer arrived in the afternoon to check for prints in both of their hotel rooms. He easily found prints for Spenser. In Blackwell's room, strangely, there were no fingerprints on any surfaces in the room, but the tech finally managed to pull a couple of partials from the metal clasps on a small overnight bag. There were no fingerprint records on file for the woman in the GRU or general Russian criminal data base. As for the man, there was some difficulty as they only had partials on a couple of fingers. It would likely be the following morning before conclusive results were available. General Klemenko had the initial report on his desk by the end of the day. It noted that Cathleen Spenser and her friend, Robert Blackwell, had flown not to St. Petersburg, but to Ekaterinburg, two days earlier. Gennady took out his personal cell phone and called Nikolai. "Your two friends have flown to Ekaterinburg. They are watch listed to see when they fly out of there. The male is using the name of Robert Blackwell. Is that enough information for you?"

"Yes, General, thank you very much. I owe you a favor." He heard a click at the other end.

Nick turned to the two junior trainee gangsters who were with him at a restaurant. "We've got an identification for Karl Beck. He's going by the name of Robert Blackwell. He and the woman flew to Ekaterinburg two days ago. You two get on the next plane out there. I want you to physically go visit the hotels used by foreigners and if there's no one registered as Spenser and Blackwell, ask the staffs if anybody's seen an old, white-haired guy with a good-looking American woman half his age. This guy's clever. He may have changed names again, but there can't be that many Americans who go to middle-of-fucking nowhere Ekaterinburg! They gave us the slip in Indiana. That isn't going to happen on our turf."

EKATERINBURG

In the late afternoon, Blackwell went down to check once again his email to see if Bob had sent any further news for him on the Interpol warrant or if there might be an offer of delivering to him a new passport. When he got back upstairs, he broke the bad news to Cathleen. "Per Bob's email, the Interpol warrant is officially out for one Robert Blackwell. And there's a big debate still going on about whether I get sent help or I'm on my own. Good thing your grandfather still has friends in low places."

"Aren't they considering the ramifications for the Group, if you're arrested for the Norway killing?"

"That's the calm analysis of the situation, but the fact that I brought this problem upon myself by using the Blackwell documents without permission -- that's what's governing their thinking. And as for ramifications, remember, I'm really KGB officer Parshenko. If I'm arrested, the Group would quickly leak that little fact to the world press and fingers would be pointed at evil Russia, not some hypothetical private group of retirees in America."

"Nice bunch you're working for."

"I'm liked on a personal basis, but professionally, the organization comes first. They don't know why I'm here or how serious is my situation. Obviously, to some of their minds, delivering to me yet another American alias passport might just be digging them a deeper problem -- if I am arrested. This isn't a business for the faint-hearted."

"Any indication whether the issuance of this warrant has hit the news?"

"It doesn't look like it. I checked a variety of websites and there's nothing about it. Fortunately, a four-month old killing when there's only a grainy picture of a suspect isn't much of a story, but I obviously can't now get on an international flight in that name."

She went over and gave him a kiss. "Oh well, I bet Yuri will give you a job driving his car part-time and we can just settle down here in the Urals!"

"I think once we get our hands on those encyclopedias tonight, I could do a little better than that. Why, I could buy my own used car and go into business by myself!"

"You've turned into such a capitalist."

"Changing topics; we've been lucky so far at avoiding Viktor's people, but let's not press our luck. I have one more errand to do to get ready for tonight, then I suggest we stay right here in this room, until time to go to the university tonight." "Sounds like a good idea to me. Besides Viktor's guys, I'd prefer not to run into Mr. Nokamura again!"

He put on the *Dynamo* soccer club ball cap he'd purchased down in the gift shop and left the suite. He took the elevator straight to the basement and went out a service door. He walked the mile or so to find the bicycle shop he'd noticed the day before. He bought a large, old-fashioned bike with a large sturdy basket on the back, perfect for hauling heavy sacks of potatoes or even a number of books. Russian bicycles weren't made for recreational riding, but for work. He also bought a heavy chain and lock, then rode the bike over to the university campus. He locked it to a tree around the back of the library and hoped bicycle theft was not a major problem in Ekaterinburg. He made one last stop at a small all-purpose store, then grabbed a taxi back to the hotel.

Once back in the suite, he reviewed one last time with Cathleen the plan for that night. It was a fairly straightforward set of actions and in twenty minutes there was really nothing left to discuss.

"You hungry?" he asked.

"More nervous than hungry, but I suppose I should eat something."

"Let's order room service."

Once their sandwiches and coffee arrived, they settled onto the sofa with the nice view of the city. Robbie then turned to a completely different subject.

"Maybe we ought discuss into whose house we should move, once we get back to Bloomington."

"Yes, I suppose we should discuss that." She was pleasantly surprised by his bringing up the subject. "You do have the bigger place and it's certainly more conveniently located to campus than mine, but it's a weirdly designed house. We might want to look around and see what else in the neighborhood might be on the market."

He thought she was politely resisting the idea. "I mean, if you want to... I guess, I shouldn't take it for granted that you want to move in with me... It's just that..."

Cathleen found it slightly humorous that a man who was so smooth in planning international espionage events was stumbling around like an undergraduate student in bringing up the subject of her moving in with him. She didn't want to torture him any longer, so she interrupted his rambling, with "Yes, I do want to move in with you."

"OK, we'll find a real estate agent when we return and start looking for a new place. We might even be able to afford something a little larger, if tonight goes well." He gave her a little smile.

"I like how you skip over the few 'little details' ahead of us, before we can get back to Bloomington," was her final comment on the subject.

He suggested that they try to get some rest, but both were too excited to sleep. The possibility in a few hours of having in their hands millions of dollars of jewels was not a thought easily pushed out of their brains. They lay on the bed, half dozing, half dreaming. The alarm buzzed at midnight. Blackwell dressed in the black pants and shirt he'd bought that afternoon. He put on his ball cap to cover his white hair and stuffed the black leather gloves in his back pocket. He picked up the cheap canvas bag he'd also bought that day and they were off. They took the elevator to the basement and went out the service exit. It was two miles to the university, but Blackwell didn't want to risk taking a taxi -- in case there were any serious police inquiries afterwards. He was hoping that a robbery of a few books of no apparent value from a library would not be considered the crime of the century by the local police, but that was no reason to be sloppy. With luck, the police might think the theft had only been some sort of prank and let a few days go by before seriously looking into the matter.

Upon arrival at the front of the library, they stood embracing for twenty minutes, leaning against a nearby building's wall. This gave them a good view of the library entrance, to check for any sign of life inside the Administration section of the building. A young couple walked by at one point, so Cathleen and Blackwell started kissing -- a simple, non-verbal explanation as to why they were standing there at two in the morning.

"I see no sign of anyone, let's move," he whispered to her. They walked around to the back, retrieved his bicycle and positioned it under the window that he had discreetly unlocked during his previous visit to the Reference Room. He prayed that no one had noticed and relocked it. He stood up on the bike while Cathleen steadied it. He gently pushed on the window. It moved. He pushed it as far open as he could, then gave a jump which allowed him to get a good grip on the bottom of the window sill. He pulled himself up and through the window. Cathleen tossed the canvas bag up to him, then took the bike and moved off to the cover of some nearby bushes.

Blackwell took out his small flashlight and quietly navigated his way to the wall behind the Reference Desk. He paused for a moment and listened. There were no sounds of any kind within the building. Lenin continued to sternly stare down from his portrait, but made no cry for help. Blackwell placed all sixty-five volumes of the Great Soviet Encyclopedia, 1926 edition, into the bag. He dragged the 150 lbs or so of books back to the window. He spread his feet, bent his knees and gave one large grunt to get the bag up to the window. He lowered it out the window as far as his arms allowed, then dropped it. He hurried back to the shelf and grabbed up an armful of various other books. He tossed them out the window as well. He lowered himself out the window and dropped to the ground. With her help, he got the bag up into the basket. They left the other books where they'd fallen, to create the impression that these few had been dropped while making off with all the others.

"God, you were in there forever. What were you doing, reading each volume!"

"There were a lot of books."

They walked the bike off into the night, under a clear sky filled with stars, and into a nearby park. They soon found a place Blackwell was searching for -- an area with lots of bushes. He spotted an opening between two of the willowy bushes and shoved the bike deep into the vegetation. They had a nice hiding place for the bike and them. It was nearly 3:00 a.m. He tore off some of the branches to make a sort of bed for them, mostly to try to keep Cathleen reasonably clean.

"Do you think there are really diamonds hidden in those spines?" she quietly asked.

"I guess there's only one way to find out," was his calm reply. "We ought to confirm there are jewels in them before worrying about getting them out of Russia."

"Do you have a knife with you?"

"Yes." He took out his small flash light and fished around in the bag till he found the volume he was looking for -- a Geographical supplement he'd noticed while filling the canvas bag. It wasn't likely to be missed from the set. He opened the book, then took the small pocket knife and sliced into the spine from the inside, while she held the light. He was finally able to break open the spine from top to bottom and out tumbled five good-sized diamonds onto the ground! Even in the low light they sparkled with fire.

"Oh my god! It's all true," excitedly whispered Cathleen.

Blackwell also noticed hidden in the spine a bit of tightly rolled paper about four inches long. He put it into his pants pocket and scooped up the diamonds from the ground. Step one was successfully completed. They lay down and she snuggled into his arm, her head upon his chest. She didn't think she could possibly sleep, lying next to millions of dollars of diamonds, but within minutes, she was asleep.

WEDNESDAY

Sunrise comes early in that part of Russia in July. By six, the birds were chirping and the two of them awoke at about the same time.

"It's daylight, let's get out of here." He pushed his way out of their sylvan den first, to check to see if anyone was around. Murphy's Law was working against him that morning. A *babushka* with a young child in hand was coming along the path just as he exited. She started to give him a curious look, wondering what he'd been doing in the bushes. He immediately reached down as if zipping up his fly and started staggering forward as any good Russian male who'd been out on an all-night drunk would do. She started giving him a good piece of her mind, as she moved quickly away with her grandson, but at least she didn't start hollering for the police.

Once she was out of sight, he pushed his way back into the bushes to help Cathleen bring the bicycle out. They had about two hours to kill. They walked their bike with its priceless treasure out of the park. They finally found a place open that early, calling itself the "French Cafe", which had outdoor seating and offered coffee and rolls. Cathleen went into to make the purchases while he guarded the bicycle. A minute later, she placed a paper sack full of *ponchiki* in front of Blackwell. They were fresh out of the fryer and still warm. He bit into one and memories of his childhood flooded into his brain. The coffee was terrible, but the delicious, Russian equivalent of the doughnut more than compensated.

He carefully pulled from his pocket the rolled up note he'd found in the binding of the book . "While we're killing time, we might as well have a peek at this." On the yellowed piece of paper was handwritten Russian, in ink. He handed it to Cathleen to see.

She took a quick glance. "I have a terrible time trying to read handwritten Russian. Perhaps you'd have better luck."

He took out a pair of reading glasses and started examining the note, assuming at first that it was by Ivy. However, it didn't look like any handwriting of hers he'd previously seen, nor was it terribly literate. It seemed more like the writing of a semi-educated person and it looked masculine. He quickly concluded that this was clearly not written by the well-educated Ivy. He slowly read through the note, guessing at some of the words. Finally, he mumbled in Russian, half out loud, the equivalent of "holy shit." He turned to Cathleen.

"I'm guessing this was written by Yurovsky. He says Princess Anastasia didn't die that night in July with her family because she was pregnant with his child and he couldn't stand to see his unborn child murdered. He substituted a local woman who occasionally cleaned at the Ipatiev House for Anastasia that fateful night. He got her drunk on vodka and put her in the fancy clothes of the princess, telling her it was a big prank. There was only one dim light bulb in the cellar, when they took the prisoners downstairs at 2:00 a.m. In all the chaos, panic and shooting, the other guards didn't notice the switch. Yurovsky then took Anastasia to a local women's monastery and there she stayed till their son was born seven months later. Anastasia died within a few hours after giving birth. The nuns knew that she was of an upper class family and had agreed to protect her from the Bolsheviks, but had no idea she was a Romanov. The son never knew his true origins and by 1938 was studying to be a priest at a small rural church in *Shirokaya Rechka*, a village south of Sverdlovsk. The boy had the name of Nikolai Yakovich Petrovsky."

"That has to be a hoax," was all that Cathleen could manage to say.

"If it is, it's a damn good one. Look at the age of the paper. And the phrasing of the sentences is that of a man who perhaps went to school till maybe the age of 10 or 12 -- that's what education Yurovsky had."

"The yellowing paper might mean only that it's an old hoax."

"That's true, but who would be trying to pull off such a hoax and why?" responded Blackwell. "Presumably, only Ivy, Yurovsky and the bookbinder could have placed this with the diamonds. Can you see any motivation for any of them to attempt such a hoax?"

"Nothing immediately comes to mind, but I guess there's a way to confirm the validity of such statements."

"How?"

"By checking at this monastery and this church. The Russian Orthodox Church was always very good about keeping records and this part of the Soviet Union was never touched by the invading Nazi armies, so their church records should still be around."

"I suppose we might have time yet this morning to make a quick trip to that little village before going to the airport, if I can get hold of Yuri to take us there. I'll try to get hold of him while you're taking care of mailing our books."

They killed almost an hour at the cafe and Cathleen was able to use the bathroom to clean up a bit. The next hour they spent walking and sitting at various bus stops, slowly making their way to their destination, while continuing to debate the authenticity of the note.

At a little after 8:00 a.m., they arrived at the American Consulate. Blackwell unloaded the heavy bag at the front gate and rode off on the bike, leaving Cathleen to explain to the local guard why she was there.

"I'd like to speak with Cultural Affairs Attaché Powell, please," she stated in Russian. He seemed a bit skeptical of admitting her to even the outer waiting courtyard till she showed him her American passport. He picked up his phone and made the call. He refused to help her with her bag, so on the street she remained.

Several minutes later, Attaché Powell came rushing out the front gate. "Dr. Spenser, how good to see you!"

"Please, call me Cathleen."

"Do come in, come in. I don't know why they made you wait out here on the street."

"Well, this was about as far as I could get with this heavy bag full of books and you're fellow here behind the glass informed me that wasn't his job."

Powell gave the local guard a dirty look and then reached for the bag himself. "I'll carry it for you."

"Do be careful, it's terribly heavy I'm afraid."

His first attempt to lift it with one hand failed. He then put all his might into the effort with both hands, while trying to appear as if it was not a problem. He got it as far as the inner waiting room, when he spotted two local employees and assigned them the task to bring the bag further. The Marine Guard on duty did a cursory inspection, confirming that it was indeed only a bag full of old books.

Once Powell, Cathleen and her bag were settled in his office, with two cups of coffee before them, she began her story.

"You know that flea market over on Pushkin Square, where they sell a bit of everything, don't you?"

Powell nodded positively, though he'd never stopped there in his life.

"Well, I found there this morning this marvelous old set of the Great Soviet Encyclopedia. It's the 1926 edition, the first one to come out, but then you knew that, of course."

Another untruthful nod from Powell. "Of course."

She took out a volume and handed it to her admirer. "As you can see, it's in excellent condition."

"Was it terribly expensive?" he enquired while thumbing through the first few pages.

"No, it was a steal really. The man who sold it to me claimed that it had been his grandmother's, but who knows the truth when you buy things at such markets."

It was still unclear to him why she had brought the pile of old books to show him. "Yes, well, you've certainly gotten a real bargain, I'm sure, " he mumbled vaguely.

"Oh, Terrence -- may I call you Terrence?"

"Terry, actually."

"Terry, this is such a find. Our curator of antique books in the Lilly Library will be ecstatic when she learns that I've acquired them. The entire original set!"

Terry was trying to share her enthusiasm. "Yes, quite a find! And thank you for bringing them here to show me."

"Well, you did tell me that if I ever needed anything, you were here for us visiting scholars. Thank goodness I met you yesterday. Terry, my hero!"

Terry almost blushed, though he was as confused as ever about why she'd brought the books to the Consulate. "And just exactly how can I help you?"

"The problem is the weight. You can imagine what sort of extra baggage fee the airlines would charge me for 150 pounds or more, on top of my own suitcases. And you must know what a small salary assistant professors receive." She reached over and touched his arm and gave him her best smile. "I was wondering if there was any way that these might be shipped out by the Consulate, back to the Lilly Library in Bloomington? What do you call that system, your diplomatic sacks?"

"Diplomatic pouch," he corrected her.

"Oh, you diplomats and all your terms. The Library will probably put a front piece in the first volume, noting the kind assistance of Attaché Terry Powell in acquiring the collection." She was actually wasting her breath at this point. She'd won him over soon as she touched his arm.

"It's a bit unusual, but I think I can consider it a special case for you," he beamed.

She provided him the address for the Lilly Library at Indiana University. He promised her that the set would be in the next diplomatic pouch. "Our bag goes out by plane every Monday, so it will be in Washington by Wednesday or so of next week, and out to Bloomington by UPS within a week or two after that."

"You are a genius! Well, I suppose I shouldn't take up anymore of your valuable time." She stood to leave.

"Perhaps we could have lunch today. My treat."

"I'd love to, but my plane leaves for Moscow this afternoon." She gave him a hug and a kiss on the cheek. "My hero!"

She met up with Blackwell at a bus top three blocks from the Consulate.

"How'd it go?"

"He'll personally wrap each book in velvet. They'll go out in the diplomatic pouch this coming Monday."

"Dare I ask how you achieved this?" he teased her.

"For a kiss on the cheek. God knows what that man would do in return for sex! Did you get hold of Yuri?"

"Yes, and he knows exactly where the church is at *Shirokaya Rechka* and said that there is only one women's monastery around here, so presumably that's the one we want. It's in the same general area as the church. He'll be waiting for us at the service entrance of the hotel in about a half hour, so we need to get moving."

They left the bike sitting behind the bus shelter, the chain and lock in the basket. A taxi took them to within a few blocks of the hotel.

MOSCOW

General Klemenko started his days early at the GRU Headquarters. He'd already had breakfast and several cups of coffee by the time that his aide, Alex, knocked on his door and entered carrying two folders.

"Good morning, General Klemenko. I have two rather interesting and confusing reports for you to see." He laid the first one down on the general's large desk. "The partial finger prints believed to belong to the American, Robert Blackwell, had a match in the Russian files, but at first it seemed impossible. According to Records, they have an eighty percent match to a dead KGB officer, named Nikolai Parshenko. He was killed while trying to defect some twenty years ago.

"Have they been drinking this early in the morning in the Technical Section?" Klemenko laughed at his own humor.

"Yes, Sir, I was ready to dismiss it as well, until we received a coded message this morning from our long-time agent, UMNITZ, informing us that former KGB Colonel Parshenko was still alive and had traveled to Russia, using the alias Mr. Blackwell."

"What," practically shouted the general. "Let me see that report."

UMNITZ reported that he hadn't been able to send or receive coded messages for over a week because of a computer problem, but finally he got it solved and the simple facts were that Parshenko was not dead, as thought for twenty years, and he traveled last week to Moscow under the cover of being Chicago businessman, Robert Blackwell. The purpose of the trip was unknown.

General Klemenko read it twice. "Immediately advise our Ekaterinburg office of the basic identifying details of these two Americans and tell them that Blackwell is a known enemy of the state, is to be considered dangerous and should be shot upon sight. No need to put at risk any officer's safety to try to capture alive. And don't go into whether he might be Parshenko."

Alex stood motionless, in silence. He'd never heard such an order before.

"Have you gone deaf, major?"

"No, Sir. I will send the instructions immediately." He saluted smartly and exited the office.

It had been a long time since Klemenko had even thought about Parshenko. He had been presumed dead for a long time. He should go back to being dead. Klemenko had no need for that old story to be revived and start people talking again about how the wife and child had been killed, or precisely who had ordered the assassination. He also wondered how his partner in crime, Nikolai, was tied in with Parshenko. Did he even know that the man he called Karl Beck was Parshenko? In any case, he'd wait to see how things played out before he bothered telling Nikolai anything more. Even with the finger print evidence, there was plenty of room for error and this might all be nonsense.

EKATERINBURG

Cathleen and Blackwell again used the service entrance to re-enter the hotel. They'd packed most of their things the night before, so after quick showers, they were ready to depart with a few minutes to spare. The phone rang.

"Mr. Blackwell, it's Pavel down here at the Front Desk."

"Yes, Pavel. I was about to phone you to ask you to prepare my bill."

"I thought you should know, I just had a phone call from someone claiming to be from the GRU -- wanting to know if I had a Mr. Blackwell or a Miss Spenser registered here. I told them that our computer was down and to phone back in about twenty minutes."

"Thank you very much Pavel."

"Not a problem. When it's not the FSB, it's those bums from the GRU, all coming around, shaking down the manager for money or free dinners. Fuck'em all!"

"Your uncle is waiting for us now at the service entrance around back. Perhaps, it would be best if you'd bring the bill up to our room and then we'll be gone."

"I'll be there in two minutes."

Blackwell put down the phone and turned to Cathleen. "Someone claiming to be with the GRU just phoned the hotel, asking for us by our names. Pavel is on his way here now and we'll slip out the basement entrance."

"Sounds like we're getting out of Dodge just in time."

"Dodge? We're in Ekaterinburg." He gave her a puzzled look.

"Never mind. But remind me to buy you a book of American expressions when we get home. Do you think it's Viktor's people pretending to be with the GRU, or really the GRU?"

"It's impossible to know, but bad news in either case, since whoever they are, now have the name of Blackwell."

Pavel arrived with a baggage cart, as well as the bill. "I'll help you with the bags. I wouldn't want any of the staff downstairs to think you were trying to sneak out the back with your luggage without paying." He gave them a big smile.

Blackwell signed the credit charge and handed the form back to Pavel, along with five of the lovely hundred dollar bills. "You've been a great help. If anyone does show up here in the next few minutes looking for us, stall as long as you reasonably can, then tell them I checked out. You didn't see how I left."

Five minutes later, the two were in Yuri's car and on their way to the church, south of the city.

No sooner had Pavel returned to the Front Desk then two young men came walking through the lobby. They'd just arrived on the early morning flight from Moscow. They both wore leather jackets, even though it was summertime and certainly looked like a couple of Mafioso thugs.

Pavel greeted them. "Good morning, gentlemen. How may I assist you?"

"Do you have a Miss Spenser or a Mr. Blackwell staying here?" Pavel debated how to respond. They didn't look like the type to believe a story of his computer being down.

"Let me check those names for you," seemed the wisest response. "What was that first name, Spenser?"

"Yes, Cathleen Spenser."

Pavel drug it out as long as he could, as he'd promised Blackwell. "I'm not finding anyone. Is that Cathleen with a C or a K?"

"What the hell difference does it make?" responded one of the thugs, who was obviously losing his patience.

"To a computer, it means everything. No, no Cathleen Spenser with either a C or a K for the first name. What was the next name?"

"Robert Blackwell -- and there's only fucking way to spell Robert."

"Ah yes, we did have a Mr. Blackwell staying with us, but I'm afraid he already checked out earlier this morning."

"Where did he go? Did he have a car or take a taxi or what?"

"I'm afraid I couldn't say. I wasn't on duty here at the desk when he checked out. Perhaps the doorman out front might remember if he left in a taxi."

The two headed back to the front door. In case they weren't happy at learning nothing from the doorman and returned, Pavel called for one of his colleagues to come out from the back office to take over for a few minutes, claiming he needed a cigarette. Pavel figured that his uncle and the two Americans would be safely gone from the hotel by now.

After Pavel saw the two Mafioso fellows drive away, he returned to his post, much relieved. However, no sooner than he was back behind the Front Desk than the GRU officer phoned again. Pavel responded that there was a Robert Blackwell staying there, but no Cathleen Spenser. The GRU man said not to inform Blackwell of their call, and that they'd be over shortly. Pavel's bravery had reached its limit, even for $500. He went into the manager's office, explained that he was feeling quite ill and had to go home. Pavel couldn't guess what was going on, nor did he want to know and had no intention of being around when the GRU showed up.

Driving along in his car, Yuri inquired of his passengers, "Did you two do anything exciting on your last night?"

"No, we had a quiet dinner up in our room and enjoyed the nighttime view of your lovely city."

Yuri pointed off to his left. "By the way, that's the site of the Ipatiev House that I mentioned to you." There was a tour bus parked there and a dozen or so people were out on the sidewalk taking photographs of the golden-domed Church on the Blood that had been built where the famous house had once stood. "It's ironic," added Yuri, "that it was Yeltsin who oversaw the destruction of the original house back in 1977, when he was still a nobody out here in the Urals, and then the church was built while he ruled Russia."

"Very interesting," replied Blackwell, as he gave Cathleen's hand a squeeze.

"We'll be at the church in about 15 minutes." Yuri was old and wise enough to know that if Blackwell wanted him to know why they were making a trip to an old, unimportant rural church, he'd tell him. So, he asked nothing.

Yuri pulled up to the simple entrance of the church grounds and his passengers exited. The iron gate was closed and there was no way for the car to go any further. The two entered the grounds on foot. The grounds were full of large and very old birch trees and obviously well tended. Blackwell guessed the church itself was well over a hundred years old. Fortunately, Cathleen had a scarf to place over her head. It was indeed a modest little church, somewhat in need of repair. On this occasion, Murphy was smiling on Blackwell, for a priest was just coming out of the church as they walked towards it.

"Good morning Father. What a lovely church you have here."

"We're small, but I try to honor God as best I can. You're foreigners?"

"Americans," responded Cathleen. I'm a professor at Indiana University and I promised one of my colleagues that since I would be in Ekaterinburg, I would stop and check on someone she thought was a distant relative who might be buried here."

"Certainly. Your Russian is very good."

"Thank you for the compliment."

"Please, let me show you our church."

"We'd love to see it." They didn't have much time, but they had to be polite to Father Dmitry, who was at least seventy years old.

"Our young priests today don't want to come to such small churches in the countryside, but for me, this is a wonderful place, with good people. It's been my home for almost fifty years. Even the Communist Party in the old days left me alone out here in the wilderness."

"You were lucky," commented Blackwell.

"Well, the Sverdlovsk Communist Party First Secretary's grandmother attended our services and even quietly brought her great grandson to be baptized here, so we had sort of an understanding." He gave Cathleen a wink.

There was room for perhaps fifty parishioners in the church. Its interior plaster walls were painted white. It was a simple, yet lovely old church. After a quick tour of his church, Father Dmitry asked, "so who is this person you want to check on?"

His name was Nikolai Yakovich Petrovsky, supposedly he was training to enter the priesthood around Sverdlovsk in 1938. Do you recognize that name?"

"Yes, I did know him. He was an exceptional man. Anyone who spent time with him could tell that there was something special about him. He'd been born right here in the area and raised as an orphan. His mother died in childbirth I think he told me one time. He was a parish priest in this area, or sometimes it's called a 'white' priest. By that, I mean he was married. As I recall, he died in the mid-1980s. Come, I'll show you his grave."

"Did he have children?" asked Cathleen as they entered the small graveyard area that was reserved for members of the clergy.

Father Dmitry pointed at a simple marker in the ground. Here he is, with his wife, who as you see outlived him by a few years. As for children, yes, I believe he did have two daughters."

"Are they still alive?"

"One girl died as a child, but the other girl is a nun over at the Women's Monastery. Sister Anastasia is her name and she is the *Igumeniya*, the head of the monastery. You must have driven by it on the way here from Ekaterinburg. She is slowing down and not in great health. Well, who of us of such an age isn't?" He laughed.

"I believe we did see a monastery off in the distance while riding here."

"It's a lovely place, but I'm not sure how much longer it will be an active monastery."

"Why is that?" asked Blackwell.

"Like many things in this world, a lack of money. There has been some talk of the city buying it and turning it into a tourism center."

"That would be a shame." Cathleen noted down the dates of birth and death for Nikolai and his wife. "You have been very kind, but we have to catch a plane shortly, so I'm afraid that we must be going."

Blackwell had slipped back inside the chapel for a moment and pushed a $100 bill into the donation box. He rejoined Cathleen and Father Dmitry at the front gate.

"Are either of you by any chance of the faith?"

"No, Father, but we would value your blessing for a safe journey," responded Blackwell. Father Dmitry said a brief prayer over them.

Once back in the car, Yuri informed them that they had to start for the airport immediately, if they didn't want to miss their flight. There was no time left to stop at the monastery. There would be no conversation with Sister Anastasia. That was frustrating, but with Viktor's people and possibly the GRU closing in on them, they couldn't safely stay another day. They had to make today's two o'clock flight.

Thirty minutes later, the car pulled up to a guardhouse by the cargo entrance to the airport. Yuri got out and went over to the guard. From their greeting, it was clear they were old pals. The two chatted for a minute. Yuri stuffed something into the guard's shirt pocket and they shook hands. He returned to the car. "It's all taken care of." He drove them directly over to an old IL-76. The co-pilot was waiting at the bottom of the stairway. Yuri made the introductions of "Mr. and Mrs. Smith." The co-pilot took their bags up into the plane, while they made their farewells to Yuri.

Cathleen gave Yuri a big hug. "You've been so kind."

"You two be happy," replied the old man, with a tear starting to form in one eye.

Blackwell gave him a firm handshake and the two climbed up the metal stairway. The co-pilot followed them. The door was closed and a ground crewman pulled away the ladder. Blackwell handed the co-pilot an envelope with the additional $700. He stuffed it into a pocket and pointed at two jump seats attached to the bulkhead. The "Smiths" attached their seatbelts and the plane started taxing out to the runway. "I feel like Ilsa and Victor Lazlo flying out of Casablanca," quipped Cathleen.

Once airborne, they returned to the topic obviously on both their minds. "You still think that note is a hoax?" asked Blackwell.

"It does seem more believable now that we've talked to Father Dmitry, but nothing is one hundred percent certain. Yes, there was a Nikolai born at the monastery, who became a priest. Those facts are true. Whether he was the son of Princess Anastasia... well, who knows? It would cast a different light on why Yurovsky made a number of pilgrimages back to Sverdlovsk, ostensibly for reunions with his fellow murderers of the royal family. Maybe, he really came back to the area to see how his secret son was doing?"

"I guess there's really no way to ever know the truth of the note," added Blackwell.

"Only DNA testing could prove or deny such a story and can you imagine the chaos and fighting that would create among the currently known Romanov descendents? They already argue over who is the rightful heir to the non-existent throne as it is, and all of them have only rather roundabout bloodline connections. Sister Anastasia would be a direct descendent and the real imperial highness, if it were all true."

"Yes, but you know what I think of DNA testing. I do find it quite a coincidence that Nikolai named one of his daughters Anastasia?"

"Are you suggesting Nikolai did actually know who his mother really was?"

"Just one more mystery," replied Blackwell. "Perhaps my biggest problem is with the idea that Anastasia and Yurovsky had a sexual affair in the first place. The differences between them. The conditions under which they met."

Cathleen gave him a hard look. "It's called rape. A woman doesn't have to be in love with a man to have his child."

Blackwell could tell from her look and the tone of her voice that he'd unintentionally touched upon a sensitive point with Cathleen. "But if that had been the case, surely she would have told people about it?"

"Not necessarily. She could have been too embarrassed. I'm afraid you men don't understand very well the psychology of rape for a woman. Or, given their already precarious situation of being under house arrest, she might have felt that telling her father would have made things even worse."

"You seem quite knowledgeable about this. Was there ... I mean were ...?"

"No, not me." She paused for a long moment. "My mother was raped by an English soldier in Belfast. She never told anyone at the time because she knew what her father would have done in retaliation and probably gotten himself killed in the process. So, she moved to Boston, where I was born some months later."

"I'm sorry. I didn't mean to pry about a part of your life you obviously preferred not to talk about with me."

"I was going to explain it all to you one day. Today was as good as any other."

"So, there never was a Mr. Spenser?"

"Oh, there was a Bernard Spenser. My mother's first employer and eventually her husband. He treated me as if I had been his own daughter. I never knew he wasn't until many years after his death. When I turned eighteen, mom decided it was time for me to know the truth about my past. Grandpa still doesn't know and never will."

They both closed their eyes and tried to sleep for the rest of the flight. They still had to get Blackwell out of Russia, and hanging like a cloud over them was still the question of what he would do about the assassin of his family.

CHAPTER 11

MOSCOW -- LATE AFTERNOON

The plane with its special human cargo made a rough landing two hours later in Moscow. Blackwell hoped there were no fragile products on board. Obviously, the ability to make smooth landings was not a criterion for flying with this airline.

The co-pilot reappeared once they had taxied to a stop near a hanger. "Wait in the plane until I come for you."

"Is there a problem?" asked Blackwell.

"No, we just need to wait for the local manager to pick up the manifest sheet and leave. He's an asshole and would want a share of the fee."

Blackwell smiled. "Understood."

A few minutes later, the co-pilot returned and gave them a thumbs up. "He's gone. And I called a friend with a taxi. He's waiting just outside the gate over there."

They walked the hundred meters to a truck gate for the airport. The exit for Cathleen and Blackwell out the control gate of Domodedovo airport was without challenge. Airport security is designed to check on people coming in, not going out. As promised, waiting outside the gate was a taxi. Blackwell told the taxi driver to take them to the Leningrad train station. They still had their rooms waiting for them at the Hotel *Metropol*, running up hefty credit card charges, but returning there seemed an unwise move. Keeping the rooms, however, did serve the purpose of possibly making whoever was looking for them think they hadn't yet returned to Moscow. Upon arrival at the station, surprisingly, the driver only charged them the correct fare for the long ride into the city.

They took their bags and headed into the station, as if they were going to catch a train. "Another false trail?" asked Cathleen.

"You're catching on. It's the little details that add up."

They simply walked straight through the large terminal and out another exit. Fortunately for them, a train from St. Petersburg had recently arrived, so there were hundreds of people going in every direction. "There's what I'm looking for," commented Blackwell. Since the end of the USSR, capitalist hustling was just as prominent in Moscow as in major tourist cities all over Europe. Thirty or so men with small signs lined both sides of the exit out of the station, all touting bus tours, cheap motels and "special" massage parlors.

The age-mismatched couple weren't that poorly dressed, but they certainly looked tired and bedraggled. Blackwell approached an older man with a handmade, cardboard sign in English -- "cheap room."

"What sort of room do you have and how much?" he asked, speaking English.

"Nice room in our apartment, very clean. My wife prepare you breakfast. Only 25 American dollar, two people."

"Where in the city?"

"At metro stop *Tulskaya* -- not far."

"We're agreed," replied Blackwell in Russian and reached out to shake the man's hand. "What's your name?"

"I'm Igor. You speak Russian?"

Blackwell tried to speak haltingly with a bad accent. "A little. My mother spoke Russian."

Igor took two of their bags and led them away. Walking several yards behind Igor, Cathleen whispered to Robbie , "You sure this is safe?"

"Perfectly. Given the poor economy, this guy is probably unemployed and the only way for he and his wife to make a few rubles is to rent out part of their apartment. And the best part, the names Blackwell and Spenser show up on no computer records that anyone can check."

"It's amazing how one can travel and lodge completely off the grid in this country if you wish."

"It's not only in Russia," he replied, "if you know how."

The Metro was crowded, but it wasn't yet the evening rush hour when it would be a crush of humanity pushing into every car. They reached the man's apartment in about 40 minutes and met his wife, Maria. She showed them the spare bedroom, which was small, like all older apartments in Moscow, but as promised, it was clean and quite adequate for their needs.

The name Smith had worked well enough on the plane, so they stuck with being Mr. and Mrs. Smith. Cathleen pretended to know only a few words of Russian, which would minimize the amount of questioning of her by an inquisitive Maria -- who clearly found the age difference of the couple interesting.

"Here is the $75 for three nights." Igor took the bills and immediately handed them to Maria. Like in most Russian families, it was the wife who ran the family finances.

"My Maria or I are always here to let you in. You came from St. Petersburg?"

"Yes, we were there for several days and on Saturday we fly home to America, to Chicago."

"Would you like some tea," offered Maria.

"Perhaps later. Now, I think we should start exploring your city, as we only have two days here."

Igor gave him a small sheet of paper with the address of the apartment and the home phone number, should they get lost. The two made their goodbyes and exited back out onto the streets of Moscow.

"I wouldn't have minded some tea actually," commented Cathleen.

"Yes, but do you know how hard it is for me to pretend to only speak a little Russian badly! I had to get out of there."

They returned to the Metro and traveled to the *Universitekski* Metro station and then proceeded on foot away from the center of the city along *Leninsky Prospekt*. Being the heart of the summer, there were ice cream vendor carts practically every block. The couple bought two cones of strawberry and were enjoying the stroll, looking in the various shop windows. They were almost to Number 87.

Blackwell stopped under a tree in the block before his target. "I don't know if you want to come any further with me, or if you should, in any case."

"I presume you're not going to kill him this very hour, are you?"

"No, just checking out the neighborhood." He wasn't certain if she was teasing him or not.

"Then I suppose I'll keep you company. With me on your arm, the *babushkas* will just think that you're a dirty old man, rather than an assassin." She gave him a big grin.

They entered the large complex. Fortunately, Blackwell had the precise *korpus* and apartment number as well, otherwise it would have taken a long time to find the desired apartment out of the hundreds and hundreds at Number 87. The door of the building he sought was propped open with a rock, so he could walk right into the small ground level foyer and found a mailbox labeled with a faded piece of paper "Verchagin, V." Blackwell stepped back outside and glanced around at the surrounding buildings, checking for any sort of security cameras. There were none. "That's all I need for now. Let's go find a decent restaurant, but away from the tourist spots."

Back near their Metro station, they saw a place called the *Praga*, even though there seemed to be nothing particularly Czech about the fare listed on the menu posted in the window. The menu was only in Russian. A good sign this wasn't a place frequented by Western tourists and thus not a place that whoever was looking for them, might be checking.

They entered through the double glass doors. It looked reasonably clean and there were a number of people eating, so they decided to give it a try. They got a table off in a corner of the restaurant. At Igor's apartment they were trying to pass themselves off as Americans who barely knew Russian. Here, the idea was to appear to be locals.

Once they'd ordered and received their soup, Cathleen raised the remaining delicate subject. "So, you're still planning on killing this man?"

"Yes, I am."

"Would you prefer not to discuss this?"

"I don't mind discussing it. I've told you I love you and that I want you in my life. It would be ridiculous that I wouldn't be willing to discuss anything with you, especially something as important to both of us as this."

"OK, so just for the sake of argument, let me ask, what does killing this man achieve for you?"

He closed his eyes in thought for a few moments. "Call it justice. The Russian government certainly won't do anything against him, since the KGB ordered his actions. Call it revenge if you like. You Americans don't seem to believe in revenge anymore, but I do. I promised my dead wife and son that the man who killed them would pay."

"And getting this revenge will make you feel better?"

"Yes, it will. And in whatever after life there may be, I think it will calm their souls as well."

"Alright, even if I accept those two points as valid reasons to kill him, what about the danger of you getting caught? You and I have a future together that we're both looking forward to, correct? You're putting that future at risk aren't you?"

"So you think that means I don't truly love you? That I love my dead wife more than I do you, and that fulfilling a promise to a dead woman is more important to me than our future life together? It's not that way at all. It will be hard to explain to someone not in the espionage profession, but you need to understand that when I weigh the pluses and minuses of an operation, I never think there is any way I can fail."

"You can't fail? You apparently 'failed' in Norway didn't you?"

"Failed? No. Could it have come off better? Of course. But my assignment was to kill that mullah. I did that and though the alias name has been compromised, I have not been caught."

"So, by your way of thinking, you don't think you can fail in killing this Verchagin?"

"No. You need to understand what is the mentality of all good intelligence officers in the world -- Russian or American or French. We all believe when it comes to a work-related matter, that we will always outwit, outmaneuver and outrun our opponent. If one doesn't have that absolute self-confidence, a person should never go into this line of work."

Cathleen could see that there was no talking him out of his plan. She could even see a certain logic to his thinking, particularly about the value of revenge. Her Irish ancestors had long been firm believers in revenge. "Is there anything I can do to assist you?"

"No, you'll have no part in this." He gave her a little smile and added, "and if I turn out to be wrong about the not failing thing, you get on the first plane back to America. Understood?"

"My god, I haven't even moved in with you yet and already you're giving me orders!" She gave him a wink.

He reached across the narrow table and took her hand. "I love you."

OSLO

Mansour parked his car at a cockeyed angle out front and rushed past the colorful carpets in the sales portion of the store. "They've got a suspect," he practically shouted to Mohammed the Elder and Karim.

"For Abdul's killer?"

"Yes, I came directly here from Police Headquarters. Deputy Commissioner Knudsen told me in strictest confidence that by checking at all the hotels in Bergen and showing a photo of a man who was photographed entering the cruise ship with a large bag, they've concluded that their suspect is an American named Robert Blackwell."

"Do they know where he is?" asked Karim.

"Not yet, but they've issued an Interpol warrant for his arrest on the suspicion of murder. A check of international flight records show that he flew to Moscow a few days ago."

"Any other news?"

"Knudsen has started taking Arabic lessons. He greeted me today in Arabic. His accent is atrocious!" responded Mustafa.

They all had a good laugh and Mustafa was dismissed. Once he'd left, the two members of the leadership debated what, if any actions, were required.

"Perhaps we should alert our Chechen colleagues? He could be on his way to kill Dzhokar in Moscow." suggested Karim.

"Maybe. It would at least be a good gesture on our part to the Chechens," responded Mohammed the Elder. "Can you arrange for our Chechen boy to safely phone Dzhokar and warn him?"

"I can. No one in the Norwegian police understands Chechen, so we don't have to worry about being intercepted. But he only likes to be phoned late in the evening. I'll arrange it for later tonight."

"Have him tell Dzhokar that if he can somehow find Blackwell in Moscow and kill him, we will greatly appreciate it. And that if we get any further details on Blackwell's location, we will phone again."

MOSCOW

Karim had been correct. No one in the Norwegian police could speak Chechen. That was not the case with the Russian *Service of Special Communications and Information,* formerly an independent agency named FAPSI, but now a component of the FSB -- the new name for the former internal security components of the old KGB. Because of the years of fighting in Chechnya, they had dozens of Chechen interpreters in their equivalent of America's NSA. They easily intercepted the call that night to Dzhokar, because the "clean" cell phone he was using had been supplied to him a few weeks earlier by an FSB informant. The FSB monitored every incoming and outgoing call the Chechen made on that phone. A complete translation of the interesting phone call from Oslo would be on the desk of an officer in the Counterterrorism Department of the FSB by morning.

CHAPTER 12

THURSDAY MORNING

Despite telling Maria the night before that neither of them were big breakfast eaters, when they exited from their room in the morning, she had bowls of kasha, fruit, fresh bread rolls with a pot of home-made jam and a large pot of hot tea ready for them.

"My goodness", commented Cathleen, "this is marvelous. I won't have to eat again till dinnertime!" Blackwell translated her compliment into Russian for Maria. They struggled through several more minutes of him "trying" to translate between the two ladies, until Maria gave up and returned to the kitchen. Twenty minutes later, the two were out the door, supposedly for a day of tourism. At the Metro stop, they went their separate ways. Cathleen headed off to locate Paddy's Pub, somewhere near the Kremlin, where they were to meet "Shaun" on Friday afternoon to get the new passport. Blackwell headed again for No. 87 *Leninsky Prospekt* to learn as much as he could about the movements and habits of Verchagin. He would need some background information, in order to plan his own assassination of the assassin. Retired or not, Verchagin was most likely still a very cautious and alert man. He and Cathleen were to meet back at the room around noon.

Upon arrival at the apartment complex, he went to the entrance of Verchagin's building and rang his buzzer. He didn't plan on confronting him at that very moment. He just wanted to confirm whether he was home or not. Blackwell got no response on the intercom system, though there could be several reasons for that, including a likely one in such an old building, that it hadn't worked for years. He went back out into the courtyard area and sat on a bench. He kept an eye on the windows and balcony of what he calculated was probably apartment 22 on the second floor.

A minute after he sat down, one of the *babushkas* with her granddaughter came and sat down next to him. "Who are you looking for?" she directly asked. "I saw you ring a buzzer, but I guess they're not home."

"That's correct. I was looking for Mr. Verchagin. Have you seen him around today?"

"Today is Thursday, isn't it? He goes somewhere every Thursday till about noon."

Blackwell wondered to himself why they even had a police force in Russia when they had the *babushka* patrol monitoring everyone! "Do you know him well?"

"Well enough, I suppose. He's lived here for maybe 12-13 years. You a friend of his?"

"No, I've never met him."

"Then why are you looking for him?"

Blackwell had come prepared for such a question. "Well, I live in St. Petersburg and my mother died recently. As I was going through her old papers, it turns out that Mr. Verchagin and I might actually be distant cousins. I thought I had no living relatives. I had to travel to Moscow on business and decided to come find out if we are, in fact, related. You know much about his family and past?"

"Very little really," she replied, then proceeded to provide everything except his pension number. "His wife died of cancer three years back and their one son was killed in an automobile accident about seven years ago. He's all alone now -- just spends most days sitting in that apartment. He'd be thrilled to learn he had a relative. His arthritis is terrible and he has kidney problems. I think he's just waiting to die." She crossed herself. "Can't blame him really, he has a rather miserable existence."

"Do you know what he did before he retired?"

"He was always a little vague. Something to do with the military, he once told my husband one evening when they were drinking together to celebrate Victory Day over the Nazis. Anyway, he doesn't seem to have a friend in the world, so he should be happy to learn of you."

"Did he ever mention living for many years out in Vladivostok?"

"No, I'm pretty sure he was born in Moscow, spent most all of his life here and will probably soon die here."

"Oh! I'm afraid then that I'm on the trail of the wrong Verchagin. My mother's letters were clear that my cousin had worked for many years out in the Far East."

"That's too bad, for both of you," the old lady commiserated.

"Well, you've been very helpful. I wouldn't mention my asking about him to Mr. Verchagin. Might depress him to think that he almost had a cousin."

"You're right and he seems depressed enough. Good luck on your search."

"Goodbye."

Grandma had been a wealth of information. She'd naturally gossip to every other old lady in the building about the interesting man from St. Petersburg, but she probably wouldn't tell Verchagin himself about his visit. Her information had put him in the mood to walk and think, so he opted to return on foot to his rented room. It had certainly shattered his mental image of a still dangerous foe, who would have to be stalked very carefully. He also considered what Cathleen had said to him the evening before about going after Verchagin.

He began to talk to Olga as he strolled. *"Well, that was a bit of a surprise wasn't it. It looks as though Verchagin is more miserable alive than he would be dead. I was prepared to kill the SOB, but that might actually be doing him a favor. I'll have to think about this a little more. But I will have my revenge for his killing you and Pavel."*

He found Cathleen in their room. Maria was chopping and cooking in the kitchen. Igor was still off somewhere. Blackwell wondered what Igor did when he wasn't hustling motel clients?

"How was your day, Mrs. Smith?"

"Excellent. I found Paddy's Pub easily enough, so we're all set for Friday. How'd your reconnaissance go? Did you find Verchagin?"

"Better than finding him. I found and chatted with one of his elderly female neighbors, who told me a lot about him."

"What is it with you and *babushkas*!"

"Best source of intelligence there is in Russia." He proceeded to tell her all he'd learned about Verchagin's rather sad life.

"And what is your next move?"

He didn't answer for half a minute or more as he stared down at the wooden floor. "I'm going to let the bastard live and suffer. He's so miserable that killing him would be doing him a favor, not punishing him. I do wish there was a way, however, to let him know I've found him and why I'm letting him live."

"God, remind me to never get you really mad at me. You are one hard man."

"I told you I wanted justice and revenge. Those can be achieved in my mind by letting him continue to suffer, not only by killing him."

"I see your point. If you feel satisfied with that solution, I certainly am. Then all that's left on our to-do list is to get the fake passport and get the hell out of this country!"

"There is actually one more problem. Viktor Litvinov and his thuggish friends still know our true names and where we live. If they don't find us here, they'll just come looking for us back in Bloomington."

"You're right. I've been so focused on our immediate problems, I hadn't thought about what happens once we're back home again in Indiana. You're the devious one between the two of us. What's your plan?"

"I'm thinking about it. Can I have lunch first before I have to come up with some clever solution?"

"Sure, as long as you're buying. Let's go eat."

They soon found a small café, which was packed – always a good sign. "Does it seem strange to be back in Moscow after all these years?" she inquired, in between bites of the rather bland *pelmeni*.

"It certainly has brought back many memories -- some good, some bad."

"Care to share any?"

"I've thought about my dead parents. And about many places that were important to me as a young man – a certain hockey rink where I played, where I met my wife, the hospital where our son was born."

"Those all sound like pretty good memories."

"Those are, but there have been others. Some thoughts have been about getting old and of having spent so many years alone since losing Olga and before finding you. Those are twenty years I can never get back. And I've thought about whether my defection was all worth it. Perhaps

I should have just stayed in Russia, stayed in the KGB, rose in the ranks along with all the other hypocrites – at least my wife and child would still be alive today."

"I've only known you a few months and your real background for a few weeks, but whether you're Nikolai or Karl, I know you well enough to say that you couldn't have lived that way for the past twenty years. You're not that cynical in your heart and soul to have led such a hypocritical life. You took a course of action that was best for you and your family at that time in history. Just because there was tragedy for your family along that path doesn't mean it wasn't the right choice."

He reached over and touched her cheek. "How did such a young woman become so wise? Let's hope I have again chosen the correct path, with you by my side."

By mid-morning Thursday, Captain Kosygin of the FSB's Chechen Section within the Counterterrorism Department, had received the Russian translation of the previous night's phone call from Oslo. He knocked on the door of the section head, Major Federov. "For once, the intercept people actually sent us something worth reading. You want the whole thing or just the juicy bits?"

Federov's glare gave him his answer, as his boss leaned back in his chair.

"Unknown Chechen Male No 1, in Oslo, called Dzhokar last night and told him that a fellow named Robert Blackwell, who'd recently assassinated Mullah Abdul in Bergen, is now in Moscow. That the Norwegians had an Interpol warrant out on Blackwell, but that Dzhokar should be extra careful in case Blackwell had come to Russia to kill him too. But if he had a chance, the 'brothers' in Norway would appreciate his killing Blackwell."

"I know who Dzhokar is, but what do we have on Mullah Abdul or this Blackwell?" asked Federov, as he clasped both hands behind his head and put his feet up on his cheap metal desk.

"As for Mullah Abdul, he was linked with a terrorist group in Norway, called the United Jihad of Europe -- till somebody shot him a few months ago. The phone call pretty much confirms what we already thought -- that Dzhokar was connected with the suicide bombing of the police station down in Chechnya four months ago by the UJE."

"And what do know about Blackwell?"

"Not much really. His documents say he is a sixty-four year old American and the Norwegians just put out an Interpol warrant on him in connection with Abdul's murder. He made a brief trip to Odessa last fall for a few days. At about that time, documents linking an Algerian businessman residing in Odessa to the Algerian GIA terrorist group, were anonymously delivered to the local newspaper. That might be purely coincidental."

"The FSB doesn't believe in coincidences. So, should we arrest this Blackwell, or give him a medal? What else?"

"According to flight records, Blackwell flew into Moscow a few days ago, then out to Ekaterinburg, where he presumably still is."

"Who the hell would he go to kill in god-forsaken Ekaterinburg? I hear people out there commit suicide from boredom, but assassination?"

Captain Kosygin shrugged his shoulders. "That's all we have. Should we notify Norway?"

"The hell with the Norwegians. This has to be some sort of mix-up. Who ever heard of a sixty-four year old assassin! OK, send a message to our Ekaterinburg office, but downplay the possibility that the Blackwell there is the one being hunted. I doubt it is, but it will at least give those useless alcoholics out there something to do."

CHAPTER 13

THURSDAY AFTERNOON

EKATERINBURG

Despite the low-key phrasing of the message to the FSB office in Ekaterinburg about Robert Blackwell, Colonel Petrov, the local chief, took it very seriously. This might be his ticket out of the dumping ground of the Urals. He immediately pulled twelve officers off of all other security investigations. This was to have top priority -- even above going out and shaking down local businessmen for "donations" to the colonel's favorite charity -- himself.

Within an hour, one of his officers had learned that Robert Blackwell had stayed at the Regency Hotel until just the previous day. When the FSB officers showed up to ask questions, no one on the staff bothered to tell them that the GRU had been there the day before, asking about the same man. Russian citizens had learned decades earlier, not to go volunteering information to a security officer, so they certainly did not bring the fact up themselves. Nor had the local GRU office bothered to officially inform their FSB colleagues of their investigation or vice versa. Both considered it none of the other's business.

Fortunately for the FSB, no one had yet cleaned the suite in which Blackwell had stayed, as it wasn't booked again till Monday. Colonel Petrov immediately sent all three of his technicians over to the hotel, with orders to gather fingerprints and do every other test they knew on the room. They found literally no prints on any surface in the room, where normally there would be prints of guests, but they got lucky. Underneath the sofa facing the large window, they found a glass on its side. Presumably, it had rolled under there and not been noticed by the guests of the room. According to registration, only Blackwell stayed in the room, but a check of the room service orders clearly indicated that two people had been staying there. The investigators got excited that they might be on the trail of two assassins, until further questioning showed that the other person had been a young, attractive woman with black hair. Further questioning led them to the barman who'd watched an attractive, black haired woman try to pick up one of the Japanese businessmen. The investigators concluded that most likely the woman was a prostitute, who Blackwell had picked up somewhere along the line.

Being military officers, no one from the GRU the day before had bothered to question the staff about Blackwell. Once the GRU men had learned that Blackwell had already checked out, they simply went back to their office and reported that fact to GRU Headquarters in Moscow. Independent thinking and initiative were traits that could only get one in trouble in Russian military intelligence. The FSB officers on the other hand, were police investigators at heart, and spent a lot of time talking to the hotel staff. It wasn't long before they got hold of Pavel and through him, his Uncle Yuri. From Yuri, the FSB learned about the two "unofficial" passengers on the cargo plane to Moscow, on Wednesday afternoon. For a "donation" of the amount Blackwell paid Yuri to arrange the flight, the FSB interviewer offered not to arrest Yuri for assisting a wanted man. Yuri had expected such a proposal and claimed from the start that Blackwell had only paid him $400, so Yuri finished the day with $300 still in his pocket.

More interesting for the FSB, they heard from Pavel about the visit of a couple of young, tough guys in cheap leather jackets inquiring about Blackwell and the woman the day before. Late that day, Colonel Petrov sent the fingerprints with a courier on the evening flight to Moscow and cabled in a lengthy report to Moscow Headquarters, alerting them that Blackwell was presumably back in Moscow.

MOSCOW

When Cathleen and Blackwell returned to the apartment after lunch, they found Igor at home instead of Maria. She'd gone out to do the daily shopping. Given the small size of refrigerators in the older apartments of the city, one couldn't store that much, but it was also tradition. Russians went shopping practically every day. Cathleen went straight to their bedroom to take a little nap. The stress of the last few days had exhausted her. Blackwell stayed in the living room to chat with Igor.

"What work did you do before you retired, if you don't mind my asking?"

Igor inhaled one last time on the remaining half inch of his cheap, Russian brand cigarette, before stubbing it out in the ash of the many that had gone before it. "I was a police detective, but I was too honest for being a policeman in today's Russia."

Blackwell found it amusing that of the ten million people in Moscow, he'd found an ex-policeman's home in which to hide! "That must have been interesting work, although I take it, at times, a little frustrating."

"Frustrating! Every damn senior police official in Moscow is on the take. You can arrest all the petty criminals you want, but the police don't touch any of the crime families and their operations."

"So you retired?"

"I was unlucky enough to arrest late one night the son of one of the major Mafioso bastards in this city. He'd beaten to death his girlfriend in front of five witnesses at this club. What was I supposed to do, brush off his coat and let him walk away? Daddy wasn't happy his little boy had to spend a few nights in jail, before he was released for lack of evidence, when the five witnesses developed amnesia. The word on the street was that daddy was going to have killed whoever had put his son in jail. Fortunately, I had a captain who liked me. He told me to immediately ask for retirement before I had an 'accident.' I'm brave, but not stupid. I retired. I just wished I'd shot dead the little prick instead of only cracking his head with the butt of my gun when he resisted arrest. I'm alive, but you can't live on my meager retirement check, so we take in tourists like you."

"Well, it's better than many a motel I've stayed in," replied Blackwell, trying to make the guy feel better. "You have any other little jobs to make money?"

"I work now and then as a night watchman at a warehouse out at the end of *Leninsky Prospekt* -- they call me whenever they need a substitute during vacation times or somebody's sick. It's a warehouse full of computers. In fact, I'm there the next three nights."

"Well, you're out of all that corruption. You have a nice apartment and a good wife. Lots of people worse off than you are my friend."

"True. Well, I need to get some sleep before I go on duty tonight. Help yourself in the kitchen, if you or your wife want to make some tea."

"Thanks. By the way, do you carry a gun at this job?"

"Of course. I still have my old Makarov handgun. Any punk comes into that warehouse when I'm there, I'm going to shoot him dead and then worry about where to hide the body later."

Blackwell gave Igor a puzzled look.

"I mean, I'll just dump the body somewhere instead of wasting people's time by calling the police. There's enough dead bodies found every morning in Moscow, nobody would care if there's one more."

"A practical approach. See you tomorrow."

"See you."

Blackwell leaned back in the comfortable chair and turned his mind again to the problem of Viktor Litvinenko. If it was only Viktor, he might be able to buy or threaten him off, but he clearly had colleagues and connections clear into Russia itself. He had to be part of a Russian gang, though his personality certainly hadn't struck Blackwell as a mob member. He checked his metal pocket watch for the time and decided that a phone call was in order. He left a note for Cathleen, saying he'd gone out for a stroll, then quietly let himself out the door. He walked to the *Tulskaya* Metro stop and made his way back to the Leningrad train station, where they'd first met Igor.

As in most major European cities, there was a PTT call center, within the train station. The FSB or city police might "live" monitor international calls from such centers made by a few specific people they were watching, but it would be days or weeks before anyone actually listened to the recordings of the thousands of other calls made from there every day. He dialed Viktor Litvinenko's home number in New York City. It was only a little after nine in the morning there, so hopefully, he was still at home.

After a number of rings, a sleepy voice answered, "Hello."

"Viktor, this is Professor Beck calling."

There was several seconds of silence. "Yes, Professor, how are you?"

"I'm in Russia and I'm losing my patience at being followed by your friends."

"My friends? What? You're in Russia?"

"Viktor, I don't have time to play games." he stated in a cold voice that immediately got Viktor's attention. "Now you start telling me exactly what your part in this is, or I promise you, when I return soon to America, I will teach you a whole new definition of the word pain. You have no idea who you are messing with."

Nick had always scared Viktor, but Beck raised his level of fear to being absolutely terrified, and didn't doubt for a moment what Beck had just told him. Cowardice and honesty seemed to be his best course. "After you visited me, I went to see Nikolai Tsimbal at a club out in Brighton Beach. He's the American representative of a certain family in Moscow, if you understand me?"

"I understand. Keep talking."

"Because of certain things my grandmother Ivy had told me many years ago, I connected your questions with the Romanov jewels. I told Nick of my suspicions. If anybody's been following you, it's him, or his people, not me. I swear."

"Why did you go to Nick?"

"I owe him $20,000 in gambling debts. This was my way out, if he could get you to tell him where the jewels are. You do know don't you? You've found them?" Viktor asked with excitement in his voice.

"Yes, I've found them. You tell Nick that I want to make a deal with him. The jewels for the safety of me and the woman."

"I don't know if I can reach him. I believe he's in Russia right now himself."

"I have complete faith in you Viktor, that you can contact him. You tell him that at midnight, Friday night, for him to come to a computer warehouse out at the end of *Leninsky Prospekt*. I'll be waiting inside the warehouse with the jewels. I want to meet directly with him, and hear from his lips a promise that we'll be left alone after the exchange. And tell him to come alone. That surely he has the balls to meet a woman and an old man without a bunch of bodyguards."

"You want me to say that to Nick!"

"You tell him that word-for-word. And tell him that if he isn't there at that time, I'll just disappear with all the jewels and start a new life in a new country."

"I'll do my best to reach him."

Blackwell put down the receiver and went over to pay the charge to the cashier. He thought that went fairly well. He was almost smiling. It was nearly six when he reached the apartment. It was Cathleen who immediately let him in when he knocked.

"I was getting worried. Where have you been?"

"I had to make a phone call to Viktor and set something in play."

"Did Viktor admit that he's been having us followed?"

"It's a little worse than it being Viktor. Viktor brought in as a partner, a Brighton Beach Mafioso named Nikolai Tsmibal, who has connections all over Russia. Tsimbal knows about the diamonds and flew over here personally to hunt for us and the diamonds."

"Oh great, so we have the Russian Mafia on our trail?"

"Just one family actually."

Usually, she appreciated his sense of humor, but this sounded bad and her face showed it. "And what else did you and Viktor discuss?"

"He's to set up a meeting between me and this Tsimbal for tomorrow night." He quickly gave her the outline of the plan he'd come up with for dealing with Tsimbal.

"I hope you know what you're doing," was her final comment.

"Get your purse and let's go down to the heart of the city. We'll be rather busy tomorrow night, so this is really my last chance to look around Moscow. I doubt I'll ever be back to my Motherland again after this, and there are some places I'd like to see one last time".

They took the Metro to the center of the city and then walked around for several hours, as evening crept in and the city's lights flickered on. When he'd left twenty years earlier, Moscow had been rather drab and cheerless, especially at night. Now, all the neon advertising, architectural lighting on buildings and better street lights made the city look like most of the other major metropolitan centers of Europe. Russians had been schizophrenic for centuries over wanting to think of themselves as Russians, not Europeans, but to judge their degree of modernity, they always wanted to look like Western Europe.

It was a clear night and the temperature had come down to an agreeable level. There were thousands of Muscovites and foreign tourists out enjoying life. Some people they passed were hurrying to specific places, but many like them, were just aimlessly strolling around the city, on a pleasant summer's night. It stayed light at that time of the year till almost midnight. Blackwell had always thought that Moscow was at its loveliest in the lingering twilight of summer nights. They walked once more over the cobblestones of Red Square and past the Kremlin, admiring the colorful, onion domes of St. Basil's. They wandered down the old Arbat, now a pedestrian street. They walked arm-in-arm, but mostly in silence. Cathleen could sense that he was reliving old memories, probably memories that involved his dead wife and son. She gave him his privacy. They bought *shashlik* for their dinner from a street vendor and went and sat down along the embankment of the *Moskva* River. Many other couples were doing the same, in that romantic setting. A large dinner-boat glided past, with its bright lights and the sound of dance music drifting over the water to the shore. The band was playing *Love Me Tender*. Blackwell smiled.

He finally felt like talking. "It's such a shame what is happening with Russia. We Russians are really a good-natured and wonderful people, but we never seem to be able to govern ourselves well. We put up with the czars for 800 years, then the communists and now little more than a thinly veiled dictatorship – a cozy conglomerate of crooks, oligarchs and egotistical politicians. At least with Marxism-Leninism, there was an ideological belief that all the sacrifices were leading to a better society. Today, it's just greed and personal desire for power. I want no more of Russia."

Cathleen would have liked to have tried to cheer him up somehow, but sadly she agreed with most everything he'd said about current day Russia and its prospects for the near future. "Perhaps things will eventually improve," was the best response she could manage. "What's on our schedule for tomorrow, other than getting your new passport?"

He described to her briefly his plan for dealing with Nikolai Tsimbal.

"I think this will all work out, but in case something does go wrong, know that I love you very much."

She'd been leaning up against his shoulder. She put her finger up to his lips. "Shhh. I'm with a man who doesn't fail, remember. I'm not worried and I love you too." He gave her a long kiss.

"Let's go home. We need a good night's rest." Blackwell helped her to her feet.

"Oh, we're going home and we're going to bed, but it isn't rest that you're going to be getting, mister!"

"Viktor, it's Nick. Stefan at the club tells me you desperately need to speak to me?" Viktor had been calling the Brighton Beach club number every hour on the hour since Beck had called him, asking for word to be gotten to Nick to call him immediately.

"Professor Beck called me this morning from Moscow, with a message for you."

Nick put down his glass and told the others at his table to be quiet. "And what is the message from our shy professor?"

"He said he has hundreds of those 'items' we're looking for and wants to make a trade. Said he's tired of being followed and wants to make a deal with you for his safety."

"And how does he know of me?"

"He knows people have been looking for him and the girl. He thought it was me behind that."

Nick snorted into his cell phone -- as if anybody could be afraid of Viktor. "And this old professor so frightened you with a phone call from 6,000 miles away that you immediately gave him my name! Yes, well, I can see why he suspected that there must be somebody with actual balls chasing him. So what is this deal he wants to make?"

"He'll trade all the 'items' for a promise directly from you to him that after he gives you what you want, you'll leave him and the girl alone. He wants to meet you alone Friday night at midnight, at some computer warehouse, at the far end of *Leninsky Prospekt*. And I'm just quoting him, so don't get mad at me -- he said that surely you've got the balls to come meet an old man and a girl without all your bodyguards. Said if you don't come, he'll just disappear to another country and that's the last we'll see of the 'items' or him."

Nikolai's eyes narrowed. "If he calls you back, you tell him that we have a deal and I'll come alone." He ended the call without waiting for a reply from Viktor. He turned to his three colleagues. "We're going to kill that asshole we've been chasing all over the country tomorrow night."

CHAPTER 14

FRIDAY

Captain Kosygin of the FSB Counterterrorism Division knocked on his boss' door around ten that Friday morning, holding an official red folder. "We received a three-page report this morning from Colonel Petrov out at Ekaterinburg. It has about three paragraphs of facts; the rest are all adjectives, describing the brilliant work of Petrov."

Major Federov snorted. "Typical. Give me the three paragraph version."

Captain Kosygin filled him in on Blackwell's activities in Ekaterinburg, including how two young Mafios were also looking for Blackwell and about there being a woman with him, maybe a prostitute.

"Well, even an assassin needs some entertainment when he's not killing someone. Visiting a non-existent book store and an old, rural church is a little harder to comprehend."

"I've saved the best for last. Our Records Section this morning ran the prints that Ekaterinburg sent to us last night and they got a perfect match for Mr. Blackwell. He's really Nikolai Parshenko."

"Ah, now we're getting somewhere. And who is Parshenko?" asked Federov as he stubbed out a cigarette. His fifteenth or so of the morning.

"Parshenko was a member of the KGB's First Chief Directorate."

"Was, you say? I presume he's long since retired?"

"I guess you could say he was retired. He was shot and killed twenty years ago, while trying to defect to the Americans in Prague."

"What bullshit is going on here?" Major Federov sat straight up in his chair.

"The Records people checked them twice and I went down myself and had the director personally show me the prints taken from the hotel suite to those on file for Parshenko. They sure looked like a match to me."

"That does it. I don't get paid enough to sort out this kind of craziness." He picked up the phone and called to General Mishkin's office, the chief of the Counterterrorism Directorate, and asked for an appointment as soon as possible.

He put down the phone and turned back to Valery. "The general is at a meeting at the Kremlin. They'll call us as soon as he returns and is available to see us. Stay close."

Blackwell and Cathleen had slept in. Friday would be a big day. Some already knew that, others would only learn it as the day progressed. Igor awoke and came out to the living room about noon. He would grab another nap in the early evening, but he couldn't sleep more than about four hours at a time anymore. Maria was out doing errands, so he made himself a light lunch, sat down at the kitchen table and lit a cigarette. The kitchen was the center of a Russian home, not the living room. Blackwell had heard Igor come out of his bedroom and came out of theirs a few minutes later. He joined Igor at the table and accepted a cup of tea. He figured Igor was the type of fellow who preferred that you got right to the point of a conversation, so he did.

"Igor, I'm not quite the old, poor retiree with a young wife I've pretended to be."

Igor exhaled the strong, blue smoke in Blackwell's direction. "I didn't exactly believe that story, but your money was real and you're entitled to your privacy."

"I won't pretend that I'm going to tell you the whole story, but what I am about to tell you is the truth."

Igor had liked Blackwell all along and he was growing fonder every minute. A man who was so honest that he even told you that he wasn't going to tell you the complete truth was Igor's kind of man. "I'm listening."

"The head of the Brighton Beach, New York branch of the Mogilevich crime family is looking for us. They'll certainly hurt us, maybe kill us. That's why we couldn't stay in a regular hotel and register. Given the

Mafioso connections in the Russian government and police, they could have tracked us down through the computer registrations. Why he's hunting us isn't particularly important to you, but I assure you, we're the innocent victims of circumstances here.

"Brighton Beach, eh? A bum named Tsimbal is, or was, the head in New York."

"Yes, Nikolai Tsimbal is the fellow. I see you keep up with events."

"I'm retired, but I read what's going on in the world. And I assume your names aren't Smith?"

"No, but the real problem is that when we get out of Moscow on Saturday, Tsimbal does know our true names and will come searching for us in America, and he knows where we live. So, I'm going to finish this here, tonight, with your help."

"And why should I get involved in your problem?" He took a deep drag on his cigarette.

"Because you told me that you'd been an honest cop and I believed you."

Igor played with the ash from the end of his cigarette against the edge of the ash tray for a few seconds while he thought. "Yes, I was honest, but more importantly to your request, it was the Mogilevich family with whom I had the run-in that cost me my job. I'll be happy to assist screwing any asshole connected with them. What do you want from me?"

"I'll need to borrow your uniform, gun and keys to the warehouse tonight. Tsimbal is coming there for a meeting with me. I intend to kill him."

Igor laughed. "You got much experience at killing people?"

"Yes, I do."

Given the calm way "Smith" answered that question, Igor stopped laughing. He believed him. "Perhaps you can kill Tsimbal, but that kind never comes alone. Can you kill two or three?"

"I've pricked his ego. He may come alone, or hopefully, he'll at least leave the others who may come with him outside the warehouse. I'll deal with them once I've killed Tsimbal."

"Why do you need my guard uniform?"

"He'll expect a rent-a-cop to be there. Sorry, no offense."

"None taken, that's what I am anymore."

"I'll be what he expects, an old man on the night shift as the watchman.

He's never met me face-to-face. By the way, do you hopefully have two handguns?"

"I do. One's my old service piece, a Makarov, and the other is a piece of crap the guard company gave me."

"Good, I'll need two. And I need one more thing from you."

"What?"

"You indicated yesterday that you knew how to dispose of a body. Once I come back here safely, I'd like you to then go to work and dump the body or bodies somewhere."

"I can do that. In fact, I have the perfect place. I'll dump them just before dawn outside this nightclub run by the Mogilevich crime family and pin a note on one of them that says 'Stay out of the Ace of Hearts' -- that's another club, but one that's run by the Ovenko crime family. There's already bad blood between Ovenko and Mogilevich. They may think that somebody in the Ovenko family killed Nikolai."

"Good idea. I've spent about all the cash I have on me, but when I leave Saturday morning, everything left in my pockets is yours."

"OK, plus anything I find in Tsimbal's pockets is mine as well. No offense, but that bum will probably have a lot more on him than you carry."

"None taken. We're agreed." They both reached across the table and shook hands.

Cathleen and Blackwell arrived at Paddy's Pub promptly at two o'clock, as directed by her grandfather. It was made to look like a 1920s Irish pub, complete with "antique" wooden bar and a brass foot rail. The wall behind the bar had shelving all the way up to the ceiling, full of bottles of every brand of whiskey made in Ireland or Scotland. There was a CD of Irish jigs and reels playing and the two bartenders on duty appeared to be imported, genuine Irishmen. Despite it being the middle of the afternoon, the place was quite crowded -- mostly with foreigners. Blackwell couldn't understand why people who'd traveled to see Russia would spend time in a totally fake Irish Pub? Cathleen made her way straight to one of the bartenders and asked if Shaun from County Kerry had by chance arrived? The bartender pointed to an elderly gentleman at the end of the bar, enjoying a pint of Smithwicks. He was a short man in his mid-sixties, with pale skin. He had faint traces of red in his eyebrows and sideburns.

He looked like a Hollywood depiction of an elderly, Irish leprechaun. Cathleen and Blackwell approached him together.

"Are you Shaun?"

"Are you the girl with the cutest tits in all of Ireland?" he asked with an Irish accent so thick you could have cut it with a knife.

"That's me -- all three of them are cute."

"Your grandfather sends his regards." He emptied his glass. "Order me another one darlin', while I go take a piss."

Blackwell leaned over and whispered in her ear. "That's the bona fides phrase your own grandfather set up? About whether you have cute tits?"

"It didn't seem out of place in a pub like this did it?" she replied with a big grin.

"Any idea why your grandfather chose this location?"

"Because one of his old comrade-in-arms owns it. Flynn had been a finance man for the IRA and had lots of money hidden away when the fighting finally ended. It had been stolen from English banks and they weren't about to give it back, so Flynn decided to do something useful with it. He opened a string of these pubs across Europe and gave jobs to all the IRA boys who wanted one immediately, or for some, once they'd gotten out of prison."

Shaun returned from the toilet and found a fresh pint in front of him at the bar. "So, this is the man who has a little travel problem is it?"

"Yes, I'm ...", Blackwell started to say, but Shaun cut him off.

"Oh, for sure, you're Ryan O'Brian. I'd have recognized you anywhere." He lowered his voice a bit. "And I've your documents in me pocket that prove that's who you are." Cathleen darlin', you stay here and have a drink, while Ryan and me go into the back for a few minutes and take a photo." Shaun took his beer with him.

They passed through the manager's office and into a small storage room. Shaun pulled down a screen for a white backdrop and took out his digital pocket camera. "That white hair does make you stand out a bit." He took a look at the passport. "It says here that you have red hair. Well, that's a bit unbelievable isn't it, for someone your age! We'll just make it bit of a faded brown. He took out a spray bottle from a cabinet. "Close your eyes." He sprayed the washable hair dye on the front half of Ryan's hair. "Just tilt your head back a little for the photo, so that only the sprayed part shows." He quickly took a couple of pictures.

GENE COYLE

"This will wash right out, won't it?"

"Ah, sure, you can use that sink over in the corner, while I print out one of these."

In five minutes, Blackwell had his white hair again and Ryan O'Brian's passport had a lovely photo in it and the whole page had been laminated.

"Here's the can of the dye. Don't forget to spray yourself before you go to the airport tomorrow. And make sure you memorize your birth date and address in Dublin."

"Got it."

"Here are your airline tickets. Be in front of the *Rossiya* Hotel tomorrow, at 10:00 a.m. sharp, to get on a bus with your tour group -- Erin Travel. Two hundred and fifty of your fellow countrymen have been over here for a week, sampling the booze and the women. Two hundred of them will already be pissed when they board the buses. After the Russian Passport Control lads at the airport have to deal with a couple hundred people all named O'Brian, O'Ryan and O'Flynn, they won't give a shit who they let out of the country. Just try to be towards the back of the pack when you get to the Control windows."

"Thank you. Always a privilege dealing with a professional."

"Remember, once you're in Ireland, destroy this passport. Don't try to travel into America with it. It isn't that good of a forgery, but it'll get you out of this backward dump."

"Anything else?"

"Don't come back here for any reason, cause I'll be gone and no one here will admit they know you. Also, her grandfather said for me to tell you that if you ever make her sad, he'll come and cut off your nuts. Understood?"

"Understood."

"Have a safe trip."

When Blackwell returned to the bar, he slipped the can of hair dye spray into her purse. "Let's leave now." Once out on the street, he explained to her the instructions about the tour group tomorrow.

"Sounds like they're as thorough as you are."

"It's an excellent plan and this forgery looks first class."

"One task done and one to go tonight. Anything else you want to see or do around the city today or have your nostalgia desires been satiated?"

"I'm going to take the Metro out to where this warehouse is located and have a quick look around in the daytime, to get a lay of the land. What about you?"

"I suppose I ought to stop by the State Library and explain to the Director of Foreign Research how some emergency is calling me home. I'll probably want to go back there someday and I don't won't to leave him annoyed. After he supposedly worked so hard to move forward the dates of my research, I don't want to just not show up with no explanation. It's only a short walk from here, then I'll head straight back to the apartment and wait for you there."

"OK. I'll see you in an hour or so." He gave her a quick kiss and then moved off into the crowd of pedestrians.

General Mishkin returned to the FSB Headquarters in the infamous Lubyanka building around three o'clock. After the briefings at the Kremlin, he and several other generals had lunched together, before he returned to work. His aide told him upon arrival how Major Federov urgently needed to see him.

"Come in Anatoly. What's so important? Have you found Osama bin-Laden hiding in a dacha on the outskirts of Moscow?"

Federov and Kosygin, carrying the red folder, stood at attention in front of the general's desk -- a desk said to have been used by the infamous Beria, before he himself was shot. The major gave Mishkin a quick version of all the events surrounding one Robert Blackwell, who per the fingerprint match, was supposedly a dead KGB officer named Parshenko. "Nikolai Parshenko was shot while..."

General Mishkin interrupted him. "I know who Parshenko was. I worked for him once upon a time. "Give me the file to read through carefully. Please wait outside." They retired to his outer office and took seats. Mishkin lit an old-fashioned, unfiltered Russian cigarette. He could obviously afford any imported brand there was, but he was a man of tradition and preferred the Russian brand he'd been smoking since he was fourteen years old. He put on his reading glasses and opened the folder. Fifteen minutes later, he lit another cigarette, then spun his leather chair around so that he could look out a window at the city. Yes, he had known and quite liked Parshenko, had even been to his house for a party once and met Olga. More than liked, he had respected the man, until his defection. He didn't have an objection that Nikolai had been shot while trying to defect. The death of the wife and son, however, had left a bad taste in his mouth. He'd always been a little skeptical about the story of the death of Nikolai, as it was all unconfirmed, public reports out of America about his having died in the hospital. But the leadership of the KGB had bigger problems in the early 1990s, like keeping their jobs or there even being a KGB, so it was much easier to report to the Kremlin that Colonel Parshenko was dead and move on to other issues.

The general also knew something that the major and the captain did not.

There had been rumors in the last few years of operations happening in different places of the world, such as the killing of the terrorist Abdul, for which no Western country's service had taken credit and not even Russian penetration agents of those services had heard about. And given his rank and friendships, he would have known if Russia had carried out some of them, no matter how many stamps of ABSOLUTE SECRET would have been on the government file. But what if there were no "government" files? This had been a possibility discussed that very day among his fellow generals. Could there be a "private" player in their age old game of espionage? If there was, having a talented and supposedly dead man like Parshenko on your team could be a real asset. "I guess we owe you something for what happened to your family," he mumbled to himself. Mishkin smiled, stubbed out his cigarette and buzzed his assistant. "Send those two back in."

Major Federov and Captain Kosygin returned and again stood at attention. This is nonsense. Parshenko is dead and the FSB doesn't believe in ghosts, do we?"

"No, Sir," they both quickly answered, wondering where the general was headed with this.

"That idiot out there, Petrov, has screwed something up. First thing Monday, send one of our fingerprint techs out to Ekaterinburg, to get new samples from that hotel room."

"Yes, Sir. In the meantime, general, should we put out an alert to the police and the Border Guards with a description of this man and woman?"

"Let's wait till Monday, when we have the new fingerprint samples. We wouldn't want to look foolish, would we, major?" General Mishkin then opened another red folder on his desk and lowered his eyes to it. A clear indication that the discussion was over. The two subordinates gave each other a look and departed. Mishkin thought to himself, "You better have your ass out of Russia by Monday old friend." He lit another cigarette.

Ten minutes later, Mishkin's aide informed him that General Klemenko of the GRU was phoning on a secure line. He'd long thought Klemenko was a horse's ass and that the rumors about his Mafioso connections were probably true. Unfortunately, the FSB had no charter to investigate senior military officials. He looked at his watch, to see if maybe it was late enough on a Friday that he could get away with having his aide claim he'd already gone for the day. No, no point in putting off till Monday what could be dispensed with today.

"Yes, put him through." It was a few moments till the two aides made the connection. "Hello, Gennady, my old friend. How are you?"

"I'm fine and you?"

"Good as I deserve at my age. What can I do for the GRU today?"

"Well, I've got a rather odd situation to which I could use the assistance of the FSB. It's not a big deal, but we're looking for a fellow traveling as an American. Naturally, we could eventually find him, but figured it might be accomplished quicker if we combined resources."

Mishkin knew that if Klemenko was asking for FSB assistance, it must in fact, be a big deal. "Always glad to assist our colleagues in the GRU. What are the details?"

"The man's name is Robert Blackwell. Has he come to your service's attention by any chance?"

Mishkin almost choked on his cigarette smoke. "No, I don't recall anything crossing my desk with that name recently. Of course, one of my sections might have something on him that they didn't realize was important enough to bring to my attention. Just what has this Blackwell fellow been up to?"

Gennady knew he couldn't play too cute with Mishkin. "Well, why he first came to our attention is rather minor, but there might be a terrorist angle. And here is the crazy part, his finger prints seem to match a long dead KGB officer named Nikolai Parshenko. You remember that name?"

"Rings a bell, but I can't recall the details," lied Mishkin.

"Well, I can fill you in on the details later, though I'm not spreading the Parshenko angle around too widely, but what I would appreciate, is if you might immediately add him to your terrorist watch list? Have your boys keep an eye out for him."

"Certainly, certainly. Have your aide send the details of his description, etc. over to my aide, and we'll get right on it."

"Thank you. Have a good weekend and give my regards to Tatiana."

"Same to you Gennady and please pass my best to your Ludmila."

He hung up and buzzed his aide. "You'll be getting some material from General Klemenko in a few minutes, over the secure fax. Be sure to bring it to my attention, first thing Monday morning. Take no action until I've seen it."

"Yes, Sir. No action until you've seen it."

"I'll be going home in a few minutes. Please bring in anything that needs my signature yet today."

At the State Library, Cathleen asked to see Director Gagarin, the official with whom she'd met on her first visit there the previous week. His secretary phoned into him and announced her arrival.

"He'll be able to see you in just a minute, if you'd like to take a seat."

"Thank you." Cathleen took a seat and started thumbing through the Library's own bimonthly journal of recent publications dealing with Russia.

Inside the director's office, Gagarin pulled from his wallet a phone number. "Andrei? This is Dimitri Gagarin at the State Library. You came by last week asking about Dr. Cathleen Spenser. Are you still looking for her?"

"Yes, I am. You've heard from her?"

"Is it still worth the $500 you mentioned?"

"Yes, yes, you'll get your money. What have you learned?"

"She's sitting in my outer office right now, but I don't know why she's come by and I may not be able to stall her here for long, so move quickly."

"I'll make it a $1,000, if she is still there when I arrive in fifteen minutes."

"She'll be here," replied Gagarin, a man always in need of extra money to supplement what he considered his insufficient library salary to provide him the lifestyle he merited. He didn't know why Andrei wanted her and didn't really care. He'd found most visiting Americans to his library since the end of the USSR annoying and never satisfied with one thing or the other about his facilities. He wished they'd all just stay home. The fact that he kept the old name plaque on his desk of the "Lenin Library", not the newly designated "State Library", spoke volumes about Gagarin's political views. After leaving Cathleen cooling her heels for about five minutes, the director buzzed his secretary. "Please show in Dr. Spenser."

"Dr. Spenser, please have a seat. I'm so sorry I kept you waiting, but I was on the phone to a colleague in Kiev. I believe we have everything set for you to start your research on Monday. Just a couple of forms for you to sign, but you can do that on Monday if you prefer." Gagarin lit a cigarette, leaned back and blew a cloud of smoke above his head.

"Unfortunately, I'm afraid I won't be able to do any research on this trip at all. I received a call yesterday from my mother in Boston. She's having some medical problems and there's really no one there to look after her, so I'm going to have to return immediately to America. I just wanted to stop by to thank you for your efforts to get things worked out for me. I didn't want to simply disappear, without letting you know the reason why."

"That's too bad. I hope it isn't anything too serious."

"I hope not. Well, I know you're a busy man, so I won't keep you."

"No, it's always good to have a chance to chat with one of our visiting scholars. In fact, I'm curious how you found the process of checking on what materials we had on hand for your research. Was the process clear and easy?"

Cathleen found Gagarin's friendliness a bit unexpected, given that during her first call on him, he'd acted like it was a great inconvenience to be bothered with a visiting researcher at all. "Yes, the email exchanges with your staff in advance of my coming, to define my field of research, was quite straight forward."

"Forgive me for being so rude. Would you like some tea? I usually have a cup about this time of day."

Cathleen looked at her watch. "Thank you, but I really need to be getting along to arrange for my departure this weekend." She noticed that a few small beads of sweat had appeared on Gagarin's temples and he lit another cigarette.

"Naturally, I understand, but before you go, one more question for you. Would you say that the level of interest in Russian Studies in America has continued to fall?"

Cathleen gave him a vague answer of "maybe", which led to a rather pointless follow-up question by him. She was about to stand and make her farewell, when his intercom buzzed, which he immediately picked up. "Yes, please send them in."

A few seconds later, the outer door opened and in came Andrei accompanied by two other men in black leather jackets. None of the three looked like they'd read too many books in their lives, unless they were from a prison library, thought Cathleen. The door closed behind them.

"Cathleen Spenser?" asked Andrei.

She looked at Gagarin and then back to Andrei. "Yes, I'm Dr. Spenser."

"Someone wants to speak with you. You'll come quietly with us."

"I'm going nowhere with you," she replied as she stood up. She turned again to Gagarin. "What's going on here?"

Gagarin shrugged his shoulders and held up his palms. "I think it best if you go with them."

Andrei took out a Glock with a silencer attached to it. "I will shoot you if you don't do exactly as we say." He nodded towards Gagarin's back door, which led down into the closed stacks of the library and employee-only exits. She saw that she had little choice and moved slowly towards the door. Andrei dropped an envelope on Gagarin's desk as he passed. Cathleen stopped for a second and said to the director in English, "when my friends come for you Dimitri, you'll know what a big mistake you've made. Try not to pee in your pants before they kill you."

A half hour later, she found herself sitting at a table in a sparsely furnished apartment. "My name is Nikolai Tsimbal," he said to her in English. "I've been looking for you and your friend, Karl Beck. Just what are you to him?"

She didn't know what Beck's instructions would be about being interrogated, but she knew what the IRA theory was -- say nothing. She sat there, expressionless and silent.

"I'm meeting him at midnight you know. He's going to give me all those little items, in return for your lives. You're going to come with me -- insurance that there'll be no funny business on his part. Then you two can go home to America."

Cathleen didn't believe that for a minute. They hadn't blindfolded her en route to the apartment, nor seem to have any concern about her seeing their faces. She knew from her grandfather's stories that that was not a good sign of her getting out of this alive. She calculated that her only chance for survival was if Karl was good at his profession as she suspected he was. Her secondary sense of comfort was that if she and Karl were killed, her grandfather and his old IRA colleagues would hunt down the asshole sitting across from her and kill him, very slowly. She continued her silence. She was a little surprised that no one had laid a hand on her, but guessed that they wanted her looking in good condition when the exchange occurred that night.

"Fine, sit there and say nothing. It doesn't really matter. Andrei, tie her to that chair until we leave for the meeting tonight." Tsimbal got up and left the apartment.

By five o'clock, Blackwell started getting worried. By six, he knew that something had happened to her and that she wouldn't be coming. He prayed that she had only been kidnapped by Tsimbal's people. Why had he let her go back to that damn State Library? He should have foreseen that that was a spot where they might have been waiting for her -- on the odd chance she would return there. He thought about phoning Viktor, but that would serve no real purpose. If they hadn't already killed her, Tsimbal would bring her to the meeting that night. This was one of those occasions in his profession when one simply had to have the patience to do nothing, until the right moment.

When Igor woke up to get ready for his night shift, Blackwell filled him in on what had probably happened to Cathleen. "I hope this Tsimbal brings her to the meeting tonight. If he doesn't, I can kill any others there, but will have to keep him alive to trade for her."

"I know you told me earlier that you didn't want any help on this, but I think the situation has changed. You may well need a second person."

"You may be right. Do you have a rifle?"

"I have a hunting rifle."

"You any good with it?"

"I've been shooting animals since I was twelve."

"I hope they'll bring her in with them, but if they leave her and someone to watch her out in a car, then I'll need you to shoot that person as soon as you hear any shots from inside the warehouse. I saw this afternoon there are a couple of other buildings next to the warehouse parking lot. Is there any way to get on the roof of one of those?"

"I think so. I remember there being service ladders to get up to the roofs of both of those buildings. I'd have a good angle and not a long shot from one of those -- if they pull right into the parking lot."

"OK, as soon as you've let me into the warehouse at eleven, you go up on one of those roofs and wait."

"Understood." Igor went to a closet and got out his rifle, which had a scope on it for hunting. He provided Blackwell a spare shirt, tie and cap for his "guard" uniform. He had no spare pants, but no great matter, as Blackwell had his own pair of black pants that looked official enough. They travelled to the warehouse together in Igor's old Lada, arriving at 10:45. His shift officially started at 11:00, but he told the other guard that since he'd arrived early, he might as well go ahead and leave. Blackwell waited out in the car, slouched down in the backseat, till he saw the other guard leave. A minute later, Igor stepped out the door and waved for Blackwell to join him.

He quickly showed Blackwell the lay-out of the building He then exited, got in his car and drove several blocks away to park. This was just in case Tsimbal was suspicious enough to have sent one of his people early, to watch the warehouse. Igor climbed up the ladder of the building facing the parking lot of the warehouse, found a good sheltered spot and laid down with the rifle. The rest was up to Blackwell.

Blackwell locked the door after Igor departed and set about preparing for Tsimbal's arrival at midnight. He put the cheap handgun in his belt holster and taped the smaller Makarov just above his right calf under his pant leg. He took his pocket knife, opened the blade, and taped it about waist high to a nearby water pipe. He was ready, just in case they bound his hands. He turned on a light and a small radio up in the manager's office, at the top of a flight of wooden stairs. The office stairs were about 30 feet from the pedestrian door of the warehouse. As a final step, he checked once more that the five diamonds were still in an envelope and returned it to a back pocket. These were the five he'd recovered from the Geography supplemental volume of the Encyclopedia set that morning in the bushes. Blackwell then sat down to wait. The hands of the clock on the guard desk barely moved. It was the longest thirty minutes of his life. He pushed from his brain any thought that Cathleen might die that night, as he'd let happen to his beloved Olga. Even if it cost him his own life, Cathleen was going to go home alive.

A little before midnight, Nikolia Tsimbal, along with three other thugs and Cathleen pulled into the warehouse parking lot in a large black Mercedes. They turned off the engine and lights and sat in their vehicle for several minutes, watching the area to see if anyone else was about. All appeared quiet.

"O.K., let's go get this over with. Konstantin, you wait here in the car and keep an eye out. You two, come with me. Dr. Spenser, if you please, out of the car." The three checked their weapons and exited the car.

At five after midnight, someone pounded on the metal pedestrian door of the warehouse. Blackwell walked slowly over to the window with a wire mesh cover over it, next to the door. He saw three men standing there and Cathleen. His heart rate quickened. Thank god she was alive and they were bringing her in with them. He prayed she was as cool under pressure as he believed her to be and wouldn't react in any way to him opening the door. There was an older man in front, clearly in charge, that was presumably Tsimbal.

Blackwell shouted through the window. "We're closed, go away. Come back on Monday morning."

The older man appeared much softer than the two younger, fitter men behind him. Tsimbal shouted back, "I'm here to see Beck, open the door old man."

"Who?"

"Beck. I said Beck."

"Oh, why didn't you say so." He stepped over and unlocked the door, slowly opening it a foot, so that they could see well his aged face and his uniform with badge. "Are you Tsimbal?"

"Yes, old man. Is there a Mr. Beck here?"

"Yeah, he's waiting up in the office, but he said that you'd be alone. I'm only to admit you Mr. Tsimbal."

"And who's going to stop us, old man? You?" asked one of the younger men, who laughed as he pushed past Blackwell.

"I'm just telling you what he said. And he said to give you this envelope." He handed over to Tsimbal the unsealed white envelope. He didn't even look at Cathleen.

Tsimbal slowly opened it, concealing its contents from his two young partners. Even in the dim light, he could see the five sparkling diamonds. He looked up at the guard. "You know what's in here?"

"Nope and I don't care. Beck just told me to say that if you wanted all of them, to come alone up to the office. If you don't come up the stairs alone, he said he'd leave."

"What's your role in this?" asked Tsimbal as he stuffed the envelope into his pants pocket.

"The guy gave me an American fifty dollar bill to let you in and tell you what I've told you. Then, I'm to sit down back at my desk and mind my own business."

Tsimbal pulled an automatic weapon from his coat pocket and pointed it at the guard. "That's a great idea; you go sit down at your desk, but first why don't you hand me that gun, just so you don't hurt yourself."

Blackwell handed over the revolver from his holster, turned and shuffled back over towards the desk.

Tsimbal turned to his two compatriots. "Sergei, you stay here with the girl and keep an eye on the old man. Watch yourself."

Sergei snorted. "I think I can handle him."

"Sasha, you wait just outside and keep an eye out for anything happening in the parking lot. If I shout, you come running. Otherwise, you two stay down here."

Tsimbal's thoughts were fixated on the five glittering little stones in his pocket and wondering how many more there were at the top of those stairs with Beck. He kept the gun out and started walking slowly across the concrete floor towards the wooden stairs. "Beck, I'm coming up, alone," he shouted. No reply. Just the sound of the radio playing rock music.

Cathleen played her role perfectly. She'd barely looked at Blackwell when they entered. After Tsimbal got no reaction to his shout, Cathleen looked up at the upstairs office door and cried out, "Karl, it's me, Cathleen. I'm OK. He's coming up to talk to you."

Blackwell was now seated behind the small wooden desk covered with newspapers and a thermos. His right hand was slowly pulling up his pant leg to reach the Makarov. Sergei had his gun out, but was staring at his boss, not watching the old guard. He had his other hand on Cathleen's right arm. Her hands were tied behind her.

Tsimbal had reached the first step of the stairs and shouted once more for Beck. Without rising from his chair, Blackwell put his first shot into the side of the head of Sergei. By the time Tsimbal had spun around instinctively towards the sound of the first shot, the *starik* had moved his arm and put two shots in Tsimbal's chest. As Sasha rushed through the doorway, he received two more bullets from the Makarov and fell dead to the dirty floor. There was total silence for two-three seconds, then the sound of a rifle shot from outside.

Blackwell opened the door wider so he could see out to the parking lot. A man lay face down on the asphalt, next to the car. Igor had carried out his assignment well. Blackwell retrieved his knife and cut Cathleen's hands free. She threw her arms around his neck.

"Oh my god," was all that she said. She then stepped back to look at the three dead men on the concrete floor. Karl went over to Tsimbal and removed the envelope from his pocket. "I believe these belong to me." He checked each body to make sure they were dead. Above the body of Sergei, he commented, "I thought you said you could handle me?"

There was a soft tapping on the door. "It's me, Igor. Is everything alright?"

"Yes, we're fine. Come on in."

Igor stepped through the doorway and looked around at the three dead bodies on the floor and crossed himself three times. "Son-of-a-bitch, you do know how to kill people."

"I see you took care of the driver easily enough."

"It was liking shooting a deer. The guy stepped out of the car, then just stood there."

Blackwell turned back to Cathleen. "How did these guys grab you? I assume it was at the library?"

"It was that jerk at the State Library, Gagarin, who obviously phoned Tsimbal's people and let them know I was there. I had a feeling he was dragging our meeting on and on, but just as I was about to leave, these two guys showed up." She pointed at the two younger ones on the floor. "The third man at the library stayed out in the car when we arrived here. They took me to an apartment, where this older one here told me how he'd arranged to meet you at midnight and that everything was going to be just fine. If you gave him what he wanted, he'd let us go home to America. I guess he thought I was stupid enough to believe that lie."

Blackwell gave her another hug. "You performed well. One would think you'd been kidnapped several times before."

"I figured you'd take care of them, but thank god you'd told me about how you'd be pretending to be the night watchman. By the way, you make a great bumbling, senile old man."

"What should we do about Director Gagarin?" he asked her.

"I don't suppose he merits killing, but he sure deserves something for his role in my kidnapping."

"You still have by chance one of his business cards?"

"Out in my purse, in their car, I do."

"I'll go get her purse," volunteered Igor.

When he returned a few moments later, he handed her the purse and she fished out Gagarin's card. "Here it is."

Blackwell took it and stuffed it into Tsimbal's pants pocket. "When his friends find his body in the morning, I suspect they'll pay a visit on Gagarin, looking for answers as to how Tsimbal got killed. His friends are probably of the school of interrogators who believe that once you beat a guy enough, his answers will start sounding more believable."

Cathleen gave a little smile. "Oh, grandpa is going to really like you."

Blackwell handed Igor the Makarov. "Nice gun. We'll see you in the morning back at the apartment. You can take care of the four bodies as we discussed earlier?"

"No problem, if you'll help me load them into the car. I'll use their Mercedes. You two go home and tell Maria all is fine."

Blackwell and Cathleen walked to the nearest Metro station. Forty minutes later, they knocked softly on the apartment door. Maria opened it and let them in.

"Igor said to tell you that everything is fine. He'll be home in the morning at the usual time."

She looked greatly relieved and returned to her bedroom. They went to their room and undressed.

"You think there will be any repercussions once we're back in Bloomington?" asked Cathleen.

"We should be OK now."

"You don't think Tsimbal would have shared with any others why he was looking for us? And maybe one of them will pick up on the search?"

"It isn't likely that Tsimbal told anyone more than the absolute minimum to get assistance, otherwise there would have been the danger of him having to share the spoils, if any jewels really turned up. Let's get to bed. We have a long day ahead of us tomorrow."

"I can't believe you can possibly sleep after such a shoot-out and you killed three men."

"My staying awake isn't going to bring them back to life."

She turned out the lamp on the small bedside table, but just lay there staring at the ceiling. Her mind still racing. She soon heard very faint snoring sounds coming from his side of the bed. She was amazed how easily he could go to sleep after the events of that night! She kept thinking about getting him through passport control the next day on the forged Irish passport.

CHAPTER 15

SATURDAY

The alarm clock sounded at 7:30 a.m. Cathleen felt as if she'd barely gone to sleep and now she had to wake up. She couldn't wait to get on the plane that afternoon for several reasons, but one of them was to simply go back to sleep. She rolled over and snuggled up on Blackwell's chest. He let her lay there for a few minutes, before nudging her. "We have to get up. We don't have that much time."

"We don't have to be at the hotel till ten, you know."

"I know, but I have one more stop before leaving Moscow. I'll go take care of something, while you take our bags in a taxi to the Hotel *Rossiya*."

"OK, but where are you going?"

"I have a verbal message to give to Verchagin, just to make his life even more miserable than it already is now."

"You don't think you'll be putting your escape at risk by approaching him?"

"Who's he going to call on a Saturday morning? If he calls the general phone number for the SVR or FSB and gets a weekend duty officer -- and if they even take him seriously -- it would be Monday morning before anyone digs out the old files and deals with it. We'll be long gone. Even after somebody read the file, there will be skepticism that someone he killed 20 years ago, came to his door on the weekend, to wish him a long life."

"You may have a point there, but for god's sake, don't miss the bus just so you can aggravate this fellow."

"I'll be there in plenty of time. I promise. Now, help me spray this crap on my hair, so I can become Mr. O'Brian."

After he dressed, the new "O'Brian" took his Blackwell passport into the bathroom and burned it - lighting it at the top first, so that it would burn slowly and thoroughly, like they'd taught him decades ago at KGB School. He crumbled up the ashes and flushed them down the toilet. "Goodbye Mr. Blackwell. The end of an interesting life."

Igor arrived home a little before eight. Ryan O'Brian had waited to leave until he had a chance to briefly speak with him. "Did everything go OK with delivering those four packages to that nightclub?"

"No problem with that, but can you believe that between the four of them, they only had about 300 rubles on them. What kind of Mafioso criminals only carry that little money on them?" He shook his head in disgust. The two sat down at the kitchen table and Igor lit a cigarette. He tried not to stare at Blackwell's new hair color, but couldn't resist looking.

"I know, it looks ridiculous." They both laughed. "Here is US$600 I have left, to thank you for your assistance last night. I also have a little something as a tip for our nice stay here in your home." He poured the five diamonds out of the envelope onto the table.

Igor was speechless.

"I trust you'll find a way to convert these into rubles without too many questions being asked. But I'd wait a few months, till the dead bodies are forgotten about."

"I ... I ... don't know what to say."

"Don't say anything. Consider it a gift from one honest man to another. Now, you and your wife can enjoy the retirement you deserve. No more lodgers. No more night shifts as a watchman."

"Thank you." Igor reached across the table and shook his hand.

"I have to leave now. In about thirty minutes, can you help Cathleen get the bags out to the street and hail a taxi?"

"I'll do that. Be safe."

Ryan stuck his head back into the bedroom for a moment. He gave Cathleen a kiss. "I'll see you at the hotel. I promise."

A cold chill went down her spine as he walked away from her. She had a horrible premonition that she'd never see him again, alive. The Irish, for centuries, had believed in fairies and leprechauns -- and premonitions. Her grandmother supposedly had been strong with the "gift."

It was early enough that Mr. O'Brian had no trouble in getting a taxi and fifteen minutes later, he arrived at No. 87 *Leninsky Prospekt*. He made his way straight to Verchagin's building. Several screaming children were just coming out the door as he arrived. He got his hand on the door before it latched and let himself in. He wouldn't have to buzz Verchagin, or anyone else, on the intercom to get into the building. He took the stairs to the dimly lighted corridor of the second floor. He pounded loudly on the metal door of the man who had ruined his life twenty years earlier.

"Who is it?" asked a thin, wavering voice from behind the door.

"Deputy Director of the Housing Association. It's about the complaints you've made." Given what the old lady had told him, it seemed a reasonable guess that Verchagin was a frequent complainer about something in the complex.

Verchagin opened the door. "It's about time you did something about those screaming children."

O'Brian pushed the door wide open and stepped in, forcing Verchagin to back up. He closed the door behind him. "We have several matters to discuss. Perhaps you'd be more comfortable sitting down." He pointed at a straight-back chair by the wall. Being Russian, Verchagin sat down as commanded.

"I understand you're alone here?"

"Yes, my wife died several years ago. What's that got to do with ..."

O'Brian put up his hand, in a gesture for Verchagin to stop speaking. "It must be lonely without your wife. You know, I lost my wife almost twenty years ago. And my son."

"Sorry to hear that," automatically mumbled Verchagin.

"Yes, they were shot and killed in Prague by some asshole. Beautiful city, Prague. You ever been in Prague, Valerie Ivanovich?"

Verchagin's eyes opened wide. His face became taut. "No," he muttered unconvincingly.

"Really? Think hard. A summer's day, about like today. On a narrow street, that led to the airport." O'Brian's voice had turned cold and hard. His stare frozen into Verchagin's eyes.

Verchagin knew. "No, it can't be you. It can't be you. You're dead."

"My soul's been dead for twenty years because of you, but I'm here. I'm here to kill you. Did they give you a medal Valerie Ivanovich? Maybe a promotion?"

"I was only following my orders."

"I could have killed you days ago from afar. But I wanted you to know who is going to kill you."

Verchagin started to cry. "I'm an old man, have pity on me."

"Pity? Like the pity you showed my wife and child. You know, I'm not going to kill you today. Maybe, I'll kill you tomorrow, or maybe next week. I want you to think about it coming. Think about it when you come around a corner in the dark and maybe I'll be waiting there. Or maybe some night, when you're in bed."

Verchagin had both hands over his eyes, crying. "No, no, leave me alone."

For the first time since he'd entered the room, O'Brian glanced around the room. On the walls, he saw various military plaques and pictures of Verchagin as a young man in the paratroopers and with Soviet troops in Afghanistan. He quietly backed up and opened the door -- then he was gone. He walked quickly from the building, but not at a run. People remember a man running. He walked several blocks within the housing projects before going out to the *prospekt* and hailing a taxi.

"Hotel *Rossiya*," he told the driver. He sat back and closed his eyes. He'd thought about this moment a thousand times. Thought about finding and confronting the man who'd killed his family. He'd often wondered how he would feel? Now he knew. He felt good. Verchagin was already a lonely and miserable old man. Now the bastard could add fear to his condition. Yes, he felt good. He didn't care what the priests and modern philosophers said, revenge was a good thing.

O'Brian reached the hotel with fifteen minutes to spare. He gave the driver all the rubles he still had, so he wouldn't have to bother with converting what was left at the airport. The driver was a happy man. Ryan came up close to Cathleen's side, unnoticed by her. "And do you indeed have the nicest tits in all of Ireland?" he whispered to her, with the best fake Irish accent he could muster.

She turned to him and threw her arms around him and kissed him. "I was so afraid that I'd never see you again." She was very relieved that her Celtic premonition had been false. If grandma had had the "gift", it obviously hadn't been passed down to her!

"Nothing to be afraid of my love. Just a short airline ride to Dublin, and it's all over."

When the tour guide started shouting for people to board the buses, Ryan and Cathleen got on the third bus in the line. Shaun had been right. A lot of their fellow travelers had taken one last opportunity for cheap booze at the hotel bar before boarding the buses and were in very happy moods. Upon arrival at the Sheremetyovo International Airport, they let most of their fellow travelers go ahead of them and they separated from each other. If questioned, each was prepared to answer that they had traveled alone.

By the time O'Brian finally reached the Passport Control official in his queue, the young man had already had his fill of drunken Irishmen. O'Brian slid his passport across the counter.

"Sure t'is a fine mornin' isn't it, your lordship," beamed the elderly Irishman.

The young Russian took a cursory look at the passport photo, then at O'Brian, stamped it and slid the passport back across the counter. "Next," he called out.

Cathleen was in the next line over and visibly sighed in relief when she saw that Ryan was safely through the control point. She actually got closer scrutiny by the Passport Control official than did the mythical Ryan O'Brian. They weren't seated together on the flight, but he came by for a moment shortly after their take-off to check on her. Ten minutes later, she was sound asleep and remained so for the rest of the flight.

IRELAND

Passport control at the Dublin airport for entry into the country was even more cursory than the departure from Moscow. Irish nationals simply held up the cover of their passports and were waved through. Again, O'Brian walked right by passport control with no hassles, while Cathleen underwent close scrutiny and a variety of questions as to why an American was traveling to Ireland via Moscow. When she and Ryan were reunited out on the sidewalk, she was in a feisty mood. "Bloody hell, next time I'll take the fake passport. It's easier than traveling on a genuine American one!"

"Relax. It's over now and we're safe."

"Well, we still need to get you back into America, Professor Karl Beck!"

"Let's first find a hotel and we'll worry about my getting into America tomorrow."

Once they'd checked into one of the ugly, modern hotels that dotted downtown Dublin for the tourists, Karl made a phone call back to Bloomington. It was still only morning in Indiana. He called the Slavic Department's secretary at her home.

"Hello."

"Hello, Suzanne. It's Karl calling from Ireland."

"Oh, I'm so jealous! Are you having a great time?"

"Well, I was, but I've somehow lost my passport and wallet. Will you go into my office sometime today and in the bottom left drawer of my desk you'll find Xeroxes of my passport, driver's license and credit card. Will you please fax those to me here at the hotel? I'll give you the number in a minute.

"Oh oh, you've got a problem! Will they let you back into America with just a faxed copy?"

"Yes, I'll go to the embassy on Monday and get a temporary document that will get me on the plane."

He gave her the hotel fax number and after promising her something from the international gift shop, hung up.

"See how easy that was!"

"And a Xerox will get you back into America?" asked Cathleen with some skepticism.

"I'll have to go to the American Consular section on Monday, but with the copies and a little vouching from you, they will give me a document that allows the airline to let me on the flight to America. There'll be an interview at Chicago, but it won't be much of an ordeal."

"I can't believe, it's as easy as you say."

"Do you want to spend a few days here in Ireland and go visit your grandfather or go straight home, say Tuesday?"

"I just want to go home! I'm not sure I'm ready for you and grandpa to meet face-to-face. I'll give him a call in a minute and let him know we arrived safely."

"Alright, we'll plan on departing on Tuesday," replied Karl. He wasn't sure he was ready to meet grandpa either -- after that warning about cutting off his nuts.

Cathleen threw herself down on the bed. "I can't wait for our encyclopedias to arrive. I sure hope Attaché Powell sent them in the diplomatic pouch as he promised."

"It will still be a week or two before the Department of State mails them on to the Lilly Library, so no rush in getting back to Bloomington."

The following morning, Cathleen stopped in the small travel office in the hotel lobby and booked two Business Class seats on the Tuesday flight to Indianapolis via Chicago. They also remembered to put a call through to the Hotel *Metropol* in Moscow, informing them that Spenser and Blackwell would no longer need their rooms.

"I'm afraid to see what my credit card bill will be this month!" exclaimed Cathleen.

"I suspect that soon your financial position will greatly improve," teased Karl.

True to his prediction, armed with his faxed copies from Suzanne, the Monday morning visit to the American Embassy got Mr. Karl Beck an official looking letter on US Embassy stationary. The document told the airline that they could let him on the flight to Chicago, without a passport. Beck bought an International Herald-Tribune newspaper that afternoon. While sitting at a small table, having an Irish coffee in the hotel lobby bar, he read a brief article about gang warfare in Moscow.

"Hmmm."

Cathleen had learned by now, that that was Karl's indicator that he wanted to tell her something. "What is it?"

"This article says that open warfare seems to have broken out in Moscow between two powerful organized crime groups. Four men believed to be associated with the Mogilevich group were found dead Saturday morning and the bodies of five more people, believed to be members of the rival Ovenko crime family, were found on Sunday."

"Shocking," she replied. "Thank goodness we're no longer in that dangerous city!" She slipped her shoe off and ran her toes up along Karl's calf, under the table.

By Monday night, they had sufficiently recovered with their sleep and anxieties of the previous days to enjoy going out for a farewell dinner. They both ordered the fresh trout and a bottle of Dom Perignon to help celebrate. The waiter poured the champagne and then gave them their privacy.

"I think a toast is called for," offered Karl.

"I agree. To what should go our first toast?"

"To us together, today and for years to come."

"Why Professor Beck, aren't you in a romantic mood!"

"I am indeed. This trip has allowed me to close the door on the past. And to start a new chapter with you."

A variety of toasts followed. By dessert, they had covered everyone from Czar Nikolai II and Czarina Alexandra to Ivy and Yurovsky.

"Have you given further thought as to what to do with the jewels?" asked Cathleen in a low voice.

"I have some, but let's not count our rabbits until they're born."

"It's chickens, not count our chickens, till they're hatched! God, when are you going to learn English! Alright, we'll wait to see what exactly is in the encyclopedias before we do too much planning, but I get to rip the next one open since you already cut into one back in Ekaterinburg!"

"Fair enough," responded Karl, as he waved to their waiter for another bottle of champagne.

CHAPTER 16

BLOOMINGTON

The flight home was long, but uneventful. Even getting through Immigration Control at Chicago's O'Hare Airport was relatively easy for Beck, with his U.S. Embassy letter and the faxed copies of his passport and driver's license. The hard part was the waiting over the next ten days, for the encyclopedias to arrive. Cathleen advised the staff at the university's Lilly Library that she was expecting a large box from the U.S. Consulate in Ekaterinburg. She also set about more mundane duties, like replacing all the plants in her house that had died while she'd been away. She now understood why Karl had no plants in his house. Karl returned to his project of working on a book about Ivy Litvinova's literary efforts. Cathleen got back to her research for a book on origins of Russian city government, though it appeared now it would have to be finished without the benefit of archival work in Moscow. Out of curiosity, she placed a phone call to Gagarin's office at the Moscow State Library the third day she was home. She learned from his secretary that he was out on medical leave and wasn't expected back for several weeks. The secretary explained that apparently he'd been savagely mugged by some street thugs going home one night. Karl was right -- getting revenge did make one feel better.

Finally, the much anticipated call came to Cathleen's office.

"Dr. Spenser, this is Ruth at the Lilly Library."

"Yes, how are you?"

"Fine, thanks. Several boxes have arrived from the State Department, addressed to us, but marked for your attention. Do you know what this is about?"

"Yes, I've been expecting them." She proceeded to explain -- again -- about how the American Consulate had been so kind as to ship this antique set of the Great Soviet Encyclopedia back to the university for her. "I'll be by in about twenty minutes to pick them up." She immediately called Karl and told him the good news and that she would be home shortly.

Thirty minutes later, the boxes had been ripped open and the books were spread all over Beck's dining room table. The two of them stood there for just a moment, staring at the 65 volumes. Cathleen felt like one of the characters at the end of that classic movie, when Bogart and the others all stood around the table looking at the statue of the Maltese Falcon -- wondering if it really was covered with priceless jewels.

Karl handed her a box cutter. "You get to go first. I suggest that you cut from the inside."

She opened one of the books and started slicing down the middle of the spine. Out came eight diamonds, each at least a carat in size and sparkling with fire, as sunlight came through the window and struck the stones. The next volume yielded five more diamonds and two large rubies. Neither spoke. Their gazes were fixed on the books. They sliced for almost an hour, carefully going back a second time to make sure they hadn't missed anything. In the end, they counted exactly two hundred diamonds, twenty five sapphires and twenty two rubies lying on a white bath towel.

"These aren't very large diamonds," observed Karl, as he picked one up off the table to examine it. "Do you think they're worth much?'

Cathleen gave him a look of utter amazement. She wondered how any man could live to be sixty years old and not have learned anything about diamonds! "First of all, these are quite good-sized diamonds and the color, sparkle and clarity are outstanding. The cut is rather old-fashioned, but I'd guess each of these is at least $20,000 -- more of course for these few bigger ones. So, 200 of them would add up to roughly, uh, four million dollars! I don't know much about rubies and sapphires, but they're gorgeous as well."

"Presumably, they would be worth even more, if they were known as Romanov diamonds, but that could become a little awkward to explain and prove."

Cathleen sat there and continued to run her fingers through the pile of jewels. "Do you know how exciting this is?" she asked Karl.

"You mean handling millions of dollars worth of diamonds?"

"Not just that, but the sense of history. We're sitting here handling Romanov Dynasty jewels. Jewels thought to have either never existed or to have been lost forever."

"But there's the catch," explained Karl. "If we were to tell the world about these Romanov jewels, exciting as that would be for you historians, imagine the downsides. There would be the legal battles. The Mogilevich crime family might put two and two together, with the possible consequences not only for us, but Igor and Maria."

"And then there'd be the question about Sister Anastasia. Would we also reveal her part of the story?" added Cathleen.

"As for Princess Anastasia, I hate to sound like a 'communist', but there were a number of good reasons that the Russian people rose up in revolt against the czar and the whole monarchial system. Just because what replaced the monarchy didn't turn out too well, is no reason to think anyone wants to return to having a direct descendent of the Romanovs running things. All that royalty crap is an anachronism. Sister Anastasia of the monastery probably has actually done a lot of good in her life. Would she be any more useful as Princess Anastasia, granddaughter of Nikolai and Alexandra, pretender to the throne of All the Russias? Given her choice in life to serve God, do you think she'd even care?"

"Probably not, but it will make a great story to tell our grandchildren someday, won't it."

"Don't we first need a child before we can have grandchildren?" responded Karl as he leaned over and gave her a kiss.

Two days later, Bob flew out from New York and met Karl at a cocktail lounge near the Indianapolis airport. Officially, to reprimand him for making personal use of the Blackwell documents, but unofficially, to welcome him safely home.

"Once you've gotten all the credit card charges in for Mr. Blackwell, let me know what the total is and I'll reimburse the Group's coffers."

"The boss won't admit it to you, but your trip might have worked out rather well, because now the airline and credit card records will show much more of a link to Russia than to the U.S. A trail that ends in Russia.

It'll help muddy the waters for the Norwegian police, who still aren't completely sure they're even on the trail of the right man."

"In any case, the alias documents have been destroyed and Mr. Blackwell has vanished from the face of the earth."

"The boss is a little curious as to how you traveled from Russia back to America, without a passport?"

"No comment. Seriously, you don't want to know."

"How about this Verchagin? Joan told me she passed you his name. Or don't I want to officially know about that as well?"

"Oh, he's alive and as unwell as he was before I got his name." Beck explained what he'd learned of the SOB's physical condition, and of his own logic that it was better punishment to leave alive a man as unhappy as Verchagin was, than to put him out of his misery.

"Did you even talk to him about that day in Prague?"

"Not really."

"Didn't learn who'd sent him?"

"No, nothing."

"Alright, the official debriefing is over, anything else you want to privately tell me?"

"Apparently, I did start a gang war between the Mogilevich and the Ovenko crime families, but that's probably on the plus side of the column."

"I read something about that in the international news section and had a suspicion that you were somehow involved. But what the hell was so important that you had to fly off to Russia in the first place and with your little professor friend in tow? Was this some super secret trip for Joan?"

"Is this truly off-the-record?" asked Beck, as he waved at the waitress to bring them another round of drinks.

"Hundred percent between me and you."

"Well, the short of it is that Cathleen and I discovered a cache of long missing Romanov jewels, probably worth several million dollars. Do you want to hear any of the details or is that sufficient?"

"Sure, that's enough. Why would I want any details? I only flew out here to the middle-of-nowhere to check on the weather! Start talking you stupid Russian."

Beck gave him the short version of finding Ivy's hints in the oral version of her novel, the chat with Viktor in New York City and then the visit of the three tough guys to Bloomington. Bob found that part amusing.

"Yeah, those Russian Mafioso guys should stay in Brighton Beach," commented Bob

"So we fly to Moscow, check in at the Hotel *Metropol* and begin our search there. There is a visit by a couple of thugs to the hotel looking for Cathleen. Guys I thought at the time were working for Viktor, but they turned out to be working for the crime boss, Nick Tsimbal -- Viktor had cut a deal with him for his help in return for a share of the diamonds."

"I've heard of Tsimbal -- another Brighton Beach bum."

"We take an early plane ride the next day out to Ekaterinburg, as that is where the czar's main assassin, Yakov Yurovsky, approached Ivy Litvinova in 1938, with a deal. He proposed to trade the diamonds he stole back in July, 1918, for the release of his daughter from a prison camp. We finally figured out that Ivy had had a friend place the diamonds in the spines of a 65-volume set of the Great Soviet Encyclopedia. The set was still sitting in the local university library, where she'd donated it back in '38."

Bob sat mesmerized as the story unfolded.

Karl explained how they stole the books out of the library and then Cathleen sweet talked the cultural attaché into sending them back to Indiana University through the diplomatic pouch. And how they arranged a cargo plane ride back to Moscow, just ahead of the GRU showing up at the hotel looking for them.

"How do you think the Military Intelligence Service got involved in this?" asked Bob.

"I have yet to figure that out, but they had my cover name of Blackwell, and came right to our hotel in Ekaterinburg.

"They knew you were staying at the Regency?"

"Fortunately, they phoned first to confirm I was there and a friendly desk clerk tipped me off, so we managed to slip out the back door just in time."

"You are one lucky Russian!"

"Anyway, we got back to Moscow and I paid a little visit on Verchagin, just to put the fear of God in him -- told him I planned on showing up one day of my choosing to kill him."

"Did you get anything important out of him? I mean, like how the Russians got onto you back in Prague?"

"No, I was a little pressed for time and just wanted to scare him. And strictly off the record, I did kill Nick Tsimbal and a couple of his men. I needed to take care of him; otherwise, he would have continued to pursue me for the diamonds, once I returned to Bloomington. I made it look as if a rival crime group had killed Tsimbal. That's about it." Beck left out the "minor" details of the living descendent of Czar Nikolai II and the IRA providing him a fake passport.

"Holy shit! And so you're just going to sit on 250 or so precious Romanov jewels? I know who's going to pick up today's check!"

"Actually, it might get a little awkward if we marketed them as Romanov jewels, but that's where you come in, you pigheaded Irishman."

"Oh, that sounds great! Now you want me to become an accessory after the fact to your international jewel heist?"

"If I remember correctly from that work in Amsterdam a few years ago, you know a guy who knows a guy in the diamond world, don't you?"

"Yes, Geert, if he's not in jail somewhere. What do you have in mind?"

"I want him to put most of these stones up for sale at one of the big auction houses in Manhattan or Paris. And I want the notice of sale to specifically mention that despite the similar antique cut of these stones, that they are positively NOT part of the missing Romanov jewels."

Bob smiled. "That's very clever, and will no doubt double the sale price." What does the friend of my friend get for his services for handling such a sale? That'll be his first question."

"I believe five percent would be customary for this intermediary service by him."

"He's going to want a lot more than that for handling hot diamonds."

"I defy you to show me any police report in the world that says that these jewels have been stolen or are missing. Just tell him that the seller is shy and wants the proceeds put in an offshore account."

"And what do you plan to do with all those tax-free millions?"

Beck took a sheet of paper from his inside sport coat pocket. "I'd like these amounts anonymously sent to these people and institutions."

Bob quickly glanced down the short list. "Joan will be pretty happy about this large donation to the Group, but what's this nonsense at the bottom about $50,000 for me?"

"You're still using that same piece of crap fishing boat you've had for years aren't you?"

"Yes. It runs fine."

"Bullshit, it's so noisy and so ugly it scares the fish away. Buy yourself something decent and try to put it in somebody else's name, so that in your next divorce settlement, your wife won't get it."

Jones shook his head in disbelief. "When will you get me the jewels?"

"I've got them all here in my coat. You want to see them?" He reached for his pocket.

"Not here in the restaurant, you idiot. I swear this young woman has rattled your brains!"

"You might be right about that. Let's go out to my car and I'll give them to you now. I want to get home to Cathleen."

"Just one more thing before we leave." Bob finished his drink and reached into his inner pocket and pulled out an envelope. He tossed it across the table. "Here's your new set of alias documents, in case Joan's ever stupid enough to use your services again. In fact, she may have something for you over your Christmas break. Let me go hit the head, while you pay the bill. Be right back."

Karl gave the waitress a fifty and told her to keep the change. He could afford to be generous and he was in a good mood. Although, there was still something tugging at his brain. Since returning to Bloomington, he'd continued thinking about all that military memorabilia in Verchagin's apartment. Also, how was it that the GRU, the military service, had discovered his alias name of Blackwell and why come after him at all, at the Regency Hotel in Ekaterinburg. Why wouldn't it have been the SVR people, the successor to the KGB? His eyebrows raised as he thought about something. A minute later, they relaxed and a profound sadness came over him.

"You look like a guy who just lost his best friend. With a pocketful of diamonds, shouldn't you be happy?" asked Bob when he returned to the table.

A smile returned to Beck's face, as he looked up at Bob. "Was just thinking about something I have to do later. Let's go out to my car and I'll give you my little trinkets."

They walked out to the parking lot and over to Beck's car. "Get in and I'll drive you back over to the airport."

Bob got in, talking about a fishing trip he had coming up the following week.

"You were, what, a captain when we first met in Prague?" asked Karl.

"Yep, that was a long time ago."

"And you'd recently gotten divorced, as I recall?"

"Yes, the first one. I've never been good at choosing, or at least not at keeping, wives. You're right. I probably better register this new boat in someone else's name." They both laughed.

As they neared the airport, Beck turned off into a city park. Being a work day afternoon, it was quite deserted. "So many security cameras at the airport. Better we pull in here for a minute and I'll give you the diamonds." He pulled into a secluded spot by a stand of birch trees. He turned off the engine and reached under the seat. "Got them right here," Beck said. But instead of diamonds, he pulled out his old Makarov pistol. He'd brought it along just as a precaution, as he was traveling with a sack full of jewels.

Bob laughed. "Very funny."

"Yes, very funny. Your weak bladder did you in. If you hadn't gone to the bathroom, giving me time to sit there and think, you might have gotten away with it."

"What the hell are you talking about?" Bob was starting to look a little worried.

"How did you know we stayed at the Hotel Regency in Ekaterinburg?"

"You must have mentioned the name, I guess."

"No, I'm quite sure, I simply said 'the hotel in Ekaterinburg', but then a minute later, you referred to it by name. Explain that."

"I told you, you must have mentioned it."

"No, I mentioned the Hotel *Metropol*, in Moscow. I'll tell you how you knew. Because you're Russian handler mentioned it to you. A couple of things have been bothering me. The first being, why was the GRU involved in looking for me? The second, all the stuff on the walls of Verchagin's apartment related to his military career. He'd been in the Soviet Army and then probably became a part of the GRU's assassination team. It wasn't the civilian KGB that came after me in Prague, it was the military GRU. I've always wondered how knowledge about my defection could have leaked out that quickly in Washington DC, and the assassin even knew the time and route we were taking to the airport that day. It's because the problem wasn't in Washington. The leak was right there in Prague, wasn't it? The helpful young Army Captain, Bob Jones. The recently divorced, assistant military attaché, Bob Jones. The man who kept saying, there was no rush to move us out of Prague."

"You're talking crazy," replied Bob. One small bead of perspiration had appeared on his right temple.

"There were very few people who knew I was traveling last month to Moscow at all and even fewer that I was using the name Blackwell. Everything I've just mentioned could have been coincidences, but you knowing the name of my hotel in Ekaterinburg -- that's what sewed it all together for me. And yes, I'm going to kill you right here and right now, so if you've got anything to say first, now is the time."

Bob had known Karl long enough to know that he meant what he said. "Yes, it was me. I was the source back in Prague. A GRU officer had recruited me only a few months before you showed up. The divorce had financially broken me and I'd already meet Carol, who eventually became my second wife. I needed money, plain and simple. The Cold War was over, what did it matter if I sold the Russians every American military secret I knew. But there wasn't much in Prague I could get my hands on, to pass to my handler. He was pressuring me to produce. And then you showed up that Saturday at the embassy, and I happened to be there. Just a lucky break for me. I suddenly had something 'hot' to pass -- word of a high-ranking KGB defector. At that time, you were just one more Ivan trying to buy your way into America. What did I care?"

"And you gave all the details to the GRU man and he told you to stall as long as possible our departure from Prague?"

"Something like that, but I swear I didn't know about the planned hit on you. He told me they were putting together a plan to kidnap you and your family to return you to Moscow. I felt terrible about your wife and child, that's why I've stayed in touch over the years since then, checking to make sure you were OK. Making amends, as best I could. The Russians thought you were dead and I never told them otherwise."

"Until a couple of weeks ago, when I told you I was going to Moscow -- and then you informed the GRU of my existence?"

"If you would have just told me you were off on some stupid diamond hunt, I could have continued to keep my mouth shut. But I thought you were on some mission for Joan. If you got caught and talked -- and everybody talks in the end -- and you told them about your association with me. Well, old friend, you put me between a rock and a hard place. I could look out for you or look out for me. It wasn't personal. You know how the game is played."

"Yes, I do and you know what I've always promised I would do when I found the person responsible for my wife's and son's deaths. But I will ask you one last question. You can answer it, because you are truly sorry for what happened. Or, you can answer it and then I promise I will kill you quickly. Who was your GRU handler in Prague who set up the assassination of my family?"

"His name is Gennady Klemenko, now General Klemenko."

"Thank you. Please slowly step out of the car."

They both got out of his car, while Karl kept the pistol on him. They walked over closer to the birch trees; the traditional tree of Russia. It almost looked like a rural setting back in Siberia. There was a slight breeze moving the leaves. Bob looked up at the beautiful blue sky, with a few little patches of white puffy clouds, as if they'd been painted there. He began to quietly recite the Lord's Prayer. He didn't feel a thing as the bullet entered his forehead.

"It's always personal, Bob -- that was the difference between you and me." He removed the list of donations for the planned sale of the diamonds from Bob's pocket and also took his cell phone. He left the wallet and airline ticket on the body. He didn't want Bob ending up in a pauper's grave in Indianapolis, as an unknown stiff. Karl figured he owed him at least that much. He also wanted to send a message to General Klemenko. A very sad Beck returned to his car and drove off.

"That was quite a surprise, wasn't it! The man who'd been so kind to us, who was going to take care of us. The man who'd pretended to be my friend all those years since that terrible day. Well, at least that chapter of our lives has ended. You and Pavel can sleep peacefully now."

Once Karl had parked at the airport, he gave Cathleen a call. "I have to make a quick trip to Washington, to see Joan."

"Did everything go OK with Bob?"

There was a long silence. "Not exactly as planned, but everything is good now. I should be back tomorrow. It's better I explain everything when I return and we can talk in person."

"OK, but call me when you get to D.C."

"I will." He didn't want to end the call. "I love you," he added before closing his cell phone.

Beck bought a ticket for the four o'clock direct flight to Reagan International Airport. He was first on the waitlist of the full flight. Beck knew there'd be at least one no-show. While waiting, he phoned Joan, briefly explaining that there was something quite pressing to discuss. She agreed to meet him at eight at Citronelle for dinner on M Street in Georgetown. Beck only knew it by reputation. It was a restaurant frequented by the shakers and makers of the nation's capital.

Beck had only met Joan face-to-face twice before, but he immediately recognized her as he approached a table off in a corner of the posh restaurant. All the tables were quite far apart, so as to provide the clientele a degree of privacy in their conversations. He recognized three well-known senators as he crossed the room and presumed that most everyone else present were equally important captains of industry or the political world -- at least in their own minds.

"Karl, how are you?"

"I'm fine Joan, and you?"

Karl knew from Bob that she was pushing sixty, but the tall, willowy blonde looked many years younger. Many a man during her years in government had mistakenly thought that her appearance somehow meant she was dumb. They had regretted afterwards making such a bad, false assumption.

Joan already had a glass of white wine. Karl ordered a single-malt.

"The veal here is terrific," suggested Joan as the two perused the menu.

Once they'd ordered, they got down to business. "I presume you and Bob met earlier today? Did he give you your new documents? I haven't heard from him today."

"Yes, I received the envelope. Thanks for your continued confidence in me. You won't be hearing from Bob. I killed him and left him in an

Indianapolis park around midday. I imagine the local police have found him by now."

Not many things left Joan speechless, but Karl's opening statement certainly wasn't anything she was expecting. After a long silence, she finally asked, "Unless you've gone mad, I assume you had a good reason for doing that?"

"He's been working for the Russian GRU for the past twenty years. It was he, who set up me and my family back in Prague, though he claimed he thought it was only to be a kidnapping of us, not an assassination." He proceeded to tell her much the same story he'd given to Bob earlier that day about the trip to Moscow, letting Verchagin live, finding the diamonds and also his reasoning for concluding that Bob was secretly working for the GRU -- plus Bob's confession before he shot him.

She sat in silence as Karl explained all the details. When he finished, her first words were, "I guess I should thank you for finding and removing a mole from our organization. You think the police will find any connection of his death to you?"

"Very unlikely. We'd had a couple of drinks at a lounge several miles away that had no security cameras and then we drove to a very empty park. The gun used and his cell phone are now at the bottom of an old water-filled gravel pit, miles from that park."

"His wife knew of his work with our group in vague terms, so I'll get someone to have a quiet word with her tomorrow. Give her a story of how he died bravely for a good cause. He had a life insurance policy for a couple of million dollars, with her named as the beneficiary -- that should smooth her grief."

"Bob was always very professional. I doubt he was carrying anything on him linking him to the Group or to me."

"When are you returning to Indiana?"

"I'll get a room at a motel near the airport for tonight and catch the first flight home in the morning."

"What are you going to tell your young lady at the university that accompanied you to Russia? I take it that's a pretty serious relationship between you two?"

"Yes, it is and I plan on telling her the truth."

"OK, you know best concerning her. I just wanted to know."

"She handled herself very well at certain tense moments in Russia. I'm sure she'll understand -- what I had to do concerning Bob."

"Well, you've had a pretty interesting few weeks. I'll give you some time to mentally recuperate and do your teaching thing, but if you're up for it, I may have a little trip in mind for you come Christmas time - and maybe Cathleen as well, if you think she might be interested."

"We'll see. Oh, by the way, I'll be bringing you a contribution of $500,000 for the Group's work, soon as I've sold the diamonds." That also left Joan speechless.

When Beck got back to Bloomington the next afternoon, he sat down with Cathleen and explained to her what had happened with Bob the previous day and of his evening meeting with Joan.

For several long moments she sat there in silence. "It's good that Joan was so understanding about Bob," she finally managed to get out of her mouth.

"You're not upset with me over killing him?"

"I'm very sorry that it turned out to be your friend, but we had this conversation before, when I thought you were going to kill Verchagin. Frankly, this situation with Bob is clearer for me. At least Verchagin was following orders for his country. Bob was someone you should have been able to trust and he simply sold you out for money, not for patriotism or ideological reasons. But I must say, doesn't all the deceit and betrayal ever depress you? I mean, how do you know who you can really trust in your shadowy world of espionage?"

"I guess all of us in that world like to think that we can judge people around us, but obviously we can't, all the time. Or at least, I couldn't when it came to Bob. Perhaps he was so close to me, my mind just couldn't think of him as a betrayer. I'm always suspicious of people that I consider potential enemies, but a close personal friend..." He shook his head. "I guess the only completely safe way would be to trust no one, but that makes for a pretty lonely existence."

She leaned up against his chest as he put an arm around her. "You know you can always trust me."

"I know." He pulled her close and just held her. There was no need for words.

Beck himself tracked down the Amsterdam "specialist" and made the necessary arrangements for the sale of the jewels and disposition of the money. Geert was a multi-talented individual, who could sell jewels and discreetly move money around the world -- and he was, as Karl had predicted, quite happy with a five percent commission. The auction of the jewels took place towards the end of August. The sale even made the major newspapers, given all the speculation about the similarity of these stones to ones known to have belonged to the Romanovs. They were sold in sets of ten stones each. Final proceeds were much more than either Karl or Cathleen had originally estimated. After commissions were paid, the two had in an offshore account just under 7 million dollars. Shortly thereafter, a number of generous gifts and donations started arriving at places around the world.

The Moscow Times reported that a generous benefactor had anonymously donated one million American dollars to a small women's monastery near Ekaterinburg, run by Sister Anastasia. The paper speculated that it might have been the charity of a major Russian crime figure, with a guilty conscience and hoping to buy his way into heaven. Sister Anastasia simply responded to newspaper inquiries that God, at times, worked in mysterious ways.

Viktor Litvinov found in his mail box one morning an envelope containing $100,000 and a note that simply said, "From Ivy With Love."

"Grandpa" Tommy Timmons walked into the Dove and Whistle in Belfast one day to join three of his old friends at the bar for conversation, as was their usual custom about that time of the afternoon. The barman on duty greeted him exceptionally warmly. "What will it be today Mr. Timmons?" asked the young man.

"Probably the same thing I've been ordering every day since you started working here two years ago. Has your memory failed you, lad?"

"I'm not daft; of course, I remember what you usually order. I just thought that what with all that credit now on your tab, you might be upgrading your drink?"

"What are you talking about young Brian? My credit?"

Brian brought the accounts book to him. It showed that Tommy had a 10,000 pound credit. "The boss told me that a certified cashier's check arrived in the mail from America two days ago. He thought at first it was a joke, but sure enough, the bank cashed it. The note with it simply said, it was to go on your tab."

Tommy had recovered his composure enough to say, "Tis about time that the money I was owed for me services rendered to the boys back during the dark days arrived! A round of Bushmills Black for me and my compatriots, if you please. And pour one for yourself while you've got the bottle handy, young man."

During the first Monday of classes at Indiana University, the student paper reported that an anonymous benefactor had donated one million dollars to the Lilly Library operating fund. The only peculiar condition attached to the gift was the request by the donor that a small brass plaque be placed at the library stating: Read Old Books. You Might Be Surprised At The Outcome.

Beck was attending the first faculty staff meeting of the Slavic Department for the new term that day.

"I've some really good news for us all," began the Department chairman. I received a call this morning from the IU Foundation, informing me that they have received an anonymous donation from a Russian citizen, for the exclusive use by the Slavic Department."

One of Beck's least favorite colleagues snidely asked, "Was it in dollars or rubles? Perhaps we can at least afford now to buy a decent coffee maker for the department."

"Actually, this person gave enough money as an endowment, so that the annual interest generated is anticipated to fund five graduate student fellowships per year, each worth $40,000."

There was stunned silence for several long seconds. Nina asked, "Is there no clue as to the donor?"

"Well, the only stipulation is that the five fellowships be named in honor of Alexandra, Olga, Tatiana, Marie and Anastasia. If that lets you figure out who gave the money, be sure to let me know!"

"They're to be named after the last czarina of Russia and her four daughters! Who would do that?" asked Nina in disbelief.

"Perhaps Nikolai II, Czar of All the Russias," suggested Adjunct Professor Beck. Everyone laughed.

Karl had left a message on Cathleen's cell phone for her to meet him at five o'clock in the original, stone Well House, in the heart of the old part of the campus. He was already seated on one of the century old stone benches when she arrived. The nearby bell tower was chiming the hour.

"Why did you want to meet here?" she asked.

"Several of my students have told me there is a very old tradition here on this campus."

"Concerning the Well House? Yes, I've heard that one as well," she replied with a grin, "but it has to be after 11:00 p.m. when we kiss in here -- not during the day."

"Actually, I was thinking of another tradition." He reached in to his coat pocket and brought out an engagement ring. "Will you marry me?"

She stared for a moment at the very large and dazzling diamond mounted in the ring. It was beautiful, but had a rather old-fashioned cut.

"I thought we sold all of these?"

"All but one. I thought I might need one for a special purpose, but I haven't heard an answer from you yet."

She leaned in and gave him one long, wet kiss. "Does that suffice for an answer Professor Beck?" Before he could answer, he again had his mouth covered by hers.

A number of students walking past were giggling at the passionate behavior of the "old people" in the Well House. "Geez, get a motel room," shouted one of them.

They finally took a break and Cathleen said, "How about a Christmas time wedding? That will give me time to make all the arrangements and to get my mom and grandpa here. And I have a great idea for a honeymoon."

"All that sounds fine," he replied, "except maybe for the honeymoon part. I think Joan already has an idea for a trip by you and me over the Christmas break."